MOONLIGHT CAN BE DEADLY

A DISCOUNT DETECTIVE MYSTERY

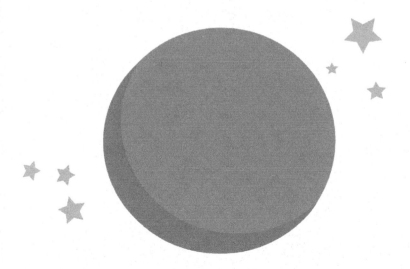

MOONLIGHT CAN BE DEADLY

A DISCOUNT DETECTIVE MYSTERY

CHARLOTTE STUART

Walrus Publishing | St. Louis, MO 63116

Walrus Publishing | Saint Louis, MO 63116
Copyright © 2022 Charlotte Stuart
All rights reserved.

For information, contact:
Walrus Publishing
An imprint of Amphorae Publishing Group
a woman- and veteran-owned business
4168 Hartford Street, Saint Louis, MO 63116

Manufactured in the United States of America
Set in Adobe Caslon Pro and Avenir
Interior designed by Kristina Blank Makansi
Cover designed by Kristina Blank Makansi
Cover image: Shutterstock

Library of Congress Control Number: 2022948574
ISBN: 9781940442471

To longtime friendships:
Lynn & George, Sonia & Paul.
With special thanks to George for
never letting us fade away.

MAIN CAST OF CHARACTERS

Penny-wise Investigations: Discount Detective Agency

- **Cameron Chandler**: single mom and investigator who can't ignore a crying stranger on a mall bench
- **Yuri Webster**: loves coffee, junk food, women, and trivia—not necessarily in that order
- **P.W. Griffin**: owns Penny-wise; startling white hair, a firm handshake, and a secret past
- **W. Blaine Watkins**: agency's blue-eyed Man Friday
- **Norm**: average in every way with the exception of his outstanding investigative skills
- **Grant**: with the agency since the beginning; dependable and calm
- **Will**: wears trench coat; prefers teasing to being teased
- **Adele**: researcher par excellence
- **Jenny**: farmer and part-time investigator who works for Penny-wise when she needs extra money
- **Penny-wise mascot**: stuffed bear dressed like Sherlock Holmes

Clients

- **Clara Ramsey**: distraught woman who wants Penny-wise to protect her niece during a full moon ritual
- **Tilly Jamison**: not the first young woman to fall for a "bad boy" or to be the object of an obsessed stalker

Cameron's surprisingly resilient and resourceful family

- **Stella**: Cameron's live-in mother whose insights often provide "aha" moments
- **Mara**: freshman year in high school; likes cooking with her grandmother

- **Jason**: Mara's younger brother; obsessed with TikTok and sneaker technology
- **No-name**: the family dog; determined to destroy stuffed endangered species

Groups with powerful leaders with hidden agendas
- **Full Moon Society**
  - **Rune Rundell**: charismatic leader admired by men and lusted after by women
  - **Ethan Jones**: unattractive man who resents Rune on several levels
  - **Professor Carter James King** (CJ): a true believer or a spy?
  - **Wylie Younger**: a regular whose description of Rune is not very flattering
  - **Larry Jackson**: Wylie's employee; more charitable than most about Ethan
  - **Riley Nelson**: a university student with no illusions about Rune as date material
- **The Green Women**
  - **Raven**: woman with unnaturally red hair and a dislike of outsiders
  - **Lark**: can spout the mission and party line word for word
  - **Phoebe Green**: Tilly's roommate; tries to be helpful but considers the three roommates "independent entities"
  - **Wren Davies**: Tilly's other roommate; dominant, defensive and detached

Major Crimes
- **Detective Connolly**: Attractive and supportive but tightlipped about his personal life

There are nights when the wolves are silent
and only the moon howls. —George Carlin

CHAPTER 1
UNDER A FULL MOON

I WAS IN A BAD MOOD as I headed through the busy suburban shopping mall to my office. It was one of those mornings when everything was off-kilter. "No-name," our dog, had been extra needy, following me around while I tried to organize breakfast for my kids, whining like I was depriving him of the attention and love he considered his due. Both of my two barely-teenagers were unusually irritating, grumbling because no one had done the laundry and they didn't have anything to wear—except all of the other clothes in their closets. And my live-in mother made an appearance to let me know I was running late. In case I hadn't figured that out.

When I finally arrived at the mall, I took a deep breath and made an effort to put what I'd endured so far this morning behind me by telling myself, "OK, this is the beginning of a good day." Then I saw her.

My guess was that she was in her early 60s, svelte, well-dressed, with nicely coifed, light brown hair that probably wasn't her natural color. She was sitting upright, her hands in her lap, making no attempt to stem the tears streaming down her face. I wanted to walk past without making eye contact, without acknowledging that she was in some sort of pain, but it's not in my DNA to ignore another person's misery. My feet involuntarily slowed down as I chalked up another notch on my off-kilter day.

"Is there anything I can do for you?" I asked as I sat down next to her on the narrow fake wood bench and handed her a Kleenex from my purse.

She turned her tear-filled eyes toward me and accepted the Kleenex. "Thank you." She dabbed at the tears on her smooth cheeks. After a few moments of silence so profound that I thought I could hear the continuing trickle of tears, she asked, "Do you know anything about Penny-wise Investigations?" She gestured in the direction of my office.

"Actually, I do. I work there."

Her eyes opened a bit wider as she seemed to see me for the first time. I suddenly wished I'd spent more time on my drab, ash blond hair earlier. Not that I ever did much more than run a comb through it. And I was wearing a jacket that had tiny lint balls growing in random patches like a virus. Not very professional for someone whose office was in a shopping mall.

"I'm an investigator." I still got a tingle of joy from saying those words. Not that long ago I had gone from unemployed PhD to an employed PI. The job was a bit more mundane than I'd hoped, but there had been a few moments of excitement and even a smattering of danger, so I wasn't complaining.

"Thank you for stopping. Maybe I can ask you a few questions?"

"Sure. But you could also come inside and talk to my boss, P.W. Griffin. She can probably answer your questions better than I can, and there's no charge for the initial consultation."

"I'd rather talk with you first, if you don't mind." The tears were slowing down, leaving white flecks of salt at the corners of her eyes.

"Not at all. Start from the beginning." I might as well hear the whole thing. I would have to explain being late to work, so I hoped she was a potential client. But if not, I would be ahead on my good Samaritan score for the day, maybe for the week or the month, depending on how long it took her to tell me her story.

"It's my niece. I think she's going to be sacrificed."

"Sacrificed?" I had visions of a young girl tossed into a volcano by two shirtless men with bulging arm muscles.

"During the full moon. On a rock altar. Like some ancient cultures did for eons, or so my niece tells me."

That seemed more like an end than a beginning to me, but I wasn't about to quibble over the story's structure when a human sacrifice was the topic. "I'm not sure I know when the next full moon is," I said, trying to put her story into context.

"This coming Saturday."

"And by 'sacrificed' you mean . . .?"

"She said they will drug her and that they don't actually rip her heart out or anything like that—" She dabbed at her eyes with the Kleenex, smudging her mascara slightly.

"I would hope not." I couldn't think of what else to say.

"But I don't like the idea of it. I'm afraid she's being too trusting."

"You think they might actually, ah, sacrifice her for real?"

3

The tears started flowing again like a stream that had been undammed. "I don't know. It just doesn't feel right to me," she said, her voice cracking like a teenage boy's. "But my niece is determined to go through with it."

I handed her another Kleenex. "How do you think Penny-wise can help?"

She took a deep breath and sat up even straighter. "I want someone to be there, to make sure nothing bad happens to Tilly."

I stood up. "I definitely think you need to talk to P.W. This sounds serious, and she will have ideas about the best approach." At least I certainly hoped she would. Monitoring a human sacrifice was not your standard fare for a discount detective agency. Probably not for any kind of agency.

After just the briefest of hesitations, the woman got to her feet. "You seem like a caring person. I wasn't sure what to expect from a storefront agency in a mall. But this is the only detective agency I know of."

It was nice that she thought I seemed caring, but the fact that we were first on her list because she didn't know of any other agency didn't say much about our reputation. I took her by the elbow and guided her to the office as she wiped her face with a Kleenex. I wondered if I should mention the mascara smudges but decided against it. She had enough on her mind and no one at Penny-wise would care.

Penny-wise Investigations is located between Ye Olde Candle Shoppe and Sew What? In the past the mall was a busy place, overflowing with people and activity, but currently it wasn't doing all that great. Several boutique clothing stores had closed their doors, as well as one of the big-box stores. There was talk that the mall owners were considering turning the mall into some sort of sports complex. Meanwhile, candles and fabrics were apparently still money-makers. And our detective agency was doing okay. We advertised "Vigilance You Can Afford" and offered gift certificates. That and our Sherlock Holmes bear mascot displayed in the window next to our front door attracted quite a few customers from the dwindling crowds.

W. Blaine Watkins, our task master, greeter and Man Friday, looked up as we came in, raising his eyebrows and cocking his head to one side like an inquisitive bird.

"This is . . .," I began, then realized I didn't know who she was.

"Clara Ramsey," she filled in for me.

"She needs to see P.W."

"Welcome to Penny-wise," W. Blaine Watkins said, his sharp blue eyes assessing our prospective client, undoubtedly noting the black smears around her eyes. "Please take a seat and I'll see if P.W. Griffin is available."

I sat down next to Clara Ramsey and turned toward her. "Do you want me to go in with you?" I asked.

"Please." She reached over and squeezed my hand.

"I'm Cameron Chandler by the way." I took out a card and handed it to her.

My colleague, Yuri Webster, suddenly burst into the room balancing a tray of coffees, a partially squashed box of Dunkin Donuts under his left arm. I jumped up to open the door to the "pit"—our collective office—for him. "One of those is for me, I hope." Flattened or not, I wanted a donut.

He gave me a wide, toothy smile and wiggled his dark eyebrows, barely visible under strands of dark hair. Then he glanced back at our prospective client and asked, "Want your coffee now?"

I reluctantly shook my head. It didn't seem right to drink gourmet coffee in front of a potential client when all we had to offer was bland office fare. Still, I could feel my taste buds protesting my "no."

The door closed behind Yuri as W. Blaine Watkins announced that P.W. would see us now. Apparently, he took it for granted that I would be accompanying Clara even though I hadn't known her name when I brought her in.

P.W. is a striking woman, tall with startling white hair and a firm handshake. She also has an incredible wardrobe, including complementary hats for her eye-catching outfits. Today she was wearing a light grey tweed dress with a jacket that had slit, three-quarters cuffs. Each sleeve had a row of gold and pearl pendant buttons starting near the neckline and ending where the cuff flared. Her gold and pearl earrings matched a gold and pearl ring. My eyes went automatically to the clothes tree in the corner where a gray hat was prominently displayed. It had a dark gray band with a large gold and pearl pendant off to one side. Perfection.

Clara seemed surprised and impressed as P.W. stepped out to shake her hand before waving her to one of the two chairs in front of her desk. The chair was red leather, perhaps a tribute to Nero Wolfe. P.W. has a complete set of Red Stout's mysteries on a lower shelf of the bookcase behind her desk.

"I met Mrs. Ramsey . . ." I began.

"Please, call me Clara," our potential client interrupted.

"I met Clara in the mall. When she told me about her situation, I recommended that she talk with you." I paused. "Should I stay?" giving one more chance to Clara to meet alone with P.W.

"Please do," Clara said. P.W. nodded for me to sit.

"Cameron referred to your 'situation.' Why don't you tell me about it. With enough detail so I understand where we might fit in. I will hold my questions until you are done explaining." P.W. believes that it is best to let a client tell their story in its entirety before asking anything that might skew their perspective or cause them to lose their train of thought. It's an approach that seems to work well, but sometimes it takes a client a long time to get to the point.

Clara took a deep breath and dove in. "I have a niece, Tilly Jamison, my late sister's child. My sister passed away when Tilly was 13. When she was dying, my sister asked me to look out for Tilly. I didn't have children of my own, and I'd always been fond of Tilly. Although I realize that no one can substitute for a mother, Tilly has been a large part of my life since then. She's nineteen now. She'll be starting her sophomore year at the University of Washington soon. In environmental studies.

"Meanwhile, like young people her age often do, I feel as though she's been searching for meaning, trying to 'fit in' somewhere. And, unfortunately, I believe she's been making some bad choices of late." She cleared her throat before continuing.

"She cares deeply about the environment and is very concerned about climate change. Which I consider a good thing. And, until recently, she's been methodical and thoughtful about deciding what she can do to help. I've tried to be supportive of both her and her cause. Not only for her but because I, too, am troubled about the state of our planet. She's done a lot more research than I have, so I've taken her suggestion on which organizations to support with charitable contributions. Then this summer she became involved in a group that has some fairly, ah, radical ideas about advocating for change. The Green Women. Have you heard of them?"

P.W. nodded yes, but I knew nothing about them and shook my head "no."

Clara turned slightly toward me to explain, "They call themselves an ecofeminist group. They consider the 'oppression' of women comparable to the 'oppression' of nature. They think that men treat women and nature as property, and they are opposed to how male dominance is impacting the environment and the world.

"I understand why that philosophy is appealing to young women, but this particular group—at least the branch in our area—also supports 'aggressive action' to ensure, in their words, that 'the Earth remains inhabitable for all organisms.' Tilly is always quoting that phrase. The problem from my point of view is the 'aggressive action' piece. It includes committing illegal acts if that's what they think is called for. Not only that, but they talk about the collapse of civilization as if it's inevitable, and they believe they need to be prepared to ensure the survival of the human race. Maybe I'm old-fashioned, but I can't help but feel that this dystopian view of society is an unhealthy way to think about the future." She turned back to P.W.

"Anyway, although her involvement with the Green Women is upsetting to me, it's not her association with that group that brought me here today." Clara paused and seemed hesitant to continue. It can be hard to share embarrassing details to strangers, even when asking for help. We waited patiently while she collected her thoughts.

"One of the Green Women introduced her to another group . . . The Full Moon Society." She sent P.W. a questioning look.

"I know a little about them, but not much," P.W. said.

Again, I'd never heard of the group. I was starting to feel like I ought to be paying more attention to what's going on in the world around me.

"Their main purpose sounds normal enough—they study the relationship between ancient cultures and the moon. But the local group is particularly interested in human sacrifice during full moon rituals. And on Saturday night, my niece has agreed to be sacrificed."

P.W. broke her own rule about interruptions to ask, "Do you mean she is willing to die during a ceremony?"

"No, it's a symbolic sacrifice. But she will be drugged. And, for obvious reasons, I don't think that's a good idea. Maybe even unsafe." Clara started to cry, again making no attempt to stop the flow of tears. They rolled down her face and dripped from her chin to her flowered shirt, leaving tiny splotch marks, like dewdrops on the petals. Her mascara drools were also inching downward. Soon the dewdrops would turn to mud if she didn't stop crying.

P.W. broke the silence, her raspy voice a gentle probe, "What would you like us to do?"

"Make sure Tilly's safe," Clara said without hesitation.

"Have you talked with her about the ceremony?" I asked.

"Yes, I tried to dissuade her not to participate, but she's convinced she wants to do it. I think it's less about a commitment to the group and more because of a young man that she seems to be quite taken with. She refers to him as Rune. I'm not sure if that's his name or just what they call him in the group."

"He's a Full Moon member?"

"Yes. The leader or one of the leaders. I'm not sure what their structure is. She doesn't actually talk as much about the Full Moon Society as she does about the other group. She really cares about the environment. But I think her interest in ancient cultures is a passing one." The implicit message was if she lives through it.

P.W. tapped her fingers on the edge of her desk, sending secret morse code messages to her brain. Then she said, "Here's what I propose. I doubt we would have any more luck than you in persuading her not to participate in the ceremony. But I can have Cameron and another investigator keep watch over her. They can try to find out where the ceremony will take place, or if necessary, they can follow your niece to the ceremony, staying out of sight unless needed. Is that an acceptable approach to you?"

Clara nodded and dabbed her face with a very limp Kleenex that was starting to disintegrate. "I would feel so much better knowing someone was there looking out for her."

While P.W. and Clara worked out the arrangement, I excused myself and went to tell Yuri about our Saturday night plans. As I grabbed my coffee and snagged a donut, I said: "Guess what we we're doing this Saturday night?"

"You asking me out?"

"In your dreams. But we ARE going out together. To view a human sacrifice under a full moon."

CHAPTER 2
FOLLOWERS OF THE MOON

TUESDAY EVENING my mother fixed one of her moderately experimental healthy meals for us: Komatsuna pasta with feta. I label it "moderately experimental" because I anticipated that she intended to pass the Japanese mustard spinach off as "greens" to my son Jason. A somewhat dubious category for him, but not objectionably exotic. Since Mara had participated in the meal's preparation, she already knew what was in the pasta, and she was undoubtedly looking forward to seeing her brother tricked into trying a dish he wouldn't have touched if he'd known what the "greens" were. Not that he would have heard of Japanese mustard spinach, but then, that was the point.

"Here's your pasta," Mara said as she placed a plate in front of Jason. She wore a pink flowered apron over a Jimi Hendrix T-shirt and jeans with shredded knees. I disliked the shabby jeans but had decided not to say anything. Although I was hoping her back-to-school clothes would be more in line with my admittedly conservative tastes.

"What's in it?" he asked, poking it with his fork.

With a straight face, Mara said, "Greens and feta."

"I don't like feta," Jason said as if everyone in the room should have known.

"It's not goat feta, it's cow feta," my wise daughter who was one year older than her brother said. "Very mild. You'll like it." Mara's lovely oval face was the picture of innocence. She was almost fourteen and looking forward to the school year starting again. I couldn't help but wonder if this was the year she would start being secretive about her talent for math and start flirting with good looking athletes with half her brain power.

"Just try it," Mom encouraged him. She had removed her apron and took Mara's from her and set them aside. I don't remember ever wearing an apron as a young girl. And I'd avoided chores whenever possible. Mara was my mother's second chance at shaping someone in her own image. Not a bad thing for either of them.

As for Jason, in spite of his growth spurt, he still seemed young in many ways. And he definitely has a young boy's picky palate. But he and I have a deal about my mother's cooking. If he tastes something and really doesn't want to eat it, he doesn't have to. But he has to give it a try and be polite. Later he can have a substitute meal, like a peanut butter and jelly sandwich. My mother tries to accommodate him if she knows there's an ingredient he detests while at the same time continuing to introduce him to healthy options to improve his eating habits.

Tonight—with everyone watching—my obedient son took a tentative, teensy bite. As he chewed, he got a "not bad" look on his face. "It's okay," he concluded.

Mara was itching to tell him what he was eating, but one "don't you dare" look from me and she kept her mouth shut.

Then I took a bite. "Delicious," I said, meaning it. I wasn't going to have to break into my secret cache of junk food later. Jason has a secret cache too, but I pretend I don't know about it.

Overall, our living arrangement works out nicely. Jason and Mara are fond of my mother, she dotes on them, and I couldn't manage without her. For these reasons, I try not to complain about her cooking or her nagging about my marital status. Currently, we have a truce of sorts about the nagging, although the cease-fire is occasionally broken when Mom simply cannot resist posting on my refrigerator what she considers to be an informative article about some aspect of life as a single mother. The articles appear pinned with two goose magnets that I have grown to despise— an arrogant bonnet-wearing goose and a smirking pig with a blue scarf around its neck. I can't throw them out because Mara gave them to me for Christmas a long time ago. Besides, my mother probably has a secret stash of replacement magnets somewhere. Maybe a miniature bridal bouquet or a Paul Rudd face.

As we were finishing our meal, I threw out a question that I didn't expect an answer to: "Anyone ever heard of the Full Moon Society?"

Jason immediately straightened up like a front-row kid who always had the answers. "They refer to themselves as the segeedooress de luna," he said. "Followers of the moon."

"That's seguidores de la luna," Mara corrected.

"That's what I said." Jason frowned. "Isn't it?"

"You mispronounced the first word and left out the la." Mara was taking Spanish and was quite pleased with her linguistic abilities.

"What difference does that make? The moon is the moon. Who says it has to be female?"

Mara rolled her hazel eyes and shook her long, chestnut brown hair to indicate how unbelievably annoying her brother was. Before they could engage in further battle over pronunciation and pronouns, I jumped in. "So, Jason, you know about them?"

"They're on TikTok," he blurted, then shrunk down in his chair an inch. He wasn't supposed to be spending unauthorized time on TikTok.

My mother scowled at him, but before she could issue a reprimand, I said, "So, who are they and what do they do?" I would deal with his online viewing habits later.

He looked around guiltily before deciding it was safe to proceed. "Well, they are a kinda weird group. They are into spooky stuff. Aztecs and sacrifice rituals, that kind of thing."

"I had a quick look at their website," I said. "It makes them look like they're a cultural anthropology study group. Although I did think their wolf howling at the moon banner was a bit strange—it looked somewhat vampirish."

"Based on what I've seen, I don't think they're a study group. They don't post much about other cultures," Jason said. "Except for the dark stuff. Like the sacrifices. Killing people by tossing them into a volcano, or clubbing them or throwing them off a cliff . . ."

"Jason," my mother interrupted. "We're at the dinner table."

"Mom asked," he said, flicking his shaggy hair away from his forehead. I needed to make sure he got a haircut before school was back in session.

"It's okay, Jason." I flashed a look at my mother that asked her to back off. "My fault for bringing it up."

"They also talk about trances and how other cultures used peyote and mescaline and magic mushrooms. Like that."

"They couldn't openly encourage people to use drugs . . . could they?" Mara said, looking to me for confirmation.

"I'm just telling you the kinds of things they post," Jason said defensively. "I think they do enactments or have meetings when there's a full moon. A friend of mine wanted to go watch, but they are secretive about where they get together."

"You weren't thinking about going with him, were you?" I asked, a tingle of fear chasing itself down my back. Was my son capable of sneaking out at night on a lark with friends? Wasn't it just yesterday that he clung to my legs when other people were around?

"Mom, come on," Jason said. I noted that he didn't actually answer my question and decided to continue the discussion once I got him alone.

"Why are you asking about the Full Moon Society?" Mara asked.

"A client's niece is part of the group, and her aunt is concerned."

"Because . . .?"

I try not to lie to my children, but my job as a PI makes it difficult at times. Sometimes there's confidentiality to consider. And I don't want them to become fearful, worrying about what could happen out there in the world. On the other hand, I don't want to be overly protective either. And in this instance, it seemed to me that a little fear might be a good thing. "They are going to perform a ritual during the next full moon. Not for real, just acting. Like a theater performance."

"Only in the woods and at night," Jason said quickly, obviously liking the idea. Like visiting a haunted house on Halloween. Or walking through a cemetery at midnight. I wasn't so old that I couldn't remember the thrill of telling ghost stories around a campfire with the darkness pressing in on you and the flames leaping toward the stary sky. But that didn't mean I wanted to encourage Jason to get anywhere near an adult group fixated on human sacrifice.

"Yes," I agreed. "Camping in the woods is one thing. But it's different when adults take an idea like theirs a little too seriously. Something could go sideways."

"You mean like someone might actually drive a stake through someone's heart?" Jason asked, eyes wide.

"No, not exactly like that."

Mom wrinkled her nose and glared at me—it was either a look of disgust or she was about to sneeze. Either way, I knew what she was thinking, that I was doing a lousy job of explaining why my son ought to stay away from Full Moon Society activities.

No-name had been lurking nearby, probably hoping for a handout even though no one was supposed to feed him from the dinner table. I was, however, suspicious that he occasionally got something Jason didn't like and wanted to dispose of. One time I found an asparagus spear on the floor. Obviously rejected by both boy and animal. Now, hearing the excitement in Jason's voice, No-name began racing around the table issuing a chorus of yips to match Jason's enthusiasm.

"That's enough," Mom ordered. To my surprise, No-name stopped, lowered his head, and, tail between his legs, headed for the stairs. I was amazed; he never responded to my commands. Then she turned to Jason. "Now, Jason, you need to keep in mind that what they do isn't like making a movie. They are fanatics, and some are obsessed with unhealthy ideas. It's not a group that you want to get mixed up with." She turned her to me. "Right, Cameron?"

"Absolutely. That's why my client is concerned about her niece."

"Is her niece a fanatic?" Mara asked.

"No, I don't think so. Well, not exactly. I mean, she seems to be attracted to somewhat radical groups. She's also a member of the Green Women. Supposedly, their goal is to put climate change issues front and center. But they call themselves ecofeminists and are considered by some to be extremists."

"Are they eco-terrorists?" Mom asked.

"Some might call them that."

"What's an eco-terrorist?" Jason asked.

"People who commit criminal acts to make their voices heard."

"Like someone camping out in a tree they don't want to see cut down?" Mara asked.

"Or blowing up part of a pipeline," Mom said, sounding very critical.

"People have been hurt during eco-terrorist protests," I acknowledged.

"But you support what they want, right?" Jason asked.

With surprising passion, Mom said, "There are legal ways to bring about change."

"Policy change can be very slow," I countered. When Mom wrinkled her nose again, I quickly added, "Not that I'm an advocate of using violence to solve social issues. But I do understand their frustration."

"So," Mara said, "Your client's niece is passionate about climate change, maybe even willing to commit illegal acts to make a point. That doesn't explain why she's a member of the Full Moon Society."

"She may be interested in ancient cultures, their rituals and myths. That's a possibility. She's a college student; it might even be aligned with some class curriculum. But her aunt thinks she's more interested in a young man who is one of the group's leaders. Sometimes young women can be attracted to, ah, men with undesirable traits."

"Can't they tell they're jerks?" Jason asked. He tended to see the world and people in black and white.

"Some jerks can be charming," I said.

Mom stood up. "I think we've about covered that topic. Who wants dessert? Mara, want to help me get the cookies?"

Like No-name, Mara instantly obeyed. What was it about my mother that everyone jumped to do her bidding? Of course, I was still trying to please her after all these years, so who was I to complain? Besides, I wanted a cookie.

CHAPTER 3
BLUE MOON

AT THE OFFICE on Wednesday morning, I was making a "to do" list for our Saturday evening responsibilities as "watchers" when Yuri arrived in a flurry of jerky movements and muttered complaints. He unloaded a pile of files on his desk and headed for the coffee machine without making eye contact. He's always pretty upbeat, so I followed him over to the coffee machine to see what the problem was.

He was pouring coffee into his mug with the fornicating penguins around the bottom. PW had warned him not to bring the mug into meetings with clients, so he had a spare that he seldom used. It sported depictions of birds. And if you didn't look closely, you might have thought he'd purchased it from Audubon. Scrutinized up close you realized the birds all looked slightly demonic, with razor sharp beaks and evil intent in their eyes. One, a vampire finch, had a drop of blood on the tip of his beak.

"Good morning," I said.

Yuri looked at me and took a sip of coffee before saying, "Sorry, no donuts this morning."

"You okay?"

"Frustrated." He waved me to the conference room. Once inside he said, "My Facebook page has been hacked. And I didn't notice right away. Not until people started telling me about the strange messages they were getting from me. I didn't want to shut it down completely and start over again, but do you know how hard it is to get through to anyone for help?" He took another sip. "And then Blake stuck me with a crappy assignment."

"Sorry about your Facebook page. Jason can probably help you with that."

"Hey, good idea. Kids know those kinds of things, don't they?"

"As for the assignment, you know Blake tries to rotate the undesirable ones."

"I know, but I'd rather be working with you on the 'sacrifice' case."

"You will be with me Saturday night, won't you?" My other colleagues are competent and reliable, but this was Yuri's kind of thing.

"Yeah, I put my foot down about that."

I had to smile. You don't "put your foot down" with either Blaine or P.W. But if Yuri wanted to act like he had, that was okay by me. "What will you be doing before then?"

"Tracking down a missing cat. Penelope. Otherwise known as Penny."

"Let me guess, she's an orange tabby."

Yuri nodded.

"Well, I think it's nice that people care enough about their pets to hire us to find them."

"But we both know that with missing pet cases it comes down to one of three things: they were picked up and are in a shelter, they're dead—probably hit by a car or snatched by a coyote—or they will come home on their own before anyone can track them down."

"Pet owners have special relationships with their pets; they need to feel like they've done everything they can to find a missing animal." I wondered if I'd feel that way if No-name ran off. Of course Jason and Mara would, so I'd have to do my best to find the unnamed, untrained and ungrateful animal.

"So, what's on your agenda for today?" Yuri asked, sounding slightly mollified by our conversation.

"My main goal is to see if I can learn more about the Full Moon Society members, especially the guy responsible for Tilly committing to the ceremony."

"I checked them out online and noticed that the Full Moon Society doesn't have the Saturday event listed on their website."

"I don't think they advertise the re-enactments, only the discussion group meetings. And according to Jason . . ."

"Your son, Jason?"

"Yeah, he and a couple of his friends find all of the ritual stuff fascinating. He's looked into them on . . ." I paused, sorry I'd started the sentence.

"On?"

"Now don't laugh. On TikTok."

"Hey, there's a lot of good info on TikTok."

"Anyway, the discussions are held mostly in libraries. Maybe they screen potential re-enactment participants. Jason thinks they have a secret handshake or password, like the Freemasons. Who knows? But someone at the Green Women introduced Tilly to this Rune guy. Will and I are going by their headquarters to see if someone there can give me his full name so I can look him up."

"Sounds like we'll be truly undercover on Saturday."

"Undercover and out of sight.

"Unless something happens."

"I think it will be more like a bad Halloween party than anything, don't you?"

"Probably. But that doesn't change my day. You'll be out there interviewing the Green Women while I'm chasing down leads on Penelope, otherwise known as Penny."

I laughed. "Now I get it. It's about the women." Yuri enjoys chatting up women, although he's careful to keep it professional.

"I am a single, available male," he said, giving me a meaningful look.

"Maybe you'll meet a single woman out walking her cat," I said with a snicker. "Well, back to work." I stood up to leave.

"You do know it's a blue moon this Saturday, don't you?" Yuri said.

"Is that significant?"

"In relationship to the ritual they are going to hold? I'm not sure. It might just be an added draw. Real blue moons are considered rare; they only occur about every two and a half years. But events such as forest fires and dust storms can turn a moon blue."

"So . . . why do I need to know that this Saturday is a blue moon?"

Yuri gave me a toothy chuckle.

"Oh no," I groaned. "You're into moon trivia now, aren't you?"

"The first drawing of the moon through a telescope was on July 26, 1609, by Thomas Harriot . . ."

"Watch me leave," I said. "Feel free to keep spewing insignificant facts about the moon after I'm gone."

I slipped out the door and closed it behind me before he could follow. I always act as though I'm annoyed by Yuri's trivia obsessions, although sometimes I find the minutiae he spouts amusing. Like knowing that butterflies fart but most birds don't. Or that 85 full-size chocolate bars can be a deadly dose. Or that dolphins sleep with one eye open. Or that pigs don't sweat. Not exactly useful information, but for some reason I remember facts like these when other more relevant details slip my mind.

Will was waiting for me at my desk. His dark brown hair looked freshly trimmed—by a barber who learned his trade in the 60s. A self-proclaimed expert on self-defense, Will makes an effort to stay in shape, but a fashion plate, he isn't. You won't see him or his wardrobe on the cover of GQ.

"I hear I'm going to meet some 'green' women today." He was grinning like he'd made a joke.

"You do know about the blue people of Kentucky, don't you?" I asked.

He hesitated, perhaps trying to decide whether I was pulling his leg. Yuri teases Will all the time, even though it's clear he's not fond of being teased. But Will's beige, belted trench coat is a bullfighter's red cape to Yuri's sense of humor.

"It's for real," I said. "Although I was introduced to them through a book of fiction."

I smiled. "Sorry, your comment made me think about the book—I really enjoyed it." I grabbed a piece of paper off my desk. "Here's some facts about the Green Women that I found online. They are supposedly egalitarian, so we won't know who the movers and shakers are until we talk to a few of them."

"If they are truly egalitarian, won't they all be equal?"

"Aren't you the idealist," I said. "And we don't necessarily have to talk to any of their movers and shakers; we just need to see what we can find out about Rune and maybe get a feel for the group in the process. We may learn something that Tilly's aunt will find useful in dealing with her niece."

On that note, I grabbed a jacket and we headed out. Fortunately, Will had on a fake leather jacket that he probably thought was trendy. I had a feeling the Green Women might be even less charitable than Yuri about a noir detective trench coat.

We took the light rail downtown to avoid traffic and having to pay exorbitant fees for parking. When we got off the train we headed for the escalator to the street above. Inevitably, it was out of order. We trudged up the steep stairs, emerging into the daylight in an area of the city where the homeless outnumbered visitors.

We passed a parking lot with a sign that warned people parking there not to leave valuables in their car. The sign had been vandalized. As had the box where you were supposed to leave your parking fee.

The Green Women's headquarters in Pioneer Square was in an ancient brick building near a park filled with tents belonging to homeless people. Most of the tents looked new, probably donated by some organization. I suspected it was an attempt to make the place look less unattractive to the visitors who frequented the art galleries and restaurants in the historic neighborhood. The tents did give the area a campground flavor, although there were a few structures pieced together with surplus lumber and dilapidated tarps that detracted from the overall effect. And, if the goal had been to help the homeless, the city would have also provided toilets. Local businesses and public buildings tried to keep the homeless out. In the long run, none of it made life better for anyone.

We entered the building with its dimly lit entry and chose the stairs over an elevator that looked old enough to have been original equipment. The Green Women were on the second floor. There was a large poster of a polar bear floating on a tiny ice floe far from shore on the door to their office. The bear was standing upright holding a seal. A penguin clung to his leg. STOP CLIMATE CHANGE was printed in large block letters at the bottom of the poster.

We pushed the door open and stepped into a large room that appeared to be both office and base of operations for the group. The walls were covered with posters depicting climate disasters and animals in distress. A banner strung across the back wall said: "The Green Women—Save our world for future generations!" As I looked around, I also saw pictures of protests—women carrying signs, women challenging politicians, women getting arrested. Another sign said: "Women Unite! Fight for what you believe in!"

There were half a dozen women at a long table near the back of the room. They were focused on several large sheets of chart paper spread out on the table. More chart papers were lying on the floor. I could make out handwritten bulleted lists, in different colors, like brainstorming notes.

As we walked toward them, Will cleared his throat to get their attention. Or maybe he was experiencing post-nasal drip and trying to get rid of the phlegm. Either way, they all looked up from what they were doing.

"Hi," I said. "This is impressive." I gestured at the posters and pictures on the walls. "We've read about your group and are here to learn more about what you've got planned." We had decided in advance that we couldn't reveal our real agenda because that would draw attention to Tilly, and in turn, to her aunt. Clara had shown us a picture of Tilly, so I knew she wasn't one of the women working on the charts. Tilly had curly golden hair, a grown-up version of Shirley Temple. There was no one in the room like that.

"You reporters?" a women with unnaturally red hair asked. It was one of those sculptured haircuts that looked professionally windblown.

"No. We're just citizens interested in what you're doing to fight climate change."

The woman with the red hair nodded to a younger woman with a fresh complexion and wide blue eyes under a clump of blond hair that stood almost upright on the top of her head. The rest of her hair was barely visible, stubble growing back after being shaved.

I glanced at Will. Egalitarian, huh? Not in the strictest sense. The others went back to their work as the young blond woman came out from behind the table. "My name is Lark," she said. "We have a room over there where we can talk." She pointed to a door near the corner of the room. It turned out to be an office with a number of folding chairs propped against the side wall. She sat down behind the desk, looking pleased with herself for being in the power position, while Will and I unfolded chairs for ourselves and placed them across from the desk.

"What would you like to know?" she asked when we were seated.

"Have you been in the group long?" Will asked, easing into the real reason we were there.

"About six months."

"How large is the group?"

"There are about 30 full-time members and quite a few we can call on for rallies."

"The group has quite an impressive local reputation," I said. A little praise can sometimes loosen tongues. Lark beamed but didn't say anything.

We went on to ask about past and current projects, whether she'd participated in any protests where things got heated, and finally managed to steer the conversation around to connections with other groups.

"I understand that some of your members are also associated with the Full Moon Society. I'm curious because the two groups seem so different," Will said.

"Oh, there's no connection," Lark said with conviction. "That group is male dominated. Women, not men, are the curators of nature. There are parallels between the oppression of nature and the oppression of women, you know." She looked at me and not Will as she spoke. The words sounded memorized.

"Men do control most of the large corporations contributing to the pollution of our planet," I agreed.

"You could join us," Lark said. "Or," glancing briefly at Will, she added, "You could make a contribution."

"I'm considering a contribution," I said. "But I admit to being concerned about the rumored links between the Green Women and the Full Moon Society."

"I assure you, there's no connection," Lark said. "None at all."

"Then why do you think people talk as though there is?" Will was trying hard to get some useful information from her.

Lark hesitated. "One of our members has a boyfriend in the group. That's the extent of a connection." Then she rolled her eyes and added, "His name is 'Rune'—can you believe that?" I was tempted to point out that some larks were on the threatened species list, and, given the nature of the group's mission, some might consider that a bit strange too.

"Is that his real name?" Hint, hint. "Is he like one of those celebrities that only has a single name?"

"That's what I've heard him called."

I turned to Will and raised my eyebrows. He shook his head. We weren't getting anywhere. I was about to thank Lark for her time when she glanced at her phone and abruptly stood up.

"I'd better get back."

I still wear a watch and find someone looking at their phone for the time even more annoying than a not-so-subtle peek at a watch. I'm not sure why.

"We appreciate you taking the time to answer our questions," I said as we folded up our chairs and leaned them against the wall.

Lark handed me a card. "If you want to make a donation, you can contact Raven."

"Is she here today?" Will asked.

"She was the woman you spoke with when you first came in. Do you want me to bring her in here?"

I wasn't prepared to make a donation of any size, so I was relieved when Will said, "Not today, but we'll think on it."

As we left, the other women in the room barely looked up. Whatever they were doing it held their full attention. I couldn't think of any way to peel someone off in order to chat with them. Apparently Will couldn't either. We exchanged looks and, by silent agreement, left.

To get to the light rail, we had to make our way past several people asking for handouts. Yuri always gives anyone who asks at least a dollar. Will's approach was different. He denied them eye contact, ignoring them completely. I always try to acknowledge them as individuals even though I don't give anyone on the street money. Each year near Christmas, my kids and I sit down and decide which groups we want to give donations to. My mother and dad always did that with me; it was a tradition I've tried to maintain with my children, even when we barely had enough money to live on after my husband died and left us penniless. I'd thought about divorcing him when the kids were young, but I'd always considered him a good provider. I had no idea that he gambled our money away on bad stock market investments. I only found that out after he had his fatal heart attack.

While waiting for the next light rail train, Will turned to me and said, "Not worth the time, was it?"

"No. But I found it interesting. I think Tilly's aunt is right to be a bit concerned." Then I laughed and said, "You didn't get much eye contact, did you? How did it feel to be both invisible and responsible for the collapse of our world as we know it?"

"I definitely did not feel any love . . . even when Lark answered my questions, she looked at you."

The train pulled up and we got on board. We managed to get two seats together, but we were facing backwards as the train slowly moved out of the tunnel into the open. It always feels disorienting to me to be seeing familiar landmarks rapidly receding instead of moving toward them.

"In retrospect, you probably should have asked Adele or Jenny to go with you," Will said.

"Maybe, but I doubt it would have made a difference. I don't think they care for outsiders, period. Unless they have big bucks to donate to their cause."

"It's too bad they feel that way. I mean, I support advocating for climate change legislation. Although I'm not even tempted to give to that group. That redhead, she was a bit scary, didn't you think?"

"You mean 'Raven.'"

"I wonder if they are all named for birds. I mean, isn't a 'bird' in British slang kind of sexist?"

"I didn't think much about it before now, but Tilly's roommates are Wren Davies and Phoebe Green. Phoebe and Green both, a twofer for her."

"Wonder if Tilly has a secret bird name."

"Maybe they're assigned a name during an initiation. Or after participating in a protest. I can think of all sorts of possibilities. It might be a way to signal their commitment to the cause. Taking flight in a new direction."

"Or winging it," Will said.

"Isn't there some myth about birds flying to the moon? Something to do with migration?"

"Never heard it, but if Lark was telling the truth, there's no link between the two organizations. Except for Tilly and the mysterious Rune."

"Maybe Raven calls herself that because she wants to be thought of as a powerful figure who can transform the world. Like in Northwest Coast Native mythology," I said.

"She seems more like a red headed woodpecker to me. Did you know they will destroy other birds' nest and even puncture duck eggs?"

"Bird trivia?! Now you're sounding like Yuri."

"Ouch. You sure know how to hurt a guy."

CHAPTER 4
MOONBEAMS

WEDNESDAY AND THURSDAY flew by. I didn't learn much more about the Full Moon Society, and Yuri failed to find the lost cat, Penny. I wasn't too worried about not knowing much about the group we would be following on Saturday night; it seemed like a straightforward assignment. We would follow Tilly and the others to the site of the ceremony, watch from afar for any signs of trouble, and return home in the wee hours. Mission accomplished. For Yuri, finding Penny was more problematic.

I took Friday off to take the kids school shopping. The older they get, the more expensive their tastes. Jason doesn't care about clothes in general, but he likes the technology that goes into the always evolving tennis shoe. When I was growing up a sneaker was a sneaker, some colors more appealing to me than others. But in today's market, there's a lot to choose from. Tennis shoes with fancy names and claims compete for consumer attention and dollars. My son had his heart set on a pair that was billed as "futuristic" and ready for "apocalyptic environments." Although he is usually very fact focused and linear, having the right tennis shoe is one topic about which he is completely irrational.

I finally gave in and let him become part of "the brave new world of footwear." But I had to skimp on the rest of his clothing needs to avoid going into debt.

Mara, on the other hand, is picky about every article of clothing she wears. I gave her a budget and let her do her own shopping with a friend that we took with us to the mall. I did, however, warn her that if she purchased anything that didn't pass the "mom test," I would make her take it back. She simply gave me that teenage look that every parent knows far too well and set off with her friend to spend my hard-earned money.

On Saturday I slept in, or tried to, so I would be prepared for our late-night vigil under the full blue moon. No-name managed to open my door and jumped up on my bed to either see if I was okay—or to ruin my morning. When I pushed him away, he barked. Like Lassie trying to get someone's attention. When I finally gave in and got up, he ran to the door, looking back to see if I was following.

"Jason," I yelled. "Your dog needs to go out."

When he didn't answer, I went down the hall and knocked on his door. He still didn't answer, so I turned the knob and peeked in. There he was in front of his computer with his headphones on. Since I'd been awakened by his dog and hadn't had any coffee yet, I was tempted to go over and yank his headphones off. Instead, I counted to three, went over and tapped his shoulder with two fingers, gently, just to get his attention. But he leapt up like I'd shot him. "Mom!" he yelped. "What are you doing?" He pulled off his headphones but left them dangling around his neck.

"I'm letting you know that you need to attend to your dog. That's the deal, right?"

He didn't respond right away. Perhaps he was considering asking if he could do it later, then apparently thought better of it. A smart kid, at times.

While Jason took No-name for his morning constitutional, I staggered into the kitchen to make myself some coffee. Maybe I could take a nap later.

My mother appeared like an apparition out of nowhere, suddenly there beside me while I was waiting for the coffee to brew. "What's up with all of the barking?" she asked. She was dressed for one of her weekend breakfasts with friends. She isn't as flashy as P.W., but she likes clothes and looks good in them. Her nut-brown hair had new blond highlights.

"Love your hair," I said.

"Thanks, but that doesn't answer my question. Is something wrong with the puppy?"

"Jason forgot to take him out, and he was trying to get our attention."

"I guess that beats having him piddle on the carpet."

Mom hadn't been in favor of getting a dog, but after Yuri showed up with him as a gift for Jason and she saw how thrilled her grandson was with him, she had caved. But even though the dog is maturing rapidly, at least physically, she still refers to him as "puppy" or "that dog."

"Don't forget that I'll be gone this evening," I said. "Not sure what time I'll get home."

"That's right—there's going to be a human sacrifice under a full moon. How could I forget?"

"Not funny." I poured my first cup of coffee of the day. It smelled delicious.

"What do you wear to an event like that?"

"Yuri and I will be dressed in black. I don't know what those not hiding in the shadows will be wearing."

Mother shivered. "I feel sorry for that young woman's aunt. But I'm sure you and Yuri will keep her safe." She patted her perfect hair and said, "I'm off." She didn't disappear in a puff of smoke, but she vanished around the corner before I could say goodbye.

I ordered a large pizza for an early dinner. One half with Jason's preferences—pepperoni, sausage and olives. And one-half catering to Mara's vegetarian tastes. Mothers don't have favorites, or if they do, they have to wait until the kids are away to indulge themselves.

Then I took a nap.

Will was watching the small house where Tilly lived in case she left early. We didn't know how far away they would go for the ritual, but there were a fair number of wooded areas near Seattle that we considered good possibilities. We also weren't sure of the timing, although we leaned toward midnight, even though the moon was full at 11:12 pm. Midnight seemed more "magical" than 11:12. Our plan was to follow her to the location, tag teaming with Will to stay undetected. Once we were there, Will would leave and we were on our own.

At 9:00 I got dressed in my Ninja outfit and drove over to pick up Yuri at his condo. Since Yuri has limited driving skills, I avoid having him drive. Especially at night when other drivers may not be able to respond quickly to his unexpected deviations from normal driving.

Like me he was dressed in black, including a black

backpack that I hoped contained some quiet snacks. We were prepared to slink and creep around undetected, a couple of detective panthers on the prowl.

"Guess what?" he said as he got into the passenger seat and put on his seatbelt. "Penny showed up. Her owners are thrilled."

"She showed up on her own?"

Yuri sighed. "I was actually re-canvassing the neighborhood and saw her head toward the house. It was tempting to grab her and pretend like I'd found her."

"But you didn't."

"No. I was afraid to even approach her for fear she'd get spooked. So I called her owners and told them she was on their front porch. Then I waited until they took her inside."

"It was a happy ending."

"It was a waste of time."

"Let's hope tonight is also a waste of time and a happy ending."

We'd anticipated Tilly would leave her home around 10:00, but we'd left early. When we arrived at 9:20, my phone rang. The call from Will ended abruptly when he saw us pull up behind him.

We had made it just in time. There was a car parked near a streetlight in front of the small house where Tilly lived with her two roommates. There were three people waiting in the car, a young man in the drivers' seat and two other men in the back. Tilly came out wearing a dark coat with a long, white dress billowing out from under it. The ethereal fabric swirled around her legs and her curly hair glimmered as she walked toward the parked car out front. She got in on the passenger side and leaned over to kiss the driver. My guess was that the driver was Rune. Rune, the man who was about to drug and sacrifice her in a make-believe ceremony. Not to appease the gods or atone for supposed sins, but to entertain a group of people seeking a bit of excitement.

We gave them a small head start before pulling out. Will was right behind us.

There are a lot of nature preserves and parks near Seattle. We anticipated the group would choose one of them for their ceremony. Although they were closed to the public at night, we didn't think that a chain across an entrance was going to be a deterrent for the Full Moon Society. Most people think that violating park regulations isn't a serious offense. They are apparently unaware that criminal trespass can involve a hefty fine and even jail time. Especially if alcohol or drugs are involved. But, unless the Society participants called attention to themselves by making a lot of noise, it was doubtful anyone would complain.

When we'd researched the possibilities, we had identified the most likely locations, so we weren't surprised when they ended up at a 3000-acre park tucked in an area known as the Issaquah Alps. It was only a stone's throw from a residential community, but there was easy access to the many cultivated trails that meandered through the park's heavily treed hills and valleys. It would be easy to find a private spot and stay out of sight. The hard part for us would be following Tilly and friends while avoiding Full Moon Society stragglers who knew where the ceremony was taking place.

I parked a few hundred yards down the hill from the main entrance to the park's large parking lot. Will kept on driving past us. He was no longer on duty.

"I've done some hiking here," Yuri said as we headed up the hill. "But I don't remember seeing any large, open areas close to the road for holding this ceremony."

"When I was here with the kids last summer, I remember a clearing with an apple tree in it. It was on a side trail to the right, not too far into the park. Next to a creek if I remember correctly."

"Did the clearing come with a large rock appropriate for human sacrifice?"

"There are some large rocks here and there in the park, but they don't need a clearing with a big rock for the ceremony. All they need is a clearing and a platform."

"I don't know, I think they need a rock for authenticity."

"What about one of those Styrofoam boulders that landscapers use? Or maybe they'll cover a platform with expandable foam spray and make it look like a rock. Not authentic, but by the light of the moon it may look real enough."

"They should hire you for their next reenactment."

It was a dark night, except for the light from the moon. Very few stars, and no streetlights. From where we'd parked, we couldn't see the park entrance. There were a few flashes of light, but that was it.

"Maybe we should have brought your dog. In case we lose them," Yuri said.

"He's so well trained; I'm sure he would have been a big help." We've been meaning to send No-name to dog training school, but we've been as slow to do that as we have to agree on a name for him. Instead, we've let him run wild, dragging around his stuffed animals. He'd recently destroyed an orange pangolin, proving just how endangered they were. Now he was working on demolishing his second ring-tailed lemur, minus the tail that had only lasted a day.

As we crested the hill we saw Tilly and her companions maneuver around the posts that held the chain across the road to the parking lot. Two of them had flashlights.

"Glad they have flashlights," Yuri whispered in his library voice. "That will make it easier for us."

"Unless they leave the main trails and go off into the brush. Without using our own flashlights, I'm not sure how we'd manage that," I whispered back.

"Hey, no one said this was going to be easy."

"But I always hope." Somehow, when we'd talked about it earlier, a walk in the woods at night had seemed more like a lark than an ominous encounter with nature. Now, actually being there, trees that were so approachable during the day cast menacing silhouettes across our path. To the right, the woods was a black, impenetrable wall. Once we reached the trail, there would only be the occasional strand of moonbeam to use as a guide and to tease out whatever lurked in the shadows.

Behind us a couple more cars pulled up. "Maybe we should wait until everyone passes by, follow at the end instead of trying to stay close to Tilly," Yuri said softly.

"What if we lose her?"

"You honestly think there will be someone other than these whackos tramping around in the woods at this hour?"

"But what if the latecomers don't know where they're going? What if they get lost? Let's stay with her. We can slip into the woods if they start to overtake us."

"Okay. But be prepared to move quickly if we have to make an exit."

We sidestepped past the chain and started up the main trail, following the flickering lights of those ahead. I kept stumbling over roots and rocks, suppressing the swear words that struggled to get out. Several times I heard a mumbled curse from Yuri who was undoubtedly experiencing the same difficulty walking on a forest path with only shafts of moonlight to show the way.

The trail veered slightly to the left and started up an incline. Nothing too steep, but I started to worry about how far and how much uphill there was going to be. I wasn't in the best of shape for a real hike.

Then the lights ahead suddenly disappeared. Darkness enveloped us. Yuri reached out and grabbed my arm. We paused, listening hard. Voices from behind seemed to be gaining on us. "Off the trail," he hissed.

I put the thought that he sounded like Gollum out of my mind and pushed through some thick underbrush that wrapped around my ankles and grabbed my clothes. We almost collided with a couple of evergreens, barely managing to get far enough away from the trail by the time the newcomers drew even with us. Their lights bounced along the trail we had just left.

Someone scanned the woods with their flashlight, illuminating the area around us. For a heart-stopping moment I thought our evening of surveillance was going to end before it began. But the group continued on their way without anyone yelling for us to come out and show ourselves.

Then their lights disappeared.

But this time we were able to determine that they had taken a sharp right turn off the main trail. All we had to do was untangle ourselves and hurry to catch up.

We both stumbled at the turn-off because we weren't expecting such a steep descent. Even if this was the trail I remembered from the trip with my kids, everything felt different in the dark. After about twenty feet the trail leveled off. I could hear the whoosh of water cascading across rocks. It was definitely the trail I pictured from last summer.

"Be careful," I whispered to Yuri. "I think there's a drop-off on the creek side."

Yuri risked a brief look with his flashlight and verified that one misplaced step and we could end up tumbling down a short embankment into the creek. In which case, we'd either attract attention to ourselves or, if no one heard the splash, we'd end up spending our surveillance in cold, wet clothes. Neither option was appealing, so we took each step with care and managed to stay on the curving path.

As the woods thinned, more moonlight found its way through the trees. In the distance we could make out what appeared to be a clearing. As we drew nearer, the meadow became more and more visible. Toward the back of the clearing there was a circle of lit torches illuminating a large, mostly flat-topped rock. The flames from the torches flickered in the light breeze, sending sparks upwards and forming eerie dark shapes that danced on the ground.

I couldn't help thinking that it was a great place for the ceremony they'd planned. Right down to the perfect rock for the sacrifice. Someone had done their homework.

There were about twenty people gathered behind the torches. Some were smoking what smelled suspiciously like marijuana, the aroma of burnt rhubarb tickled my nose. Tilly in her white dress and the man I thought might be

Rune were standing to one side of the rock. The man was wearing some sort of costume, a mishmash of what could have been Aztek or Mayan or just something he found in the thrift shop that looked old and a bit exotic. Leather leggings peeked out from under a long cape and several long strands of chains with large beads dangled from his neck. A wide, gold bracelet caught the moonlight as he gestured.

We heard voices from more people coming up the trail, so we hurried past the gathering to a clump of trees just beyond the clearing. There wasn't much cover in the area; we wouldn't be able to move around much. Fortunately, we had a good view of the rock from our hiding place.

"Wonder what time it is?" I whispered to Yuri.

"I'm going to look." He pulled out his phone, turned away from the meadow and hunched over. I saw a flash of light out of the corner of my eye. Yuri quickly turned it off. "Eleven forty-five," he said.

Suddenly the group started moving around, and for an instant I thought we'd been spotted. But they were simply staging the event. Someone positioned candles on one end of the rock. Another person placed a floral crown on Tilly's head. A man wearing a long tunic with fur trim and some sort of feather headdress was standing nearby holding what looked like a large wooden cup. Next to him was another man wearing a mask and some sort of animal crest headdress. He had a small drum hanging from a strap around his neck and was thumping it with random strokes. Da-dum. Da-da-dum. Dum-da-dum.

Several men and women in hodge-podge costumes came forward and began chanting. I couldn't make out the words. Whatever they were saying wasn't very coordinated. Some were shaking rattles in time with the chants. One of the men had what looked like a ceremonial spear with feathers hanging from it; another had a bow, but I didn't see any arrows. A few of the women were carrying what looked like medieval slings and some held strange looking clubs. I wasn't sure women were even allowed to participate in most ancient ceremonies, let alone possess weapons. Although I did remember reading about Aztec and Mayan women warriors, so who knew? Besides, this was obviously a hybrid ritual with its own accoutrements and rules.

The rest of the participants stayed back, just outside the circle of torches. Some were definitely smoking weed. And there were flasks being passed around. Probably not ancient hallucinogens, but in keeping with the scant knowledge I had about what went on during sacrificial rituals.

The drumming became more insistent, and the chanting grew more intense and unified. It sounded like some eerie version of scat. Vocalizations without meaning but with a heavy beat. Then, the inner circle stepped back a few feet, stopping in front of the torches, and everyone fell silent. The man with the large wooden cup stepped over to Tilly and offered it to her. I may have imagined her hesitation, but she took the cup in two hands and drank from it. I found myself holding my breath, praying that we hadn't just made a mistake by not stepping in.

Then several men helped Tilly up on the rock, and she lay back, hands folded across her stomach. The chanting resumed as the inner circle of costumed men and women began dancing around the rock. The entire scene was like something out of a movie, a primitive group of people warding off an unknown evil by offering up a young, innocent woman to the gods. I had to admit it was nicely choreographed. I wondered if this was something they did on a regular basis or whether tonight was a first. Maybe the rock was Styrofoam, something they used for various ceremonies.

I kept staring at Tilly's chest, hoping to see it moving up and down so I'd know whether she was still breathing, but we were too far away. Then, suddenly a man jumped up onto the rock and raised his hands in the air, a dagger in one and the wooden cup in the other, yelling something I didn't understand. I was fairly certain it was the same man who had been standing next to Tilly earlier; the cape looked right. But he was also wearing some sort of headdress with pieces of fur dangling over his face. Yuri leaned forward as if poised to pounce.

When the man leapt off the rock, Yuri and I both let out a sigh.

Then the chanting stopped and four men came forward carrying a litter with gold tassels hanging from it. The four men were wearing jeans and long-sleeved black T-shirts and feathered headdresses. A bizarre combination of the modern and some imagined ancient society. Tilly's limp body was lifted off the rock and placed on the litter. I was still unable to see whether she was breathing or not and was wishing we had a better plan.

As they carried her back toward the main trail, everyone fell into step behind the litter, some carrying torches to light the way, as they softly hummed something that sounded like a cross between the Volga Boatman and Old Man River.

When they turned down the trail in our direction, we slipped down and to the side of the trees we were hiding behind, hopefully not visible to anyone looking our way. We had expected them to head back to their cars. Instead, they were going further into the park.

We trailed along behind, hoping no one turned around. I knew Yuri always carried a gun when we were on a field assignment, but there were too many of them to make that feel at all comforting. Even if the weapons they carried didn't look that functional.

I thought I heard a coyote and put that on my list of things to worry about.

The ground became uneven as they left the main trail and followed a narrow path that wound up a hillside. I wondered how the four men carrying Tilly were faring. But then, they at least had flashlights to guide them. And torches. What had happened to the candles? Hopefully someone had extinguished them.

Near the top of the hill, everyone stopped. Their torches lit up the area as they clustered together in a haphazard semi-circle around . . . the entrance to a cave.

CHAPTER 5
THE KILLING MOON

THE FOUR MEN carrying the litter had gone into the cave. Everyone else waited outside, holding their torches and continuing to chant something unintelligible, the sing-song droning slowly becoming more and more disjointed now that the drumming had ceased. I didn't know how long it was before the four men came out, but it felt like forever. They quickly blended into the crowd as two or three others went into the cave.

After a few minutes, I thought I saw two people come out and then two more go in. This pattern repeated itself over and over. My guess was that the cave was small; they had to bend slightly to go inside.

I lost track of how many went in and came out. Since they were all gathered around the entrance, it was difficult to see what was happening. Then, suddenly, everyone whooped, tore off headdresses and stamped their feet. I assumed that meant the ceremony was over, especially since at that point they started back down the trail, chatting boisterously, like people after a sports event where their team had won.

Yuri turned toward me and raised his eyebrows? "Did you see Tilly leave?" He mouthed the words.

"No." I whispered back, feeling a tickle of panic. Where was Tilly? Had someone stayed behind with her in the cave while the drugs they had given her wore off? We should have counted participants and kept better track of how many went in and came out.

They group was barely out of sight when Yuri said, "Come on!" and headed for the cave entrance. I got out my flashlight and hurried after him. What if there were still Full Moon Society members in there? I didn't remember seeing the man I thought was Rune hanging around. But then, the group had been facing away from us, and I hadn't been looking for him either.

I heard Yuri say "Oh my god" seconds before I saw the figure in the white dress lying on the litter on the cave floor. We both rushed over, our flashlights zeroing in on . . . the mannequin head with a poorly fitted blond wig. I quickly flashed my light around. There was no one else there. And no sign of any other way to get out of the tunnel except the way we'd come in. It was just us and the prop on the litter.

"What the . . .?" Yuri said.

"Do you think she changed clothes in here and left with the others? But if she was drugged as she appeared to be . . .?"

"It doesn't make sense." Yuri took his phone out and took a couple of quick pictures. "Okay, let's go after them."

We headed off down the trail, using our flashlights in order to go faster. At this point the goal was to find Tilly, even if we exposed our presence in the process.

When we reached the meadow where the ceremony had taken place, I glanced at the rock to see if the candles were still there. If no one had thought to put them out, they posed a fire hazard. I felt a flicker of relief when I didn't see any burning candles, but by the light of the moon I could make out something else on the rock, something that looked very much . . . like a body.

"Yuri, stop," I commanded loudly. He turned back as I sped over to the rock.

As I drew nearer, I could see a dagger sticking up out of what I was hoping was another mannequin.

But it wasn't. Nor, thankfully, was it Tilly.

Yuri came up next to me and shined his flashlight on the victim's face. The man was staring at the full moon as it looked back at him. Blood was oozing out of his chest and sliding down the side of the rock. Even while I was feeling appalled at the sight of the dead man, I was registering the fact that it was indeed a fake rock. The mind is a strange thing.

"I'm pretty sure it's the man who jumped up on the rock when Tilly was lying there," I said. "You don't think it's Rune, do you?"

Yuri pressed two fingers against his neck and shook his head. "I don't know, but whoever it is, he's dead."

I dialed 911 as we raced toward the main road in an effort to stop the ceremonial participants from leaving. And to find out what had happened to Tilly.

We arrived minutes too late. The last car was just starting up the hill. We tried to wave at them, but they either didn't see us or were ignoring our frantic attempts to hail them.

While I explained to the police that we had discovered a dead body in the park, Yuri was on the phone calling

P.W. I imagined she wasn't going to be pleased with either the timing or the reason for our call.

Nor was the officer I spoke to.

"Yes, I know the park is closed at night," I said.

"No, I don't know who the deceased is." I almost added "for sure," then decided it was better to hold back my guess for a while.

"But I do know what he was doing here and who he was with," I added.

"Well, no, I can't give you any names."

"Don't misunderstand me, I would be happy to give you names, but I don't know who they were."

"I know I said I knew who he was with, but only the name of the group, the Full Moon Society, not the names of individuals."

"I'm a private investigator. We were keeping an eye on a young woman for a client."

"No, none of the participants are still here."

"We weren't able to catch up with them in time to keep them from leaving."

"Yes, we'll wait here until you arrive."

Yuri was staring at me as I finished the call. "This is going to be hard to explain, isn't it?"

"Apparently. What did P.W. say?"

"Just to tell the truth and keep her informed."

"Well, it isn't as if we had anything to do with the murder," I said.

"I don't think that will keep us from spending the rest of the night at police headquarters."

I thought about that. Should I call my mother? Nah, I decided. She wouldn't be waiting up for me like when I was a teenager out on a date. I could call after I had a better idea of how long it would take with the police.

"Caves have been used since the Paleolithic for burials," Yuri said.

Before he could continue, I interrupted: "This is NOT the time for trivia." I was always amazed that he could spout facts like that on the spur of the moment. The few times I'd checked, he'd been right on. Then it hit me. "There's no chance . . .," I began. "No, I mean, no . . . not possible."

"Are you having a conversation with yourself?"

"Did you look at the ground in the cave?" I asked, the image of the cave as a burial site overpowering my imagination.

"You can relax. I did look at the ground. The earth looked packed down; there was no sign of any digging."

"So it did cross your mind?"

Yuri shrugged. "What can I say, worst case scenarios are my specialty. That's what reminded me about Paleolithic burials."

"If taking her to the cave was part of the re-enactment, I wonder what they did in there? And how did she leave without us seeing her?"

"We were both looking for the white dress. Obviously, she must have left with the others, but in different clothes."

"You think she left under her own steam?"

"The drug must have worn off fast," Yuri said. "Or else she was acting and not drugged."

We paced back and forth, lost in speculation. Then Yuri said, "In medieval times blue was the color of purity, not white."

"Yuri—" I warned.

"Just thinking about the ceremony tonight. They weren't too concerned with accuracy."

"I know. Even the rock was fake."

"Really? I'm disappointed about that. It was a nice touch though."

Ignoring his comment, I said, "It seems to me that whoever stabbed the man on the rock had to have done so before the cave ritual. I think we would have noticed someone sneaking off."

"Maybe our dead man stayed behind to put out the candles and collect whatever else was left behind. The killer could have anticipated that and hung back too. Probably knocked him out first. Even if he was forced at gunpoint to get up on the rock, I can't imagine him waiting quietly while someone plunged a dagger into his heart."

"It must have happened quickly. Otherwise, how did they manage all that without anyone—us included—seeing it happen?"

"We were pretty focused on Tilly . . . until we weren't." Yuri sounded bitter. "I don't think we are going to come out of this looking all that good."

I was to remember his prescient words often over the next few days.

CHAPTER 6
MOONWALK

TWO POLICE CARS came roaring down the hill, sirens screaming. We stepped out on the road and waved, then quickly jumped back out of the way. The two cars skidded onto the shoulder with flourish, like skiers angling their skis to stop after a downhill run. A tall, lean man with a narrow face got out of the first car and came over to us. "You Chandler and Webster?" We nodded.

"I take it you found a body but don't know who it is."

"Correct." We had decided it was better to let the police tell us who the victim was. In case we were wrong. We had enough strikes against us already.

"And you were out here, why?"

"We were following a young woman," Yuri said, leaving unstated that our purpose had been to keep her safe. And that we had watched her being drugged and then lost sight of her.

Three other officers joined us. They didn't introduce themselves. In the dim light I couldn't quite make out the first initial and last names on their uniforms. They seemed anxious to get on with it, so I didn't bother asking for identification.

"Okay," the first officer said. "Why don't you show us what you found." He sounded like he almost didn't believe there would actually be a body in the woods. Did they get false alarms about murders?

We headed off in the lead. They followed, the light from their flashlights bobbing around our feet, like a spotlight on a dancer's shoes. It made me want to walk faster to escape the circle of attention.

When we arrived at the clearing, I was almost relieved to see the body. For a moment I had been worried it would have vanished, like Tilly. But the costumed man was still stretched out on the large fake rock with an ornate dagger in his chest, the eerie, primal scene captured by the yellow-gray light of the full moon. In a movie, this was the point where there would have been the howl of a wolf in the distance or a shadow moving across the pock-marked lunar surface.

The three officers hesitated briefly, perhaps startled by the surreal image, before rushing past us. Yuri and I watched as they checked out the body. The lead officer's voice echoed loudly in the clearing as he called it in on his phone. I didn't recognize the code, but I had no doubt about the message.

"Hey, there's a dead animal over here," one of the officers called out from the edge of the clearing. "Looks like a dog."

The lead officer suddenly seemed to realize that they might be contaminating the scene and motioned for everyone to back off. He ordered two officers to stay behind while the rest of us returned to the road to wait for the homicide specialists to arrive.

The lead officer, who had still not identified himself by name, told us that we would need to go downtown to make statements. Since it was about a forty-minute drive, he asked for ID and took down our information before agreeing to let us drive there on our own. I assumed that meant we were not suspects.

As we headed back to Seattle, Yuri turned to me and asked, "What do you think? Should we call Clara?"

"I told her we would only call if there was a problem."

"I think a dead body and Tilly disappearing qualifies as a problem."

"Call PW again first."

Yuri called PW and put her on speaker. She signed off on us calling Clara. She also said she'd alert our lawyer to stand by. "Why?" I asked. "I mean, we didn't perform our duties with stellar competence, but we didn't commit any crimes."

"As soon as this gets out, the press is going to be all over it. I can picture the headlines . . ." Her voice trailed off, leaving the picture for us to fill in on our own.

"Got it," I said. "We were supposed to keep things safe and instead theatre became reality."

"No one should blame you for what happened."

"Should being the operative word," Yuri said.

"Just tell the truth and stick to the facts." She paused, then added: "In the end, the most unpleasant truth is a safer companion than a pleasant falsehood."

"That's according to . . .?" Yuri prompted.

"Theodore Roosevelt. A wise man. Call me if you need any more inspirational quotations." With that she ended the call.

Yuri smiled. "We can't be in too much trouble if PW is peppering us with quotations."

"It feels to me like a moonwalk," I said. "No matter what it looks like, we're moving backwards. Now call Clara while I concentrate on my driving."

Clara was understandably upset and said she would get back to us after trying to get in touch with Tilly. Yuri asked for Tilly's phone number, not mentioning the fact that we would most likely have to give both Clara's and Tilly's names and numbers to the police.

She called back just minutes later. "There's no answer on her cell; it goes to voicemail. I left a message for her to call me the instant she gets my message."

"Do you have numbers for her roommates?"

"No, I don't. Tilly said they didn't share contacts. Something strange like that."

"Okay," Yuri said. "As soon as we give our statements, the police will probably send someone over to check on Tilly. Maybe she turned her cell off for the ceremony."

"But wouldn't she turn it back on? And shouldn't she be home by now?" Clara couldn't keep the panic out of her voice.

"Not necessarily. The group may have gone somewhere together to debrief. I wouldn't be concerned yet." The word "yet" hung in the air like a bad smell.

After we ended the call, I asked Yuri if he really thought the party continued after they left the park.

"I bet it did for some of them. But as a group? I have my doubts. But that doesn't mean she didn't go off with her boyfriend."

"Unless he was the one on the rock."

When we arrived at the police station, we were shown to a dingy lobby and told to wait. So that's what we did. We waited and waited, taking turns asking the officer at the main desk about what was happening. Each time he assured us someone would soon come to take our statements. His idea of "soon" apparently came from a different dictionary than ours.

Finally, after two cups of bad vending machine coffee and as many trips to the restroom, we were waved inside and separated. A female officer motioned for me to follow her, and a male officer indicated Yuri should go with him. It felt like they anticipated a strip search.

"Sorry we had to keep you waiting for so long," Officer G. O'Dell said. "We've been waiting on a report from the scene."

"Cause of death?" I asked, trying not to sound irritable. What kind of information could they possibly have been waiting on in order to take our statements?

"I can't share any details with you, I'm afraid."

"I understand." Could I help it if my words and tone didn't match? I'd been up most of the night and was starting to feel cranky. And the fact that the vending machine coffee was sending acidic shock waves throughout my body didn't help.

Once in the tiny room with its small, metal table and two chairs, she asked if I wanted anything to eat or drink before we began. I was tempted to complain about their coffee but went for polite instead and simply declined her offer. Yuri had eaten two bags of Cheetos and a Payday from the vending machine in their lobby. Usually I can't resist Cheetos, but I was more tired than hungry.

"Now then," she began, placing a fresh notepad on the table and removing a Bic pen from her shirt pocket. "Let's start from the beginning."

The problem with starting from the beginning was that there were so many "beginnings." Did it begin when I took the job with Penny-wise? When I ran into Clara Ramsey in the mall? Or when P.W. assigned us to protect Tilly? Or, most recently, when we attended the Full Moon Society ceremony? Since I wanted to get out of there as quickly as possible, I decided to start with this evening's "beginning."

She took notes and only interrupted twice. Once to verify that I didn't see Tilly come out of the cave and once to verify that I didn't know the victim. I was glad she had asked if I "knew his name" rather than if I had any idea who he was. That made it easier to deny.

Then it was over. She smiled, thanked me and said, "That's it." Kind of like the end of a Looney Tune cartoon: "That's all folks."

"I have one question," I said. "Do you know if Tilly Jamison has been located yet?"

"I'm afraid . . ."

"I don't see how telling me whether she's been found is any kind of secret," I interrupted. "I just want to know if she's safe."

Officer O'Dell frowned. Wavered. Then said, "Wait here."

She didn't make me wait long, only a few minutes. "Sorry, but Tilly Jamison is not at home and not answering her phone. But we are looking for her."

I stood. "Thank you. I wish your answer had been different, but I appreciate knowing."

Yuri was waiting for me in the lobby. He looked as tired as I felt.

"Your mother called me," he said.

"Great. I had my ringtone off. I probably should have called her, but I didn't want to wake her up."

"I gave her a brief update and told her you would be home soon."

"Like in time to get up and go to work?"

"Tomorrow's Sunday. We don't have to work on Sunday . . . do we?"

"Actually, I'm not sure how much sleeping I can do while Tilly is still missing."

"Me neither. But I do need some shuteye or I'll be worthless."

We swapped stories about our police interviews on the trip to Yuri's and decided we would touch base tomorrow on next steps. Then I drove home, playing loud music to keep myself from falling asleep at the wheel. Mom wasn't waiting for me downstairs. She had apparently been reassured enough by what Yuri told her to have returned to her own upstairs apartment. Not even No-name cared about my return.

I went straight into my bedroom and managed to take off my shoes and my jacket before crawling into bed. The last thing I remember was asking myself, where the hell was Tilly Jamison?

CHAPTER 7
CLAIR DE LUNE

THERE WAS A KNOCKING sound coming from somewhere. It got louder and louder before I finally realized someone was respecting my privacy rather than barging in. Or else I had locked my bedroom door.

"Who is it?" I yelled. I almost added "go away."

No-name barked at the same time Jason said something, so I had to ask, "What did you say?" In spite of trying to hold onto the pleasant dream I'd been having, I felt myself coming awake.

"Grandma wants to know if you're joining us for breakfast," Jason yelled through the door.

My stomach gurgled a hunger message. "Tell her I'll be there shortly." As I pushed back the covers, I realized I was still wearing my cat-burglar outfit. No time for a shower if I wanted to get in on Sunday waffles . . . or pancakes . . . or an omelet and biscuits. They all sounded good.

I quickly changed clothes and joined my family just as Mom was putting out the oatmeal. "There are raisins, blueberries and a granola topping," she said. Although I was slightly disappointed with the heathy fare instead of the splurge I'd been imagining, it did look good.

"You look beat," Mara announced. "What time did you get home?"

I sighed dramatically. "I imagine I'll be asking you that question in a few years."

"No," Jason said. "You won't have to ask because you will have a tracker on her phone, and you will be waiting up for her."

"Not funny," Mara said. "She'll probably chip you."

Jason made a face and tightened his lips while I sensed his mind searched for a stinging comeback.

"Drop it, you two," I warned as I spooned all three toppings on my oatmeal.

Jason sent Mara a "you just wait" glare and turned to his oatmeal. "Where's the sugar?" he asked.

"No sugar," Mara said. "It isn't good for you."

I could tell from the way his lips twitched that Jason realized he now needed two comeback remarks instead of one. It reminded me of a cartoon strip in which Charlie Brown claimed that he always knew the perfect thing to say . . . but by the time he thought of it the next day it was too late.

"Have some more granola," I said. "It has sugar in it."

"No, it doesn't," Mara retorted. "Grandma makes it without sugar."

Hmmm. That explained why it was never sweet enough for me.

Mom sat down with her oatmeal, turned to me and asked, "So, what time did you get home?"

I involuntarily yawned before saying, "Not that long ago." Mara and Jason looked surprised. Because I was being honest? Or because I'd stayed out almost all night?

"What happened?" Mara asked.

Although I hadn't thought about what I was going to tell them, I knew there was no way I would be able to keep them from finding out the lurid details eventually. As soon as the news leaked, the press would be all over it. Actually, I was somewhat surprised my news junky son hadn't already heard about the body on the rock.

"Well," I said, pausing to take a bite of oatmeal. "It will be on TV news soon."

Jason stopped stirring heaping teaspoons of granola into his oatmeal and gave me his full attention. Mara and Mom were also waiting for me to tell all. I put down my spoon and quickly gave them a high-level overview, including the fact that Tilly had gone missing, ending with how long we'd had to wait around to give our statements. Then I picked my spoon up again and returned to my breakfast.

"Was it a ritual sacrifice?" Jason asked, sounding more like a member of the Adam's Family than my beloved son.

"I doubt it," I replied with my mouth full. "It happened after the ceremony."

"Have they identified the victim?" Mom asked.

I swallowed and looked at the clock. It was almost 11:00. "There's a good chance they have by now, or they will by sometime today." I took another bite. "Yuri and I think it may have been Tilly's boyfriend, but we don't know for sure."

"What about Tilly?" Mara asked. "Are you going to look for her today?"

At that moment my cell started playing Clair de Lune, my latest ringtone. It was supposed to be soothing rather than jarring. It was, so much so that sometimes I failed to recognize that it was my phone ringing. And it seemed like an ironic twist given what had happened last night.

"I just checked with someone I know at police headquarters . . .," Yuri said without preliminary small talk or even a "hello."

"Female?" I chided.

"A female resource, yes. Who told me the police still haven't located Tilly. So, I called P.W. who called Clara— and she hasn't heard from her either. I say we make a trip to her place and talk to the roommates and maybe have a look around. Want me to come by and pick you up?"

"Sure," I said in a moment of weakness. I had to occasionally let him drive, and a Sunday excursion on residential streets seemed reasonably safe. And it would give me a chance to finish breakfast. But not enough time to shower. Sometimes you have to prioritize.

I quickly informed the family what was happening and took my oatmeal to my room so I could finish it without having to answer any more questions. It was too bad I didn't have some sugar hidden away in my closet next to the Frans almond gold bar I was saving for a time of need.

Yuri pulled up in his 2019 Honda Accord just as I took the last bite of oatmeal. He seemed to have a different car every year. None of them new. And although he claimed to have never been in an accident, each of his vehicles had battle scars of one sort or another. His current car had multiple scrapes on the passenger door that looked like it had been attacked by a lion. Worst of all, the car was metallic gray—camouflaged in rain and on overcast days, most likely looming erratically out of nowhere at unsuspecting drivers.

As I walked out to his car, I noted that it was parked slightly crooked, one wheel on the curb. I got in, adjusted my seatbelt and said a silent prayer to Hermes, the patron god of travel, according to one of Yuri's trivia rants. Yuri pulled out without looking to see if there were any cars coming, the car bouncing slightly as it came off the curb.

"I'm really concerned about Tilly," he said. "She must have known her aunt would be worried."

"There may be a good explanation."

"Like, 'dazed from being drugged, I staggered off into the woods and passed out'?"

"You think we should be searching the woods for her?" I hadn't thought of that.

"No, I don't really think she could have done that without someone noticing. I think it's more likely she went home with someone. Probably Rune, if he wasn't the victim."

"Pretty inconsiderate of her not to answer her phone though. And that's not how Clara described her."

"I know. That's why I'm concerned."

The tiny one-story house where Tilly lived with two other Green Women was in a row of tiny one-story houses that had probably been built in the 50s. Most were painted white and had compact porches next to one-car garages. It was amazing to me that a neighborhood like this so close to the city had survived gentrification.

Yuri pulled into their narrow driveway, miraculously not hitting the low fence that enclosed the front yard. I saw someone peek out the window as we made our way through the open gate to the front door. Yuri couldn't resist using the brass knocker shaped like a hand to announce our arrival. The three taps didn't sound like much. Still, moments later, a young woman opened the door.

My first thought was that her hair was an unfortunate "blah" color, the personification of "dishwater blond." The other cliché that described her was "full-figured." Her thighs bulged below her hips, and she had what would never be described kindly as "love handles" clearly visible through her T-shirt. But she had a pleasant face, and she had opened the door wide.

"Hi," Yuri said. "We're friends with Clara, Tilly's aunt. Clara is worried because she hasn't been able to get in touch with Tilly, and we were wondering if she has come home yet."

"No, she isn't here." She abruptly started to close the door, as if we had said we were peddling magazines instead of inquiring about her roommate.

Yuri took a quick step forward and put out one hand to block the closing door. "We've been asked by her Aunt Clara to find her. Would you mind if we asked you a few questions?" He had on his charming face and manner, but she seemed immune. Although she didn't slam the door shut on his hand.

Another young woman appeared next to her. This one was all angles and drama. Her dark, long hair was perfectly straight and shiny, like she had just stepped out of a beauty parlor. In contrast to her professional hair, she was wearing worn jeans and a faded, navy-blue sweatshirt. "We aren't Tilly's keepers, just her roommates," she said as she nudged the other woman aside so she could close the door.

"Wait," I said. "We think Tilly may be in trouble. You might be able to help."

The two women turned away from us and whispered back and forth. I couldn't make out what was said, but when the dark-haired woman stomped off and the other woman held the door open for us, I knew who had won the argument.

"Thank you," I said. Yuri and I followed her down a short hallway into a small living room with an overstuffed gray couch, an overstuffed chair in worn red material, and a beige lounge chair with matching ottoman. Two walls were lined with bookshelves filled with books. Some of the books were on end with their spines facing out, but most were simply stacked in piles.

"I'm Phoebe," the blond said as she took a seat on the couch and pointed us to the two chairs. The other woman was standing behind the couch, like she wasn't going to participate but intended to make sure nothing happened that she didn't approve.

"I'm Cameron Chandler, and this is my colleague, Yuri Webster." I was going to explain more, but Phoebe interrupted.

"You're the two detectives, aren't you?"

"If you're asking whether we were at the ceremony, yes."

"Not much of a recommendation," the second woman said. "From what I read in the paper."

"You must be Wren Davies," Yuri said, changing the subject. "Clara Ramsey gave us your names and address. She's understandably worried about her niece."

"I'm afraid there's not much we can tell you," Phoebe said. "We consider ourselves 'independent entities.' We live together, but we don't have to answer to each other for our actions."

"Even so, I would imagine you talk to each other. For instance, it would be helpful to know the name of Tilly's boyfriend."

The two women exchanged looks. Wren said, "If you are referring to the leader of the Full Moon Society, he isn't exactly her boyfriend."

Phoebe was looking at the floor.

"What is this leader's name?" I asked, skirting the boyfriend issue.

"Rune," Phoebe said. "Rune Rundell."

"You don't happen to have a picture of him, do you?" Yuri asked.

Phoebe hesitated, avoiding making eye contact with Wren. "There's one in Tilly's room. I'll get it for you."

Wren didn't say anything but her displeasure radiated outward like circles from a rock tossed in the water. "He won't know where she is," she declared with confidence.

"Her aunt thought she might have stayed with him last night."

"Ha. That's unlikely."

"Why?"

"They weren't getting along."

"Oh." That was news. "If she didn't come here and wasn't with him, any idea where she might have gone?"

"Maybe she hooked up with one of the other Full Mooners."

Phoebe came back with a framed picture that she handed to me. I took one look and handed it to Yuri. It was a picture of two very handsome young people. Tilly with her full head of curls looking up at a young man who had his arm around her but was looking straight at the camera.

There was a dog sitting next to his feet, looking up at him as if he'd been ordered to "sit." I remembered an officer saying there was a dead dog at the murder site—could it have been Rune's? Had he been with them the night of the full moon ceremony? Yuri stood up and handed the picture back to Phoebe.

"Thanks for your time," he said. "Cameron? Any more questions?"

"No, thanks."

Phoebe walked us to the door. As we stepped outside, she said softly, "I hope you find Tilly."

We still didn't know where to look, but one thing we knew for certain: she hadn't spent the night with her boyfriend. And not for the reason Wren mentioned.

A line from a poem titled Low Tide by Edna St Vincent Millay came to mind: No place to dream, but a place to die. Rune Rundell was definitely the young man on the rock with the dagger through his heart.

CHAPTER 8
RUNE UNDER THE MOON

BY MONDAY MORNING the story had made it to the main local paper and all three local TV stations. The headline in the paper said "Human Sacrifice Under a Full Moon." Each of the three television stations had their own version of how an ancient ceremony ended in a violent death, with emphasis on the bizarre nature of the setting and the costumed participants. There was also mention of two detectives who were there to allegedly ensure the safety of participants. That wasn't actually what we had been tasked to do, but the accusation still stung. Fortunately, they didn't yet have our names. They did, however, have the victim's name. One of the local tabloids ran the headline: "Rune Under the Moon" with what looked like a stock photo of a full moon shining down on a dagger wielding figure spooking around in some trees. It's amazing what you can find online.

My son liked the sound of the headline and kept repeating "Rune under the Moon" between bites of toast at breakfast until Mara turned up some obnoxious music on her phone to drown him out, and I had to ask both of them to please finish their breakfasts in silence. Mom took that opportunity to pop in, noted that no one was talking, and immediately asked, "What's wrong?"

Both children started defending their actions at the same time. Mom held up a hand and said, "One at a time, please."

I grabbed my coffee and a partially eaten piece of toast and warned, "You'll regret that." Then I exited stage left, leaving my mother to sort out the sibling tiff that would just pop up again in some other form at another time. Like whack-a-mole.

Yuri, Will and I were in P.W.'s office debriefing with her when Clara called. P.W. put her on speaker.

"I need your help," she said, her voice pumped with desperation. "Tilly called me. She's been kidnapped."

"Kidnapped?" I repeated. "You mean like she's being held for ransom?"

We all involuntarily leaned toward the phone. The words "kidnapped" and "ransom" threatened like rainclouds before a storm.

"No, it's not like that. At least I don't think it is." We all settled back in our chairs, although the tension remained.

"You said the call came from Tilly?" P.W. asked.

"Yes. She was very upset."

"What did she say? Tell us exactly what you remember her saying."

Clara took an audible breath and spoke slowly, as if trying very hard to give an accurate and complete account of the conversation. "She sounded frantic and somewhat disoriented. She said she was being 'held against her will.' Those are her exact words—held against her will. That she didn't know where she was. Then, before she could tell me more, she said that 'he was coming back' and she would call me again when she got a chance."

"Did the call come from her cell phone?" Yuri asked.

"No, I didn't recognize the number."

"You need to call the police," P.W. said. "They are equipped to handle situations like this."

"I know that's what I'm supposed to do, but I don't want to . . . at least not yet. The press is already treating last night's ceremony as some sort of crazy cult thing. And with this on top of what's already happened . . . well, I would like to keep Tilly's name out of it as much as possible."

"Since the victim was her boyfriend . . .," I began.

"And since she was the original 'sacrifice' . . ., Yuri added.

I finished the sentence for him, ". . . she will already be on the police and press radar. I'm not sure there's any way to prevent more adverse publicity at this point."

"That may be, but I would like to try." Clara sounded firm about her decision.

"But if she's been kidnapped . . ." Yuri said.

"I want to make it clear that my recommendation is that we involve the police," P.W. said firmly. "Although I do understand your concern," she added.

"Cameron, Yuri, I know you feel like you failed Tilly by letting her get away from you on Saturday evening," Clara said. "But that's not how I see it. I didn't ask you to stop the ceremony. And from the way you've described what happened, I'm not surprised that someone was able to take advantage of the situation and steal her away. She was probably still drugged. But now . . ." She paused. "To be honest, I'm afraid the police might over-react. What if it ends up in a shoot-out? Tilly could be caught in the crossfire." P.W. started to speak, but Clara didn't give her a chance. "I know what you're going to say, but my gut tells me you're wrong."

P.W.'s hand snaked out to the skinny, unlit Russian cigarette in her antique ashtray. She massaged its slim roundness as if she could squeeze answers out of it. But the cigarette didn't give up any secrets as far as I could tell. "All right," P.W. conceded. "I'll send someone to pick up your phone. We might be able to trace the number."

"No, I want to hold onto my phone. In case Tilly calls back. I'll bring it in. I can be there in about twenty minutes."

"Okay. And if we get an address, I'll have Yuri and Cameron check it out. But if they feel they need to bring in the police, they will do so. I don't want them to risk their lives or the life of your niece. It will be their call. Are we clear?"

"I just want my niece back."

The next twenty-five minutes went by slowly. Yuri and I went to get coffee and to mark time while waiting for Clara. We were torn about whether it was our duty to involve the police or if it made sense for us to check out the location from which the call was made first.

"We're assuming Will can trace the call," I said.

"If the caller's phone number and address are publicly listed, it's possible for anyone—not just the police—to track a call. Once you have the number, there is a reverse lookup website which will display the address of the caller. I've never done it myself, but my guess is that Will can do it."

"If he does, you need to hold off teasing him about his trench coat for . . . oh, at least a month," I said.

"That's asking a lot."

I laughed. "Actually, I think he kinda liked the original bear with the beige trench coat and Sherlock Holmes cap that Jenny made as a joke. It's too bad there were so many comments about Sherlock not wearing a beige trench coat. Maybe we should see if she still has the coat—we could put it in one of those shadow box frames and hang it in the office."

"Every kid that sees him in our window seems to want one. If the detective business slacks off, we should go into Sherlock Bear production." We turned to look at the toy sleuth in his red plaid deerstalker cap and cape under the flyer that said: "For the man or woman who has everything—give them the gift of vigilance. Special rates for gift certificate detection services."

"When I first started working here, Mara wanted one."

"I rest my case."

We had just paid for our coffee when we saw Clara. We waved to get her attention and went with her back to the office. Will met us at the door. "Nothing from Tilly yet?" he asked Clara.

"No, nothing."

"Okay, let me have your phone and I'll give it a go."

"Should I come with you?"

"No need."

W. Blaine Watkins stood up. "Mrs. Ramsey, P.W. would like you, Cameron, and Yuri to join her in her office."

We went in and sat across the desk from P.W. She had removed her cobalt-blue jacket revealing a silk floral blouse with muted colors that reminded me of a Monet painting. "No more calls?" she asked, although it was obvious from Clara's demeanor that she hadn't heard from Tilly again.

"How long will it take for him to trace the call?" Clara asked.

"Assuming he can," P.W. said. "The police have more options for tracking calls," she began, but Clara interrupted her."

"No, I want to stick to what we agreed to earlier."

P.W. nodded.

I appreciated Clara's faith in us, but dealing with kidnappers was definitely not in my comfort zone, not even close. What if "he" was actually several people? What if they were all armed? And if they were holding her for ransom, why hadn't they contacted Clara? If not for ransom . . . then what?

While we waited, we took turns asking Clara questions to see if we could glean any information that might be helpful, but there were no sparks, nothing that gave us any ideas about where to start our search. Our conversation was flagging when Blaine poked his head in to announce that Will wanted Yuri and me to join him in the pit. Clara gazed hopefully after us as we excused ourselves.

"Almost there," Will said without looking up. Yuri and I watched as his fingers flew across the keyboard. "Gotcha," he said as the address he'd punched in came up on Google maps. He switched to street view. Yuri and I bent down to get a better look.

"Not much of a house," Will said. "The yard is what might generously be called 'overgrown. Its owner is listed as Ethan Jones.'"

"Is that a shed out back?" Yuri asked.

"Please tell me she isn't locked up in a shed." The image of Tilly being imprisoned in a backyard shed was like something out of a bad movie. One I unfortunately had seen on more than one occasion.

"Want me to tag along?" Will asked.

"This is just a reconnaissance. Perhaps a grab and run if it's feasible. Otherwise, we contact the police," Yuri said.

"So, that's a 'no thanks,'" Will said.

"That's a 'wish we didn't have to do this but we are going to give it a try.' You check this Ethan Jones out, okay? Or have Adele do it."

"I'm on it."

I went in to tell Clara and P.W. that we had an address and were on our way to check it out. We asked Clara if the name Ethan Jones meant anything to her. It didn't. As we took off, P.W. reminded us not to take any unnecessary chances that would endanger us or Tilly. And to keep them informed.

A half hour later we were parked down the block from the house we had seen online. There was a single row of cedar bush trees along both sides of the lot, planted close together to provide privacy. Unfortunately, every third tree was encased in brown needles that did not look like they would ever return to a living green. "Whoever lives there needs a better gardener," Yuri observed.

"Not much cover," I noted.

"Maybe we can come in from behind."

"No alley that I saw online."

"No car in the driveway," Yuri commented. "Maybe in the garage."

"There could still be a way in from the back."

We drove around the corner. There was what looked like a footpath running along the fence line in the back yard of the house on the corner. "Let's check it out," Yuri said.

"Why not."

The scrub grass path wasn't well used. It was the kind of urban track often created by neighborhood kids who preferred trails to sidewalks. Maybe it had once been an alley, although it was only about four feet wide.

Our target house was the third one from the street. There was no back fence, and the shed was only a few feet from what we assumed was the property line. The shed was weathered, its roof covered with healthy mounds of moss.

We stood very still and listened but didn't hear anything. No voices. No machines running. And, most importantly, no dogs barking.

"You take the left and I'll go right," Yuri said softly. "I'll check out the shed then head for the house. Stay out of sight and meet me back here in five, okay?"

That five-minute deadline had been optimistic. It only took two minutes for someone to shout: "Hold it right there or I'll shoot."

CHAPTER 9
TALKING TO THE MOON

THE YOUNG MAN with the rifle looked like he meant it. He was standing with feet slightly apart, the rifle butt snugged against his shoulder, with his finger on the trigger. He was aiming somewhere between Yuri and me, but it felt like he had both of us in his sites.

Yuri and I were about twenty feet apart, so realistically, unless the guy was incredibly fast, he wouldn't be able to shoot both of us before one of us could return fire. But since I didn't have a gun, and Yuri didn't have his out, that wasn't reassuring. If he shot Yuri first, I wouldn't have any options other than exercising super powers I didn't have. My mind processed the situation and several scenarios with lightning speed. Apparently reaching the same conclusion at the same time, Yuri and I raised our hands in the air.

"Okay," Yuri said, voice calm. "You don't need to shoot. And you might want to put that rifle away before the police arrive."

"I don't think it's illegal to shoot trespassers."

"Actually, it is," I said. "Unless they're inside your house—"

Before I could finish, he screamed, "Shut the fuck up!"

He focused his rifle on me, and as he did, Yuri drew his gun.

"If you shoot her, you're dead," Yuri said in his best Bruce Willis voice.

"Hey, let's put all the guns down," I said, in my squeaky frightened voice. "This isn't high noon. We have a couple of questions. Then we'll leave, okay?"

The man's eyes flicked to Yuri's gun, then back to me, his rifle still pointed somewhere in the vicinity of my solar plexus. It was hard to gauge exactly where he intended to place the bullet, but I had no doubt he would hit his target.

"No one comes creeping around from the back to ask questions."

I didn't know whether he was trying to imitate some tough guy or if he was a tough guy in real life. He was a thin, pale man with light brown hair and the narrow, pointy face of a bull terrier. But he had bulging biceps visible through his T-shirt; he was having no difficulty holding his rifle steady.

"Ethan," I said, keeping my voice as calm as I could. "Please put the rifled down."

"How do you know my name?" he demanded loud enough for the neighbors to hear. I couldn't take my eyes off the rifle, but I prayed that he had at least one nosy neighbor watching our little drama unfold who would call the police.

"We know a fair amount about you, actually," Yuri bluffed. "As does our boss who is waiting for us to report in. So, you'd have to act quickly to get away with murdering the two of us."

"Who said anything about murder?" Now he sounded a bit uneasy, but he didn't put the rifle down.

"We just have a couple of questions," I repeated. "Then we'll leave."

"About what?"

"We're looking for a young woman who you were seen with at Saturday night's Full Moon Society ceremony." Yuri overstated the case a bit by saying he was seen with Tilly at the ceremony since we didn't even know if he was a member, but it got a quick reaction.

"There were a lot of people there."

"But not all of them were seen leaving with her." Ethan hadn't denied it, so Yuri wasn't letting up.

Ethan's aim wavered, the barrel moving away from me. I suddenly realized that I had been holding my breath and exhaled my relief. Then he pointed his rifle at the ground, but he was still holding it in a way that suggested he could swing it back up and take a shot faster than we could blink.

"Okay, ask your questions," he said. "Then I want you off my property." His threat didn't sound as convincing as it had moments before.

Yuri lowered his gun too. But he kept it in the "ready" position.

"When did you last see Tilly Jamison?" Yuri asked.

For a moment I thought Ethan was going to deny knowing her, but he'd apparently fallen for Yuri's bluff about being seen with her. "When I dropped her off after the ceremony."

"Where did you drop her off?"

"At her place."

"That's strange," Yuri said. "Because she didn't make it home on Saturday night. Want to try again?"

"I'm not responsible for what she did after I dropped her off," he said. "Now if that's all . . ." He motioned for us to leave with his rifle. It took a lot of resolve for me to stand my ground rather than taking him up on his offer to leave without being shot. But I somehow managed to sound almost confident when I said,

"No, that's not all. I want to know if you are holding her here against her will."

He hesitated for just an instant. "Why would I do that?"

I felt like yelling "because you're a crazy pervert." Instead I said, "Because you think you can convince her to like you, and that you can develop a relationship with her if she just gets to know you. But I can assure you that won't work." That was the extent of my armchair psychoanalysis, but it seemed to hit its target as precisely as if I'd shot him. His face was slowly turning red from the neck up.

"You don't know what you're talking about."

"Oh, I think I do." I wasn't sure that poking the monster was a good idea, but Yuri wasn't trying to stop me, so I continued. "I know that she was in love with Rune and that . . . "

"No," he said louder than necessary. "You've got that all wrong. Rune meant nothing to her."

"No, you're the one who has it all wrong, it's YOU that means nothing to her."

Yuri had been slowly moving further and further to his right, and out of the corner of my eye I saw him pull out his phone. Ethan had been focused on what I was saying, but all of a sudden, he apparently realized what was happening and started to raise his rifle as he turned toward Yuri. But Yuri was faster. His gun was already aimed at Ethan.

"Drop the gun, Ethan Jones. Now!"

Ethan hesitated, then slowly pointed it at the ground again, but he didn't let go of it.

Yuri kept his gun trained on Ethan while giving the police our location and explaining that we were detectives who had been hired to find a missing woman who we believed Ethan Jones was holding hostage in his house.

Ethan obviously couldn't make up his mind what to do.

"Yes, I'll stay on the line until a unit gets here," Yuri said, his gun in one hand and his cell phone in the other.

"It's over, Ethan," I said, trying to draw his attention away from Yuri. "You're going to have to let Tilly go."

He looked around, a wild animal's fear of capture in his eyes. "She wanted to come home with me," he said, sounding whiny and desperate. "Rune drugged her, and she didn't want to be with him anymore."

"Drop the rifle," Yuri ordered. "The police might shoot you if they see you holding a weapon."

"What about you and that gun of yours," he said defensively. "Maybe they'll shoot both of us, huh?"

"No one is going to shoot anyone," I said. "The police are going to come and search your house. If Tilly is here, they will take her home. If not, we'll owe you an apology."

"I just told you she wanted to come home with me. I'm helping her get off the drug Rune gave her."

"It's been two days since the ceremony," Yuri said. "You're telling us she's still drugged?"

"She hasn't been herself since then," he said. "I've been trying to help her."

"Of course you have," Yuri said sarcastically. Now he was poking the monster. I truly believed at this point that

Ethan was some kind of twisted personality. And I was also convinced we would find Tilly inside. I hoped she was okay, neither physically harmed nor traumatized too much.

We heard sirens in the distance.

"Why don't we meet them around front," I suggested. If they couldn't see us they might feel compelled to search the yard with guns ready for action. There were too many ways that could go sideways.

"After you," Yuri said to Ethan, motioning with his gun. For a heartbeat I thought Ethan might make a run for it. Then he apparently decided to cooperate. Maybe he'd convinced himself he could make the police believe the story he'd told us about helping Tilly come down off of the drugs Rune had given her. Or maybe he believed that Yuri would shoot him if he didn't.

When the police pulled up in two separate cars out front, Yuri slipped his gun out of sight, but we both kept an eye on Ethan's rifle. He seemed to have forgotten it until an officer got out of the second car on the passenger side, leaned across the roof with his gun aimed in our direction and yelled: "Put your weapon down!"

Yuri and I had moved away from Ethan so as not to get caught in crossfire if he decided to resist arrest. But we needn't have worried. He raised one hand and leaned down to lower the rifle to the ground with the other.

"Just protecting my property against trespassers" he yelled back.

Two other officers were now moving in our direction while the first two hung back, weapons drawn, watching.

"I'm the one who called," Yuri said. "She and I are private detectives. We've been hired to find a missing woman, Tilly Jamison, and we have reason to believe she's in this house."

"And what makes you think that?" one of the officers asked.

"She made a phone call to her aunt from here. Her aunt is our client."

One officer reached down and picked up Ethan's rifle. I noticed that he checked to see if the safety was on, then motioned for one of the other officers to come and take it.

"It's for self-protection," Ethan said. "These two sneaked in from the alley. What was I supposed to think?"

Ignoring his question, the officer turned back to me. "Jamison. That name sounds familiar."

"She and Ethan Jones here were involved in the Full Moon Society ceremony on Saturday evening," I said.

The officers exchanged looks. "I don't suppose you are the two detectives who were there as security?"

"We weren't hired as 'security,'" Yuri said. "We were keeping an eye on Tilly."

"But your eye wandered?" the second officer smirked.

"Look, we admit we screwed up," I said. "But we've tracked her here and want to make sure she's okay. Are you going to take a look inside?"

"Do you have a warrant?" Ethan asked.

"No, we don't have a warrant. We were asked to come here because there were two men with guns threatening to shoot each other."

"That's not what I said—" Yuri began.

"But it's what the neighbor who called it in said." The officer turned to Yuri. "I assume you have a permit to carry a concealed weapon?"

"Yes, would you like to see it?"

"First, let's clear up this question about the young woman." He glared at Ethan. "If we get a search warrant, or should I say when we get one, will we find her inside?"

Ethan was obviously faced with a tough choice, either lie and hope they couldn't get a search warrant or go with the story he'd told us. He made his choice quickly. "They drugged her during the ceremony and she came home with me so I could help her recover."

"That was two days ago," I pointed out. "And she called her aunt from here and said she was being held against her will." The police looked to Ethan for a response.

"She's confused. The drugs have made her confused."

"Why don't you let us decide for ourselves," the officer said. "Can we see her?"

If I'd been on Ethan's side instead of Tilly's, I would have suggested he not say anything more or let anyone inside until he had a lawyer present. Fortunately, he thought he was smarter than the cops or us, so he agreed to let them inside.

They asked Yuri and me to wait outside, but I argued that she might need a woman's assistance, and I could see them processing the possible downside of two male police officers dealing with a female kidnapping victim. They waved the other two officers over, and they stayed with Yuri while the four of us went in, Ethan in the lead, me sandwiched between the two officers who had their guns drawn—just in case.

All of the blinds were pulled down. In the dim light, I could see it was a tidy, sparsely furnished, no frills kind of place. Not much of a bachelor pad if that was what he'd had in mind. And definitely not the kind of place to impress a young woman like Tilly.

I suddenly felt vulnerable. What if Ethan had an accomplice? Why hadn't I thought of that before insisting I should go with them? What if Ethan had another gun stashed somewhere and was preparing himself for a shootout with the police? What if—

Ethan led us through the living room to a closed door at the end of a hallway. He knocked softly and said, "Tilly, are you awake?" If it was all farce, it was nicely performed.

When there was no answer, one of the officers waved Ethan aside and slowly opened the door. I was right behind him, straining to see past his bulky uniformed body. There were no lights on in the room, but I could make out a narrow bed in the corner. And there was someone in it.

One of the officers stayed with Ethan while the other held out his arm to keep me back as he slowly approached the bed. "It's Tilly," I said. At least it looked like her in the gray-yellow light seeping through around the edges of the old-fashioned roller shades. "Please hurry."

The officer motioned for me to stay away as he knelt beside the bed and checked for a pulse. After a few seconds, he said, "She's alive."

"Thank god," I said. Thank all of the gods and fate and whatever spirits were protecting her.

"See if you can rouse her," the officer said as he got out his phone and called for an ambulance.

I knelt beside the bed and gently touched her shoulder. "Tilly," I said softly. Her eyelids quivered, but her eyes didn't open. She was wearing a T-shirt with a unicorn on the front. Her hair looked as though it hadn't been washed for days, and there was a faint odor that I didn't recognize hovering over her. "You called your Aunt Clara, and she asked us to come get you."

Tilly moaned, as if trying to speak but unable to get her mind and her mouth to cooperate.

"Don't try to talk," I said. "Help is on the way." I heard Ethan say he wanted to see Tilly, but his protests faded as one of the officers insisted he leave with him.

Then, because I didn't know what else to do, I started rambling assurances: "You're going to be fine. The ambulance has been called. And your Aunt Clara will be so happy to see you. And your roommate Phoebe will be happy to see you." I didn't mention Wren because I was fairly certain Wren wanted to remain an "independent entity" no matter what had happened to Tilly. And I, of course, didn't mention Rune. I wondered if Ethan had told her about Rune's death. Just how sick did he have to be to keep her here doped up like this? What had he hoped to accomplish? Had he been planning on keeping her locked up indefinitely?

I took hold of Tilly's hand and gave it a squeeze. It may have been my imagination, but I thought I felt her squeeze my hand back. She looked so weak and childlike lying there. No one deserved to have something like this happen to them. Rune had used a drug that must have worn off enough for her to leave the cave under her own volition. But whatever Ethan had used seemed to be more potent. Hopefully not lethal. And even if she made a full physical recovery, I'd read that kidnap victims frequently suffered lingering effects such as stress, anxiety and feelings of helplessness.

If only we had been able to prevent this from happening in the first place.

As for Ethan? Well, you can't lose what you never had. Whether he was a lovesick Lothario hoping to win over the fair maiden or a crazy man fulfilling some sick fantasy, it was over now. He'd been talking to the moon with no one on the other side talking back.

CHAPTER 10
LUNAR MADNESS

BY THE TIME the ambulance arrived, Tilly had opened her eyes a couple of times, blinked a few times, then shut them again. She hadn't said anything. They let me stay in the room while the medics checked her out and got her ready to move. One of the medics asked me several questions about her condition that I couldn't answer. I did tell him that she had been drugged on Saturday evening, but I didn't know what drug she had been given, so that wasn't very helpful. I heard them say something about pumping her stomach, but that it was probably best to get her to a hospital rather than treating her on the spot. I asked which hospital they were taking her to, and the medic yelled it over his shoulder as they quickly hauled her away.

Yuri was waiting for me outside. He said one of the officers had taken down our information and that they would be getting in touch with us, but for now we were free to go. "Let's get out of here. This whole situation makes me feel dirty."

"I know what you mean."

Once on the road, Yuri called P.W. and Clara. As soon as he told them Tilly was alive and on her way to the hospital to be checked out, Clara broke down and started sobbing. "Thank you, thank you," she kept saying over and over. I wished we were able to tell her Tilly was not only alive but conscious. At least she was alive.

"You need to know she may still be under the influence of drugs," Yuri warned. "She wasn't able to tell Cameron what had happened to her." Yuri shook his head and glanced at me to let me know he was downplaying her condition. Hopefully it was just a question of flushing the drugs out of her system. Maybe by the time Clara got to the hospital, they would at least have a diagnosis. Or, best case scenario, Tilly would be able to carry on a conversation with her aunt and tell her what had happened. And thank her aunt for her role in saving her from Ethan.

Before rushing off to the hospital, Clara wanted to know more about the man who had been holding her niece captive. We told her Will was looking into it, and P.W. promised we get back to her later with more information. That seemed to satisfy her. "Thank you again," she said.

"So," P.W. asked as soon as it was just the three of us, "why don't you tell me what you know about her condition." P.W. never missed a nuance or the hidden message behind an evasive response.

"She was really out of it," I said. "At first she couldn't even open her eyes. She managed to open them briefly right before they took her to the hospital, but she couldn't talk. I think she squeezed my hand once, so maybe she knew she'd been rescued."

"And this Ethan Jones person?"

"Borderline crazy," Yuri said. "We'll fill you in on all of the details when we get back to the office."

"Okay."

"But, in case the police contact you, you should know that there were a few, ah, bumps in, ah, making contact with him."

"'Bumps.' Do I need to get you a lawyer?"

"I don't think so, but a neighbor did call the police about our confrontation with him. He threatened us with a rifle and I had my gun out. And we were on his property. If he hadn't been holding Tilly hostage, they might have questioned who was in the right."

"Well, the bottom line is you got her away from him. That was the best possible outcome. I'm proud of you."

After he hung up, I said, "Even though Ethan got the drop on us and things were a bit messy, it probably turned out better than we could have hoped. If we had decided she was there and called in the police to handle it, there might have been shots fired."

"Still, the police aren't going to give us any medals for what we did. And after what happened Saturday night—"

"We are mere mortals, Yuri."

"Dang, I thought I was Super Yuri and you were right up there with Wonder Woman."

"Even the Greek gods had their weaknesses."

"Maybe even the gods would have had trouble dealing with someone suffering from lunar madness, is that what you're trying to tell me?"

We were interrupted in our morale building exchange by the dulcet tones of Clair de Lune. I had Yuri answer it for me. It was Detective Connolly from Major Crimes. We'd had quite a bit of interaction with him on another case, and I admit to being attracted to his sharp blue eyes and Irish good looks. The one time he'd dropped by the house to share some information with Yuri and me, my mother had started making wedding plans. But there hadn't even been a first date. And I didn't know for sure whether he was single. In fact, I didn't know if he had a first name!

"Just the two people I wanted to talk to," Connolly said.

"We're on our way to the office," Yuri said. "Can we call you back when we get there?"

"Wouldn't want to cause an accident. Call me as soon as you arrive, okay?"

Yuri was silent for a moment after he tapped "end" on my phone. I, too, was processing the exchange. "So," I asked, "what do you think he wants to talk to us about?"

"Do you suppose he's already had a report on what happened at Ethan's? I sensed some urgency in the request."

"Me too. That's what worries me."

Once at the mall we hurried past the coffee stands calling to us like Sirens with aromatic wafts of coffee instead of songs. Blaine looked up as we came rushing in. "We need to see P.W. as soon as possible."

"She's expecting you. Knock first though."

P.W. wasn't smiling as we came in. Not that she was a smiley person, but I was looking for reassurance any place I could find it. We didn't sit down. "Detective Connolly wants us to call as soon as we can," I said.

"I've heard he's in charge of the Rune investigation," P.W. said.

"It's referred to as the 'Rune investigation' now? Sounds like a movie title." Yuri's cheeky comment earned him a frown.

"Go call him," P.W. said. "Then come back and tell me about your conversation with him, and I need the details about what happened at the Jones' house." We turned around before she added, Columbo style, "One other thing. Don't offer opinions or conjecture. Stick to the facts. And if you have any concerns about a particular line of questioning, say you want to talk to me first. Got that?'

We both nodded. I could feel her comment settling in the pit of my stomach like overeating on Thanksgiving. Were we missing something? What were the red flags going off for P.W.?

"Conference room," Yuri said. We hurried past our colleagues. Only Will looked like he wanted us to stop and talk. "Later," Yuri said automatically as we headed for the small room at the back of the pit. After he shut the door behind us, he shook his head as if it were an 8-ball searching for answers.

"Do we need to get our story straight before talking to Connolly?" I asked.

"Which story? We don't know what he wants to talk to us about."

"I suppose we take P.W.'s advice—stick to the facts and keep it simple."

"Too bad you and Connolly never hooked up."

"There was never anything there."

"Hey, I know you checked out that sculpted chin of his and those cornflower blue eyes."

"Sounds like you have a thing for him."

"Even a heterosexual male can notice a handsome man when he meets one."

"Well, right now he's not a prospective friend or an old acquaintance; he's a police officer investigating a murder. And he has some questions for us that we may not want to answer. So, let's get on with it—stick to the facts and watch out for landmines."

Connolly answered on the second ring. "Thanks for calling so promptly," he said. I felt like pointing out we were law-abiding citizens who cooperated with law enforcement. Well, mostly. When we first encountered him while working on a case, we had unfortunately crossed the line a few times. But fortunately, he had let us off with some very harsh warnings. When he was angry, his blue eyes became very intense.

"What can we do for you?" Yuri asked.

"I called to give you a head's up. About Tilly Jamison."

"Tilly? We located her and she's been taken to the hospital," I said.

"I know. And I also know her aunt is your client. And that you were there the night Rune Rundell was murdered."

"We've both given the police statements," Yuri said. Then added, "But of course you know that."

"And you know that I'm the lead on the murder investigation, right?"

"Yes, P.W. told us."

"We were already looking for Ms. Jamison in connection with the murder, so when her recovery was called in, I immediately contacted the hospital. We intend to interview her about what happened on Saturday evening and about her escape with Ethan Jones as soon as her doctor gives us the okay."

"Escape?" Yuri and I both said at the same time.

"We know she left with Jones that night. We also know a few things I'm not able to discuss with you. But I wanted to make sure you didn't try to talk with her before her interview with us."

"She's the victim here," I said. "And it sounds as though you are treating her like a suspect."

"I can't discuss details with you. The reason I called is to make it clear that she's off limits to you for now. And I also have a couple of questions about anything she may have told you when you were left alone with her at the Jones' house."

"'Left alone with her'—you make it sound as if we had a cozy conversation. You do realize that when we found her she couldn't speak, she couldn't even open her eyes. She wasn't able to tell me anything."

"You wouldn't lie to me, would you, Cameron? To protect your client's niece?"

"No, I wouldn't lie to you, Detective Connolly. And if you want to know more about her condition, why don't you talk to the medics who took her to the hospital?" I was angry. There was something going on here that I felt certain was both unfair and based on misinformation. I wondered if someone had fed the police a line, and if so, why?

Yuri jumped in just in time to keep me from saying something I might later regret. "Do you have any other questions for us?" He motioned for me to calm down.

"That's it for now." Then he added, "I'm glad the two of you managed to avoid getting shot this morning."

Yuri gestured for me to keep quiet, but I couldn't help myself. "That sounds like implicit criticism." Actually, not too "implicit."

"I know I don't have to tell you that you should have called the police instead of confronting Jones on your own."

Yuri had seemed determined not to let me escalate the exchange, but suddenly he was the one to lose it. "To be clear, Detective Connolly, we had no intention of confronting Jones. We were simply trying to determine if Tilly was being held there against her will."

"Well, I don't want to argue with you about this, but I think you were pretty certain she was there. That's my point. As private investigators, you need to be clear about the boundaries of your authority."

I was trying to get my thoughts in order when Yuri took a deep breath to get himself under control before responding. And he almost succeeded. Almost. "Thanks for that advice. We'll make sure we check on boundaries the next time someone points a rifle at us."

What?! I mouthed at Yuri. I mimicked his "keep your mouth shut" motions and rolled my eyes.

"Sorry, Detective Connolly," Yuri said quickly. "I know that sounded defensive. Things did not go as planned this morning, and we're both still a little shook up."

Connolly's voice was softer and more sympathetic when he responded to Yuri's apology. "I understand. I've been there. I don't want to see either of you taking unnecessary risks. Truce?"

"Truce," Yuri said, motioning for me to agree.

"Truce."

"Okay then. I'm sure your client will keep you informed about Jamison." He paused. "And you did all right this morning." Then he hung up without waiting for a comment.

"All right?" I said. "What does that mean?"

"I think it was his way of saying we stepped over the line and were lucky we weren't shot for our efforts. Which, from his perspective, is probably a fair assessment. But he's also glad everything turned out the way it did. That no one was shot."

"First you're mad at him and now you're defending him?"

"He's a cop. He sees the world through a cop's eyes. And he sees us as impediments to him doing his job. But I still think he has a thing for you, Cameron. Otherwise, why worry about things such as 'truces' and staying safe?" Yuri wiggled his eyebrows. At times it was an annoying nonverbal poke, and this was one of those times.

"If he had a 'thing' for me as you keep suggesting, he could have asked me out. And he hasn't. So, let's not talk about him anymore. Let's focus on our debrief with P.W."

"Truce." He held up his hands in mock surrender.

Our debrief with P.W. was thorough. She pulled every detail of encounter with Ethan Jones out of us, thought about it, and in the end agreed that we hadn't done anything that was going to land us in trouble with the law. Especially since it would end up being bad press for them if they went after us when we were the ones who had located Tilly and made it possible for the police to save her from Ethan.

We were just finishing up when she got a call from Clara. We could hear muffled crying and an emotional monologue as P.W. began looking more and more upset. When she put the phone down, she solemnly announced. "Tilly is a suspect in the death of Rune Rundell."

CHAPTER 11
MOON TRANCE

WHEN I ARRIVED HOME Monday evening, my mother, Mara and Jason met me at the door. Before they could bombard me with questions, Mom informed me that we were all having pizza together, her treat. I felt relieved that I would neither have to cook nor eat something healthy. After the day I'd had, I definitely wanted comfort food. Mara looked pleased, but Jason calmly asked my mother, "You do know I don't like mushrooms on my pizza."

Mom smiled. "Let me see, one pizza with pepperoni, sausage and olives . . . and another vegetarian. Right?"

Jason and Mara high-fived and grinned.

Mom looked at me and said, "I expect you to share Jason's pizza. Mara and I prefer vegetarian."

I barely had time to change my clothes and set the table before the pizza arrived. We quickly settled in and immediately grabbed what we wanted. Well, Mara, Jason and I "grabbed," Mom carefully lifted a slice onto her plate with a spatula. And then ate it with a knife and fork.

When they hadn't bombarded me with questions at the door, I'd thought they either didn't know what had happened yet or they had agreed to wait until after dinner.

I was wrong on both counts.

His mouth full of pizza, Jason managed to say, "I heard they found that woman you were looking for." From the way he'd worded his question, it was possible they didn't know about my role in her rescue, which was probably a good thing. Maybe the police would take all the credit and refer to Yuri and me as an "anonymous tip."

"Yes," I said between bites, dabbing my chin with the extra napkins my mother had put on the table.

"Is she okay?" Mara asked.

"I think so, but she was drugged pretty heavily. Her aunt is going to keep us informed."

"I heard she's a suspect," Jason said.

I stopped eating. "Where did you hear that?"

"It's on, ah, social media." His eyes darted away from mine.

"Jason," Mom and I said together. "You know . . ."

"I do know, but I don't rely on TikTok or Twitter for all the news. I read the *New York Times*, the *Washington Post*, the . . ."

I held up my hand. "Stop, we know you read and listen to multiple news sources. Most of them legitimate. I'm just surprised, and disappointed, that Tilly is considered a suspect and that it's getting coverage like that somewhere, anywhere. She's been through so much, and I can't imagine that she had either motive or opportunity to attack Rune."

"Wasn't he her boyfriend?" Mara asked.

Mom was taking it all in. Suddenly I was fairly certain why we were having pizza for dinner—she wanted an excuse to talk about Tilly's situation without being distracted by food preparation or by appearing crass enough to be interested in the details of a lurid murder investigation.

"But they'd been fighting," Jason said. He glanced at me and added, "According to one unnamed source."

"Even if they'd been arguing about something, they were still in a relationship. There didn't seem to be any problems between them on Saturday night. She was, after all, going along with the ceremony he'd organized."

"You do know the biggest reason the police suspect her, don't you?" Jason stopped chewing, grinning with anticipation of what he was obviously hoping would be a big surprise.

"No, as a matter of fact I don't. What do your unnamed sources have to say about that?"

"Her fingerprints were on the dagger." With that stunning announcement, he took a huge bite of pizza, still managing to look pleased with himself while chewing.

"Seriously?" Mara looked at me. "You hadn't heard that?"

"No," I admitted. "I knew she was a suspect, but I didn't know why. And I don't see how that's even possible."

Mom said, "But you did lose track of her that evening, didn't you?"

"Only after they took her into the cave."

"Maybe there was a secret exit," Jason suggested, his eyes bright with the possibility.

"No, I'm pretty certain there was only one way in and out of it. There are a lot of old mineshafts in the area, but they've all been blocked off for safety reasons. Still, since we couldn't figure out where she'd gone, we checked out the cave walls and looked for another way out. We didn't find anything though."

"You didn't show us any caves when we went there," Jason complained. "I'd like to see them. Will you take us there this weekend?"

"No, they aren't that safe. And I don't think that's a good idea right now."

"Maybe in a month or two?" Mara said. "Just a peek?" Apparently this was one time she and Jason were in agreement on something.

"It couldn't hurt, could it?" Mom said.

"You want to go too?" What was with my family's morbid interest in this death? "You do realize an actual person was murdered there. It wasn't some Halloween stunt or staged drama."

All three looked momentarily chastened. Then Mara said, "You've talked about other bad things that have happened at work. Why is this different?"

"Caves are cool," Jason threw in for good measure.

"I'll think about it," I conceded. "Now eat your pizza."

Mom stayed after dinner to have a glass of wine with me. "A full moon, a human sacrifice, a cave in the woods, and someone stabbed by a ceremonial dagger. You have to admit, it's quite a story. It's easy to lose track of the fact that the person who died was someone's son, someone's friend, a real person."

"I know. And keep in mind that for me it's personal. It started out as a simple assignment. A surveillance. And now the person we were supposed to keep an eye on is being accused of murder because her fingerprints are allegedly on the dagger that killed her boyfriend."

"I'm sure there's a reasonable explanation. There always is."

"The sad thing is that she has already suffered so much."
I went on to give Mom the highlights of Tilly's rescue from
Ethan Jones, ending with, "So, if she was barely conscious
after the ceremony and he kept her drugged the whole
time, I don't see how she could possibly have murdered
Rune."

"Could she and Ethan have done it together?"

"Tilly and Ethan as partners in anything is beyond
believable. He's an unhinged creep. And not a particularly
attractive human being. Putting aside that it's an unlikely
alliance, I don't see how they could have slipped away and
murdered him before Yuri and I discovered his body. The
timing doesn't work out."

"Could Ethan have done it while they were taking Tilly
to the cave?"

"It's possible. If he did it, that's when it had to have
happened. We were watching the procession, not the
clearing. But there wasn't much time for him to murder
Rune and rejoin the group. And once they reached the cave,
I think we would have noticed him coming back. I think I
would have, maybe not though. We were really focused on
trying to see who was going in and out of the cave."

"He obviously had fantasies about her that must have
started long before the ceremony. And he knew about
her relationship with Rune. Jealousy can make people do
terrible things."

We finished our wine and called it a night. I was tempted
to call Yuri with Jason's "news," but decided it could wait
until tomorrow. I was exhausted.

In spite of all of the questions swirling through my
brain, I fell asleep almost immediately.

Tuesday morning I was getting ready to leave for the office when Yuri called to pass on a message from P.W. Tilly was still in the hospital but scheduled to be released later in the day, depending on the results of some tests. Clara was with her and wanted the two of us to come by. "I remembered Connolly's request," Yuri said, "So I asked to make certain Tilly had already talked to the police before saying yes. She has. Let's meet in the hospital lobby so we can runego up together. Okay?"

I arrived about five minutes before Yuri did. That gave me enough time to buy two coffees. When he came in carrying a coffee, I was disappointed. But he didn't seem to be: "I could use another," he said. "Thanks." He finished off the one he'd brought with him, caught himself at the last minute from tossing the full cup in the trash by mistake, and got rid of the empty cup.

Before we went up to her room, I told Yuri what Jason had read about her fingerprints being on the dagger. "I don't see how that's possible," I said, "but we should probably ask her about it. I wonder if the police mentioned it to her?"

"Maybe she handled the dagger before the ceremony and the murderer used gloves."

"Would the fingerprints look different if there was pressure put on them when the murderer stabbed Rune?"

"Like, maybe some would smear a bit? Or if there was blood over the print?"

"Wishful thinking, huh?"

"Well, we know that fingerprints can sometimes be detected even if someone is wearing gloves, depending on the gloves. And I vaguely remember a murder case where the forensics analysis proved someone other than the suspect had handled the weapon because of the location of smudges made by a glove wearer."

"My guess is that Connolly would be all over any anomalies."

"You're probably right. Let's go talk to Tilly."

Tilly was sitting up in her hospital bed when we arrived, her Aunt Clara in a chair next to it. Neither looked particularly happy. But Tilly looked a lot better than the last time we'd seen her. There was color in her cheeks and her hair had been washed. Clara saw us coming and stood to greet us. "I'm glad you're here," she said. "Tilly, do you remember Cameron and Yuri?"

Since she hadn't opened her eyes at Ethan's, I doubted she could "remember" us. But she studied us like she thought she ought to.

"Sorry," she said finally. "I really don't remember much."

Hospital rooms seldom have enough chairs for visitors, and this one was no exception. Yuri and I remained standing at the foot of Tilly's bed. She looked pale and alert. "I understand you've talked to the police," I said. Tilly nodded.

Clara said, "The two officers seemed nice enough, but I don't trust them. I think they want to close the case more than they want to get at the truth."

"What did they ask?"

"They wanted to know everything, starting from the time she arrived for the ceremony, when she left the park, the time spent at that man's house, and how she ended up here."

"I wasn't able to tell them much about what happened after the ceremony," Tilly said. "And hardly anything about being at Ethan's. It's all foggy. Except for that brief time where I came to long enough to call Aunt Clara. I remember struggling with him when he came back and caught me with his phone, but I was too weak to get away. That's where it all ended for me. Until I woke up here."

Clara interrupted. "They kept asking the same questions over and over. Like they expected her to change her story."

"They were polite," Tilly said. "But I don't think they believed me."

"It would be helpful if you told us what you told them," Yuri said.

She looked reluctant to relive the events another time, but her aunt encouraged her: "Tell them everything, Tilly. They may be able to help you get through this."

"If you were there," she began. Apparently her aunt had filled her in on what she had hired us to do. ". . . then you know probably better than I do what happened that night."

"We'd like to hear it from your perspective," Yuri said.

"Okay."

"Start with who was in the car when you left home, please."

She gave us a high-level overview of the events leading up to her being taken prisoner by Ethan. Everything she said was consistent with what we'd observed or had pieced together. There were no surprises, but quite a few unanswered questions.

"Do you know what drug was in the drink you were given at the ceremony?" Yuri asked.

"No. It made me totally relaxed and groggy, but I wasn't completely out. I knew what was happening. And when we were in the cave, they gave me something to counter the effects of the drug. But they warned me it would take a while to feel totally normal."

"You had clothes to change into in the cave?"

"Yes, Rune had someone take them there earlier. I was pretty unsteady. Ethan helped me change while one of the men dressed the mannequin."

"And you left with Ethan?"

"Yes. He told me Rune said I was to go with him."

"That's why you went with him? Because he said that's what Rune wanted?"

"Yes. I knew Rune was responsible for gathering things up after the ceremony, so even though he hadn't mentioned it earlier, it didn't seem strange that he would have asked someone to look after me when it was over. Kind of thoughtful actually. I didn't feel that great."

"We understood that you had a falling out with Rune," Yuri said.

"We had a fight about whether I should participate in the ceremony. I . . . I didn't want to be drugged, and he insisted it wouldn't be realistic if I was pretending to be drugged. In the end, I agreed to do it."

"But you hadn't broken up with him."

"No . . ." She started to cry, her shoulders shaking with grief. "I can't believe he's dead."

"I'm so sorry," I said. "And I'm sorry we have to ask you these questions, but if we're going to help you, we need to know what happened."

Clara handed her a Kleenex. She pulled herself together, wiped her face and blew her nose. "It's okay."

"Can you tell us a little more about how Ethan got you to go with him to his place?"

"I assumed Ethan would drop me off at Rune's. Then, when I got in his car he said something about my seat belt not being fastened right. He leaned toward me, and the next thing I knew he had me pinned against the seat and was holding a cloth over my nose. It smelled like nail polish, sweet yet like a disinfectant at the same time."

"Did you tell the police this?" Yuri asked.

"Yes, but they seemed to think I went willingly with Ethan. I mean, I did, but only because he said that was what Rune wanted."

"What's the next thing you remember?"

"I have some muddled recollections of being in a bed with someone next to me, talking. Then at some point, I actually felt like I was waking up. I couldn't really focus or concentrate, but I was aware there was someone in the room. And there was this voice in my head that told me I shouldn't let whoever it was know the drugs were wearing off."

"That was when she called me," Clara said.

I looked to Tilly for confirmation. "I heard him leave and forced myself to get up. I managed to make it to the other room and saw a phone on a table. I had a hard time punching in the numbers, but I managed to call Aunt Clara. Then, before I figured out where I was, I heard him coming back. He caught up with me as I was trying to find a way out. After that, I don't remember anything until I woke up here."

She leaned back and started crying again. "When the police questioned me about what happened, they acted as if I was the one who stabbed Rune. Why would they think that?"

"Tilly, I'm going to tell you something that may not be true. We didn't hear this from the police; it's just a rumor. But . . . is there any way your fingerprints could be on the dagger used to stab Rune?"

"What?" Tilly looked truly shocked.

"It may have been used during the ceremony. Did you at any time pick it up?"

"No. I hate knives. I never touched it."

Before I could ask a follow-up question, a nurse came in to see how Tilly was doing. She fussed around a bit, said the doctor would be by shortly to discharge her, and suggested we might want to leave while she walked Tilly through the check-out process and got her dressed.

We went out in the hall with Clara. "She's going to stay with me a few days," Clara said. "Just to make sure she's okay. And to keep her away from the press. Phoebe told me they've been calling her and Wren, and there's a TV van parked in front of their house."

"What do you want us to do?" Yuri asked. "P.W. said you were hoping we could advise Tilly about what to say if the police question her again. I know she felt they treated her like a suspect, but do you have any reason to believe that's what they're actually thinking?"

"I tried to tell her she was imagining things, but I felt the same way. Like they thought she was really upset with Rune and in cahoots with Ethan. I don't see how that's possible given the call she made to me and the condition she was in when they found her. But yes, I'm worried."

"Maybe you should think about getting a lawyer," Yuri said.

"I'm hoping it won't come to that."

"We know the major crimes detective in charge of the investigation," I said. "But I doubt he will be able tell us anything we don't already know. I'll give it a try though. Meanwhile, keep an eye on her. She's been through a lot in the past few days. She's going to need time to recover."

"Thank you. I can't tell you how much I appreciate everything you've done for her, for us."

In the elevator, Yuri voiced my sense of guilt: "It's just too bad we didn't prevent what happened to her in the first place."

CHAPTER 12
PAPER MOON

WE DECIDED TO HAVE a quick lunch at the Food Court before returning to the office. My mother says that breathing the air in any food court is to inhale nanosized cooking oil globules and free-floating calories. Sometimes the mismatched aroma of competing menus is a bit off-putting even for me, but the Food Court's convenience outweighs the overpowering smell of food and the echoing noise level of activity. Yuri got a burger and fries and I got a beef and broccoli chow mein. It always leaves a greasy feeling in my mouth, but I like it going down.

As we located a table away from other eaters, I caught sight of someone I thought I recognized as he disappeared into a store at the entrance to the Food Court. I almost missed the table with my tray as I set it down. "I must be seeing things," I said.

Yuri was already starting on his food. He stopped short of putting a fry in his mouth to ask, "Why?" Then the fry disappeared.

"Because I thought I saw Ethan Jones going into that sports shop.

"No way."

"There's such a thing as felony bail, but I wouldn't think they would release him until they at least take the time to investigate whether he's a danger to Tilly."

"You stay here while I go take a look." Yuri jumped up so quickly I didn't have a chance to say, "no, I'll go." Instead, he left me with our food, and I watched as he raced toward the sports shop. Although I hadn't planned it, it seemed like a good opportunity to snitch a few of his fries. Maybe he wouldn't notice, or maybe I should leave a piece of broccoli in their place.

Yuri disappeared inside the store only to reemerge minutes later, shaking his head.

"Well?" I asked when he rejoined me.

"There's a side entrance that opens onto one of those easy exit corridors. There were no customers in the shop, so I assume whoever you saw went in one door and out the other." Yuri looked down at his food, "I want my fries back."

"I didn't scarf any of your fries," I lied, unconvincingly I'm afraid.

"Yes you did—I counted them before I left. You owe me four fries."

"How about a piece of broccoli?"

"Put your broccoli away. I repeat, you owe me four fries. In fact, you probably owe me several orders of fries given that you're always helping yourself to my food."

I laughed. "Okay, next time."

We finished our lunch and, since Food Court coffee is worse than our office coffee, we picked up a couple of coffees at a stand on the way back

We weren't in the pit long before being summoned to

P.W.'s office. She wanted an update on Tilly's situation. We filled her in on what Tilly had told us about what she could remember about the ceremony and what happened afterwards. Then I mentioned that, although I couldn't be certain, I thought I had seen Ethan Jones near the Food Court.

P.W.'s hand snaked out to the cigarette in her antique ashtray. "If it was him, any chance he knows you saw him?"

I thought about her question. "I'm not sure."

"But isn't it too soon for him to be out on bail?" Yuri asked.

P.W. was tapping her cigarette. "I don't like this."

"I'm going to call Detective Connolly to ask about whether Tilly is seriously a suspect rather than a victim. Assuming he'll tell me anything. I'll also ask if Ethan is out on bail. That should be public information."

"Let me know what he says. If Jones has been released already, you two may need to take some precautions."

I'd been concerned for Tilly, but P.W.'s comment made me wonder if Yuri and I were also on Ethan's list. We had, after all, destroyed his make-believe fantasy world of romance. To say nothing of getting him arrested and possibly charged with kidnapping.

Yuri went with me into the conference room to call Detective Connolly. When he answered, I told him he was on speaker with Yuri and me. "Do you have time for a couple of questions?" I asked.

"I have time for questions, but maybe not for answers."

Yuri gave me a look that said, "Don't let him get to you."

"Fine. We basically have two questions. First, did Ethan Jones make bail?"

"Why are you asking?"

"Because I think I saw him here at the mall."

There was a moment of silence before Connolly said, "It's not inconceivable he was there to do some shopping."

"Okay, so you're saying that after drugging and kidnapping someone who might still be in danger from him and threatening to shoot us, he was let go?"

"Hold it right there. You're making a number of questionable assumptions. First, we don't know for certain that he 'kidnapped' your client's niece." I started to interrupt, but he continued talking over me. "Second, the judge granted him bail; he didn't break out. He's apparently not considered either a flight risk or a danger to anyone."

"Then why did you hesitate when I told you I saw him at the mall where our office is?"

"Well . . . it's entirely possible he is not, ah, pleased with the role you played in his arrest."

"But if he isn't a danger to anyone, why should that matter?"

"I admit here are some unresolved issues that make me somewhat uneasy about him making bail. But until we have proof that he actually kidnapped Ms. Jamison, we can't charge him with anything."

"What about the fact that she was heavily drugged and incapable of leaving on her own?

"We're looking into that."

"And what about the fact that he threatened to shoot us?"

"You were trespassing. And you were armed."

"How much proof do you need?" Now my voice sounded like a fingernail scraping across an old-fashioned blackboard, and Yuri had both hands raised, palms down, motioning for me to take it down a notch or two.

"I understand your concern. But there are some facts you are not privy to."

"Like Tilly's fingerprints on the dagger?"

"I can neither confirm nor deny . . ."

"Come on. She didn't have the opportunity to kill Rune. No way. And Ethan kept her drugged and refused to let her leave or call anyone. It seems pretty clear to me."

"Consider it from another perspective—what if they were in on it together?"

It was the same question my mother had asked, but she hadn't known the situation at the time. It seemed to me that Connolly had enough facts to recognize the absurdity of the accusation.

"Seriously? She was drugged for the ceremony. She was drugged out of her mind when the EMT came to Jones' house and took her to the hospital. Before that, she'd called her aunt and told her she'd been kidnapped. And, bottom line? Ethan Jones is a very strange guy who she had never given the time of day to before the ceremony. To top it all off . . . she was in love with the victim! In what universe does that make her an accomplice to his murder?"

"You make a convincing case. But, there are a few things you don't know."

"Then tell me so I won't feel like the police are making a huge mistake."

"Okay, keep this under your hat for a while, but there's a credible witness who saw Jones and Jamison making out. And several people overheard a fight between Jamison and Rundell."

"I know about the disagreement they had about her being drugged for the ceremony. But there's no way she made out with Jones. The witness is mistaken. Or lying."

"Until we verify otherwise, we have to pursue the possibility that Jones and Jamison were in this together. I'm very sorry. But that's the way it is."

"I expected better of you," I said. Then, before he could say anything more in his defense, I added, "Thanks for your time" and hung up.

"That went well," Yuri said.

"Sorry. I guess I lost it. But I once considered him date material, and now . . ."

"You thought about dating him? That's not the way I remember you telling it before . . ." He smiled. But the smile vanished quickly. "Still, I think it was a mistake to tick him off like that."

"I just can't see how anyone could have interpreted what happened at Ethan's as anything but kidnapping. Dozens of witnesses could testify about her being drugged for the ceremony and in the cave when Rune was killed. I don't gt it."

"But if she isn't the killer, the real killer either knew her prints were on that dagger and wore gloves to make it look like she did it, or they didn't know about her fingerprints but used gloves and accidentally involved her because she'd already handled the dagger."

"Whose side are you on?"

"I'm not saying she lied about never having handled the dagger, but her prints got on it somehow."

"Someone is trying to frame her. I don't know how, but that's the only explanation." We sat in silence a moment while I got my heartrate back to normal. "I overreacted with Connolly, didn't I?"

"Yes, it's becoming a pattern. And it isn't like you. I think you care about his opinions too much. Realistically, you can't expect him to share information the police haven't made public yet." Yuri leaned toward me. "Although he did do just that. Makes me wonder if he cares about what you think of him as a person."

"Or, he may be worried about the consequences of letting a dangerous man loose. Think how the headlines will read if Ethan attacks one of us or tries to kidnap Tilly again."

"Okay, so given what we know, and what we don't know, what do you want to do next?"

I didn't have to think about it; I knew what needed to be done. "Two things. First, I say we try to find out more about the anonymous witness, and second, we need to figure out how Tilly's fingerprints got on that dagger."

"Sure. Just so I'm clear on this. You're saying that all we need to do is identify the anonymous witness and basically, find the killer. Anything else?"

"Okay, I get your point. Maybe we should take a hard look at motive. Who would want to discredit Tilly? And who wanted Rune out of the way? See where that takes us."

"Sounds good. But I think we should start with Rune first. It's unlikely Rune's murder was the result of someone wanting to hurt Tilly. That was probably an afterthought."

"You're right. So . . . who wanted to see Rune dead? I suppose Ethan is the most obvious suspect, but I'm still not convinced he could have pulled it off in the amount of time he had. And Rune undoubtedly had other enemies."

"We may not have names," Yuri began, "but consider the larger picture for the moment. The killer had to be someone who knew about the ceremony and could either slip away unseen . . . or . . ." " . . . who wasn't participating in the ceremony but was waiting in the woods for the right opportunity."

"We need two lists: possible enemies and members who didn't attend. Hopefully there's someone who makes both lists."

"Maybe our anonymous witness makes both lists too. Unless the so-called witness simply took advantage of the situation to make Tilly look guilty."

"You have to really dislike someone to try to frame them for murder. That goes beyond pranking, more like revenge or retribution."

"You're saying that we need to consider making a list of enemies for Tilly, too."

"Yes, but I think we should start with the Full Moon Society."

"Don't you have a source, someone who could give you the name of a Full Moon Society member who might be able to help us put together those lists?"

Yuri grinned. "Unlike you, I cultivate sources rather than pissing them off." He waved me out of the room. "Give me a few minutes."

"You don't want me listening?"

"I don't want to give away any of my trade secrets."

I left him alone, knowing that he didn't want me hearing him flirt with his female "sources." He was lucky there was a fun-loving air of innocence about him. Everyone's big brother. Or little brother. Otherwise, he wouldn't have been able to get away with it. As far as I knew, he'd never been involved in a serious relationship, although he didn't lack for female companions. At one point my kids had hoped Yuri and I would get together. There was the spark of friendship but not of romance. Since good friends are hard to come by, I'm glad to count him as one of mine.

Hopefully Yuri's sources would come through with a name or two. There were a lot of unanswered questions surrounding the ceremony and Rune himself. We needed to find someone in the inner circle who could steer us in the right direction. Assuming that Tilly was telling the truth.

CHAPTER 13
MIMING THE MOON

I WAS FILLING WILL IN on what had happened with the case so far when Yuri came flying out of the conference room waving a piece of paper. "Got TWO names. Two. And one even answered his phone and can take a break at work to talk to us. Let's rock and roll."

Will rolled his eyes. "Love your enthusiasm, Elvis. Hope your lead pans out."

"I'll drive," Yuri said as he headed for the door.

I raced after him. "No, I'll drive."

"You need to relax."

"I'll drive," I said firmly. He held up his hands in surrender. "Don't think that makes up for pilfering my French fries."

Maybe it didn't make up for the fries, but it made me feel a whole lot safer.

As I drove out of the parking lot, Yuri punched in the address on the GPS for the small manufacturing firm where Wylie Younger was employed. "He sounded a bit older than I'd anticipated," Yuri said. "I think he might be a supervisor or manager; he told me to have the receptionist send us in when we got there."

"Did it sound like he has an office?"

"Yeah. Somehow I pictured these Full Moonies to be unemployed student types."

"Well, at the ceremony they did drink and do drugs like frat boys away from home for the first time."

"Maybe Wylie is young at heart."

"Or maybe participants use the full moon as an excuse to get together and let loose."

"Rocking away their troubles under a full moon." Yuri clicked his fingers and tried to find a beat that fit the words. "Isn't that a song?"

"Not one I'm familiar with."

"I think it is, but I can't quite place it. Do you know how many songs there are about the moon?"

"Spare me for now, okay?"

He hummed a few more offkey notes while snapping his fingers. "Doesn't it seem strange that the Full Moon Society exists in the first place? Unless, like you say, it's an excuse to party. I mean, if you really wanted to learn about ancient cultures wouldn't you take a class at a community college or university?"

"There's a difference between taking a class and reliving an event. Think about Civil War reenactments."

"Yeah, I've always thought that was weird."

"I think the appeal is that it's a fun social event with a little education thrown in for good measure."

"I would rather play chess in the park. Or strum a guitar in a subway tunnel. Or be a wandering mime. Or . . ."

"I got it. Strange, individual activities are your thing."

"Not that I would do any of them. Except maybe play chess in the park."

"I didn't know you played chess."

"I'd have to learn how first, I guess. But did you know that in 1968 the Soviets designed a special chess set using pegs and grooves so they could play chess in space?"

"Space trivia? What's wrong, run out of moon facts?"

"No, but it's all part of the cosmos. If you want more moon facts, did you know that a storyteller mimed a performance of the Apollo 11 moon landing to celebrate its 50th anniversary? His name was Andrew Dawson and the show was called Space Panorama."

"That's something I can't picture, and I'm not sure I even want to. Fortunately, we're here."

The gate in the chain link fence was open, and the parking lot was only about half full. The large brick building looked like it had been there a while.

"Metamfiezomaiophobia is the fear of mimes," Yuri said as we got out of the car.

"I'm not afraid of them; I just don't want to talk about it right now."

"Just saying . . ."

"Wonder what they manufacture here?"

"I Googled them. They make those overhead stow bins for airplanes."

"Looks like a big place. I wouldn't think making stow bins would be enough to keep a large operation in business."

"Hard to know. Although the abuse those bins take, maybe replacement orders are big."

There was a reception desk just inside the main door. Behind the desk was an older woman with glasses attached to a gold chain that sagged around her neck. She had on a baggy cardigan sweater and I could hear the hum of a heater behind the counter. When we told her we were there to see Wylie Younger, she gave us directions to his office: "Go in through the double doors, make a right, and it's the third door down." Yuri thanked her with sufficient enthusiasm to coax a smile.

Wylie met us at the door to his office. The receptionist must have warned him we were on the way. He didn't look anything like an unemployed student, more like an extra in a WWII film with his round, wire-rimmed glasses and his stiff demeanor. "Please, come on in and take a seat."

The chairs offered looked like they had been original furnishings, old, made of bleached wood and, as I quickly discovered, uncomfortable. But Wylie seemed pleasant enough, and willing to talk. When Yuri asked about the members who weren't there that night, Wylie seemed puzzled.

"Sure," he said, "I can give you the names of some regulars who weren't there that night. But why would you want to talk to them?"

"They knew Rune, right? As well as Ethan and Tilly. We're just trying to talk to as many members of the Society as we can." That seemed like a lame explanation to me, but Wylie seemed to accept it.

"Okay." He took a notebook out of his desk and asked for my phone. Then he took a picture of the page and handed my phone back. "That's a list of the main participants and their phone numbers. Rune thought we should be able to contact each other since some of the meetings weren't posted on the website."

He ran his finger down the list of participants. "The ones who weren't there were . . . Eddie, Vince, Deanna, and . . . Carter." Looking up he said, "All the regulars wanted to be there. It was a major event."

Yuri noted the four names on his phone. "Any idea why those four missed the ceremony?"

"Yeah, Eddie's wife is pregnant and he didn't want to leave her alone. Vince had to work the evening shift. Deanna's boyfriend didn't want her to attend. Not entirely sure why. And Carter, I don't know about Carter. He's a bit aloof. Doesn't say much."

"I assume you've talked to the police," Yuri said.

"Yes, and a couple of reporters. I have nothing to hide."

"What was your opinion of Rune?"

"As you may know, he started the group. He was knowledgeable and energetic and always willing to try something new."

"Like the full moon sacrifice ceremony."

"Yes, that was his idea. Ironic that it turned out like it did." He sounded more matter-of-fact than sad about Rune's death.

"Was Rune a likeable guy?"

"That's not one of the words I would use to describe him. As the founder, he considered himself in charge of everything. It was his way or the highway, if you know what I mean. Some of the guys didn't care for that. All the women loved him, of course. He was good looking and could charm the pants off a snake."

That phrase was a new one on me, but I got the idea. "Was there anyone in particular in the group who didn't like Rune?" I asked.

"Not that I know of."

"Did you hear of any trouble between him and Tilly?"

He hesitated. Oh, oh. "Rune liked women. A real womanizer in fact. Tilly may have been his girlfriend, but we all knew he slept around."

"Did Tilly know that?"

"Well, she may or may not have known all along, but as of a couple weeks ago, she definitely was aware of his, um, indiscretions. I overheard Ethan telling her about his latest."

"Overheard?"

"At our last meeting before the ceremony, I was outside having a smoke during a break, just around the corner of the building. They apparently didn't know I was there. Ethan said he was telling her for her own good." He made a harrumphing sound. "Heard that phony line before. My guess is that he was hoping she'd turn to him for consolation. We all knew he had the hots for her. He was always trying to get her attention and followed her around like a lovesick puppy."

"But you don't think she fell into his arms to get even with Rune?"

"I highly doubt it." He harrumphed again. An expression of skepticism or just clearing his throat?

"Ethan couldn't hold a candle to Rune in the charm and looks departments." Skepticism then.

"And he has always been a bit needy and intense. Besides, she would have had other, better options. She's an attractive woman."

"We heard that someone claims to have seen Ethan and Tilly making out," Yuri interjected.

Wylie looked surprised. "I find that hard to believe."

"You don't happen to know whether Tilly confronted Rune about Ethan's accusation, do you?"

"No, I don't."

"How did Ethan get on generally with Rune?"

"They butted heads over things from time to time, but nothing serious."

"It's our understanding that Tilly was participating in the ceremony because of Rune. So, if she was told about his other women just days before the ceremony, why do you think she went along with it?"

"I'm not sure. Denial maybe." He shrugged. "Or Rune convinced her she was his number one. To be honest, she didn't display all that much enthusiasm for ancient cultures and rituals."

"Would you describe the group's mission as educational or social?" I asked.

Wylie laughed. "Rune was into all of the details about the various cultures and their practices, but most of us were mainly having a little fun." He stopped laughing. "Until Rune was murdered, of course."

"Of course."

"I got involved initially because of my interest in astronomy," he said. "I've been monitoring the brightness of stars and tracking asteroids and studying changes in the moon for some time. Another amateur astronomer I met at a star party told me about the Full Moon Society. Said it was thought-provoking, added another dimension to the study of the moon. I went once to see what it was all about, and have been attending meetings ever since. Rune did make it interesting—just the right mix of information and entertainment. Not exactly academic, and more, ah, socializing than serious conversations. But a good group of people."

After a few more questions, Yuri said, "So, who on this list should we should talk to if we want to know more about Tilly's relationships with Rune and Ethan?"

"Well, I think you'd get the same story from just about everyone." He thought for a minute. "I don't think she had any special friends in the group, but I couldn't say for sure. One of my employees went to high school with Rune. Larry Jackson. He was there that night. If you want, I could give him a short break to chat with you, as long as you're already here."

"That would be great. Thanks."

We said our thank you's and goodbyes and followed his directions to their lunchroom. It didn't take long for Larry to join us there. He was wearing overalls and a sleeveless T-shirt. A tattoo of an eagle covered his left shoulder, its head hidden by the edge of his shirt. He got a soda out of the refrigerator and sat across from us at a rickety table covered with an old-fashioned red checked oilcloth.

"The women have always liked Rune," he said when we asked about his relationship with Tilly. "He was a chick magnet. Tilly should have known he wasn't a one-woman man."

"How did they seem before the ceremony?" I asked.

"Fine."

"And Ethan?"

"Same old Ethan."

"Can you elaborate on that?"

"He's not a bad guy, just a little odd. Tries too hard to act macho and fit in."

"Were you aware that he wanted to be more than friends with Tilly?"

"That was pretty obvious to everyone, except Tilly. Rune thought it was amusing. He knew he didn't have anything to worry about."

"At the end of the ceremony, did you notice anyone hanging back?"

Larry laughed. "Subtle," he said. "That's what the police asked me and the others I've compared notes with—was there anyone who didn't stay with the procession heading for the cave? But the answer is 'no.' Rune was getting a few things cleaned up, but no one else stayed behind that I saw. We were all into the chanting and enjoying ourselves. To be honest, most of us were a bit high."

"You didn't see or hear anything unusual?"

"Just a coyote barking. I thought that was a nice touch. Totally unplanned of course."

"Do you have any theories about what happened?"

"All I know is that it couldn't have been one of us. No one could have slipped away without being noticed. We may have been drinking and smoking a bit of pot, but we weren't completely out of it. Besides, there were a couple of detectives there watching . . ." He stopped in mid-sentence and blinked. "Not you two?"

I reluctantly nodded. "We just want to verify our own impressions."

"Not your finest hour, huh?"

"No," I admitted. "Not by a long shot."

CHAPTER 14
FLY ME TO THE MOON

WEDNESDAY MORNING I was in the kitchen getting a cup of coffee when I heard my mother shooing No-name down the stairs. "Bad puppy. Go on, scoot."

I went out to see what the problem was.

"Cameron, we need one of those expansion gates to keep your dog where he belongs."

"Not my dog, Mom. And weren't you the one who said—in front of Jason—that there was no reason not to keep the dog when Yuri brought him here as a surprise for Jason?" I'd never totally forgiven her for that.

Mom stared at No-name. He was wagging the whole back half of his body, looking up at her adoringly, as if he didn't realize she barely tolerated him. On the other hand, maybe he was using that innocent look to taunt her. No, on second thought, even if No-name was smarter than I gave him credit for, he wasn't smart enough for that. Then it hit me.

"You've been giving him food at the table, haven't you?" Mom looked somewhat guilty, but not contrite. "You're not supposed to do that. It's habit forming and not healthy for him."

"Well, I want him to like me. Just not enough to want him to come upstairs to visit."

"I'm not sure you can have it both ways. And please don't let the kids catch you doing that—I've tried very hard to discourage them from feeding him at the table."

"Buy me a gate and I'll promise to be good." Then, laughing, she added, "On second thought, I'll buy myself the gate so I don't make any promises I can't keep."

No-name nosed her slacks, leaving a wet mark. "Now look what you've done. Bad puppy."

I refrained from smiling and faded back into the kitchen, leaving the two of them alone to work out their differences.

Yuri was waiting for me at the office. He waved me into a conference room to tell me about the meeting he'd had with P.W. before I arrived. Apparently, Clara was still concerned about Tilly being a suspect in Rune's murder, but P.W. didn't want to give her any false hope, and she wasn't sure what we could do to prove Tilly's innocence. Short of finding the murderer, that is. And that was a job for the police.

"But," Yuri said, "P.W. and Clara have agreed we should talk to one or two more Full Moon Society members about Ethan and Rune. They think we might get more information out of them than the police will. Because I'm so charming, of course."

"I think we should talk to one of the women. They might have a different read on the Ethan-Rune-Tilly triangle." I smiled, "And because you're so charming, of course—who knows what they might reveal."

Grinning widely, he said, "I agree 100 percent. And my second vote goes for the aloof Carter King. It sounded like he was the only regular who didn't have a reasonable excuse for not attending the ceremony."

I pulled up my copy of the Full Moon Society list Wylie had given us on my phone. "Want to look these women up ourselves or ask Tilly for a recommendation as to who it might be best to contact? We don't have to let on that we're asking about the 'love' triangle."

"We don't have much time, so I say we punt. Throw a dart."

"Even I know those are mixed sport metaphors." I looked at the list. "How about we start at the top with the first female name, Riley Nelson."

I punched in her number and she answered before the second ring had a chance to do more than burp. And, not only was Riley more than happy to chat with us, she was a student at the University of Washington and could meet us on campus outside the Hub at 11:00. She texted me a selfie she'd taken so we would recognize her. In it, her head was tilted to one side and she was giving the camera a wide smile that flashed white teeth and narrowed her eyes slightly. In the background there were students crossing the campus Quad, looking down at their phones as they hurried by.

Then Yuri called Carter King, and I listened to Yuri's end of the conversation. "Glad I caught you in." "I understand you are a member of the Full Moon Society." "Oh, I see. Well, would you be willing to talk to my partner and me about the group? We're investigating what happened the night of the ceremony."

"Yes, I understand you weren't there, but it sounds as though you may have some insight into the functioning of the group."

"No, we are not associated with the police."

"It won't take long."

"Yes, we can be there at 1:00."

"Thanks."

"From this end it sounded like he didn't really want to talk with us."

"It seems he is a professor in some executive business program at the University. Said he's studying influencer strategies and social control theory. Wanted to emphasize he wasn't 'one of them,' I think."

"Well, if nothing else, it's certainly convenient that he and Riley are both in the same location. I say we talk to her and then grab a coffee and a snack on the Ave before we meet with the King."

"Maybe you can buy me some fries."

"If we come across a place that will sell just four, sure."

The day was overcast with a nip of cold weather to come. The walk from the university visitors parking lot to the HUB—the Husky Union Building—took us down intersecting walkways among soaring evergreens and the occasional deciduous. The leaves on the deciduous trees were engaging in their autumn ritual, fading from shamrock or basil green to pale yellow to rusty brown before plunging downward to litter the paths with their limp or crinkled corpses. Yuri had a map he'd printed and kept turning it this way and that to figure out where we were. It hadn't been that long since the last time we were on campus, and I knew exactly where we needed to go, but I let him struggle. It was fun to watch.

When we reached the steps to the HUB, I immediately spotted Riley. She not only looked like her selfie, she was the quintessential student: backpack, jeans, pony-tail, tennis shoes. I flashed on what Mara might look like a few years down the road when attending a college somewhere. It was both exciting and scary.

Riley caught sight of us and waved. We hadn't sent her pictures, but I had described us. I'm pretty standard looking, but Yuri tends to stand out with his unkept dark hair and black-rimmed glasses. She made a beeline in our direction, stopping at the top of the stairs to wait for us. After brief introductions, we went inside together and Yuri went to get us something to drink while Riley and I found a table.

"I feel so bad for Tilly," she offered after I'd explained the nature of our inquiry. "She was so into Rune."

"I heard they'd had a falling out."

"More like a come-to-Jesus meeting for both of them. Tilly had to face that he'd been fooling around with other women, and he had to accept that she wasn't about to put up with that."

"You think he was willing to change for her?"

"Well, no, I don't believe someone like him changes. But I think he told her he would, and she probably believed him. She was really hung up on him."

"What about her and Ethan?"

"That creep? He had like a double-crush on her, but she only had eyes for Rune. But even if she hadn't been in love with Rune, she wouldn't have had anything to do with Ethan. He is definitely not her type. I'm not sure he's anyone's type."

Yuri appeared with our drinks and a basket of fries. Riley and I immediately went for the fries. I told Yuri what she had said so far about the Tilly/Rune/Ethan trio. He asked, "Any idea if Ethan resented Rune because he cheated on Tilly? Or because Tilly was crazy about him?"

"Not that I know of. But I usually avoid talking to Ethan. I might say 'hello' or 'so long,' but that's about it."

"You dislike him that much?"

"No, it's more a matter of not wanting to waste my time on him."

"How about other group members. Was there anyone you know of who was upset with Rune?"

"There was some macho jockeying for top dog, but other than that, no. It's not an official club or anything. Just a group of people who occasionally hang out together."

"What about Carter King? I understand he was usually at meetings but didn't attend the ceremony."

"That wasn't surprising. He's a bit stand-offish. Doesn't come to the after-meeting parties or the outdoor events. But I don't think he had any problems with Rune."

"Why do you think he attends meetings if he doesn't want to interact socially?"

"Well, we do talk about different cultures and their religious and spiritual beliefs. Not a lot, but some. I assume he finds those discussions interesting."

"Do you?"

"Sometimes. But . . ." She grinned at us. "What can I say, it's also a way to meet men. I've dated several in the group."

"Including Rune?"

"I'd prefer not to comment on that. However, I had his number right from the start. I wouldn't have tried to domesticate him."

"I've known a few guys like that," I said, more to build rapport than as a lead-in to sharing confidences. Getting married young had prevented me from a lot of mistakes I might have made. "Good for the short-term, but best not to get too attached."

"Too bad Tilly had to learn the hard way."

"There are always a few lessons that can only be learned the hard way." That I could definitely relate to. "Anything else you think we should know?"

Riley tilted her head to one side like she was about to pose for another selfie. But instead of smiling, she got serious. "Not sure it's important, but there were rumors that Rune was fooling around with someone Tilly knew. Someone in that climate group she belongs to."

"Do you think Tilly heard the rumor?"

"I have no idea, but if she did, well, she would have gone after the girl, not Rune, don't you think? That's what I would have done."

I wasn't sure what I would have done under the circumstances. It's bad enough to have your boyfriend cheat on you; worse yet if it's with someone you know. An interesting conundrum—whether to confront a lover or a friend. If Tilly had known about the rumor, whether she had acted on it or not, it was something she hadn't chosen to share with us. And if the rumor was true, it was definitely a provocative twist in a complicated matrix of relationships.

We left Riley and headed to the Ave to grab a quick bite. We found a small Korean eatery packed with people and managed to squeeze in and corral a small table at the back as a couple was leaving. I got the seafood tofu soup and Yuri got beef kalbi, bbq short ribs. We exchanged sips and bites. Both were delicious.

We lingered a little longer than we should have and had to hustle to make our 1:00 appointment with Dr. Carter King. His office was in one of the modern buildings on campus, nestled among thick-trunked evergreens with limbs reaching out across the lawn as if trying to claim land rights.

Like its older counterparts, the building's windows were partially covered with ivy. But no amount of greenery could hide the boxy, glass design. It just didn't say "academia" to me. Rather, it screamed "corporate."

The interior was also very contemporary with glass see-through walls probably intended to make the interior feel spacious. To me it just meant "no privacy." How could you even blow your nose without feeling like you needed to be discreet? And what if you wanted to rest your head on your desk for a bit of shut-eye? Or scratch an itch? Or comb your hair? Or eat some Cheetos?

When we reached Dr. King's office, I didn't care much for the look of the glass box he occupied, but I definitely liked the way he looked. He was with a student when we arrived, so I had time to check out his office, although my eyes focused mostly on him. Grayish green shirt with rolled up sleeves, well-trimmed beard with stands of silver gray adding a touch of distinction, and a full head of wavy dark hair. Be still my heart.

"I see the way you're staring at him," Yuri said. "Like a starving woman presented with a box of chocolates. Where to begin, where to begin."

"Don't be ridiculous. I'm doing a professional assessment."

"Sure you are."

The student left and Dr. King came to the door to greet us. Although I wasn't able to guess his height within a quarter inch, I was confident he was over six-feet tall. Another plus from my 5'10" perspective. And I couldn't help but notice that his gray-green eyes matched the color of his shirt. When he opened his mouth and a low-pitched melodic voice came out, I almost swooned. Fortunately, Yuri wasn't drooling like I was, so he was able to perform the normal introductory function.

"It's good of you to see us," Yuri concluded. "We won't take much of your time; we just have a few questions." We sat down across from the professor's desk, and Yuri immediately turned to me to begin the interview. He knew I'd been distracted by the professor's looks, otherwise he would have taken the lead. He can really be annoying at times. But I had recovered sufficiently to perform my assigned duties without gushing.

"We understand you've been attending Full Moon Society meetings because of your interest in influencer strategies. That sounds more like marketing research than a model for analyzing a fringe group." See, Yuri, I can be tough and fawning at the same time.

"Actually, I see them as a microcosm of groups that come together around a single issue. In this case, supposedly an interest in ancient rituals, including human sacrifice."

"Why 'supposedly'?"

"Well, it's a rather offbeat topic, don't you agree? For a voluntary, self-selecting group, that is. Not one that you would expect people from diverse backgrounds to necessarily find attractive."

"I am surprised at the size and diversity of the group," I said. "And I'm curious how the Society came to your attention in the first place."

"Through a student. She knew my Masters is in anthropology and asked me if I was familiar with the group. She was thinking of attending a meeting and wanted my opinion."

"And had you heard of them?"

"No, but after she decided to go to a meeting and told me about it, I was intrigued. On the one hand, it sounded like they were conducting mini seminars on the rituals of ancient cultures. Their sessions apparently covered everything from acts of atonement to various types of celebrations. Animal sacrifices to appease the gods. Dancing and music. Funeral rites. Use of hallucinogens to free the human spirit. Random topics from different time periods and civilizations. And she explained that they held meetings outside during full moons and did re-enactments. She was also very impressed with their 'charismatic' leader. It appeared to have all the elements of a quasi-secret society while being open to the public. I was curious."

Yuri jumped in. "I bet you could see a professional article coming out of this, right?"

The professor gave Yuri a warm smile. "You caught me. Given the topic, it might even have had non-academic interest."

"You're talking in the past tense," I pointed out.

"Rune's death makes the whole thing problematic. I did think I could use the topic to catch the attention of people who wouldn't otherwise be interested in how groups form and what keeps them together, but I don't want to write something for a tabloid or get that kind of publicity. Still, I can use what I've learned in class as examples and perhaps grab the fleeting interest of students for a few minutes."

I somehow doubted his need to grab attention, especially from female students.

"I looked you up and noticed that you did an interview on Yale's Skull and Bones that got quite a bit of traction," Yuri said.

"I'm intrigued with secret societies and quasi-secret groups. What draws people to them, how they maintain participation, why people don't report abuses . . . They are extreme examples of single-issue groups."

"You didn't tell any of the members why you were attending their meetings, did you?" Yuri asked.

"No, I wanted to get a glimpse from the inside."

"Any chance Rune found out what you were doing and was upset with you?"

Professor King smiled again. "And I stabbed him to keep him quiet?"

"Yuri wasn't suggesting—" I began.

"It did cross my mind," Yuri admitted.

"I have tenure. I believe I could have weathered a few complaints about undercover research."

I jumped in to change the subject. "So, what did you think about Rune and his 'followers'?"

"My armchair analysis was that Rune liked being the center of attention and had organized the group as a venue for being in the limelight. His grasp of information and his ability to keep people coming back was amazing though. There are other full moon society groups in the country, so the concept wasn't unique. But it served what I consider his 'purpose' quite nicely."

"You don't think he had a sincere interest in ancient cultures?"

"Not an academic interest, but he obviously had sufficient knowledge about the topic to make captivating presentations and come up with events that were well-attended. I found his mini lectures to be fairly accurate if a bit haphazard. One of the things he was fond of pointing out was that a lot of ancient religious ceremonies used psychoactive drugs to enhance the experience. I admit that concerned me."

"Did you suspect him of selling drugs?"

"It crossed my mind. None of the meetings I attended included any alcohol or drugs. But I got the impression that some of the full moon outdoor meetings did. Part of the 'authenticity' of re-enactments perhaps."

"Do you think everyone knew the full moon ceremony was going to include drinking and drugs?"

"No one mentioned it to me, but that's one of the reasons I decided not to attend."

A student appeared in the doorway and waved to Professor King. He looked at his watch and said, "I'm sorry, but I have an appointment with a student."

Yuri and I stood. "We might like to talk to you again if that's possible."

"Certainly. Do you have a card?" He was responding to Yuri but looking at me.

"Give him your card, Cameron," Yuri said with a pointed nonchalance that called attention to his hidden agenda, at least to me.

I handed the professor a card. He glanced at it and said, "Good, I'll call if I think of anything."

"Thanks Professor King," I said.

"Call me CJ, please." He gave me a 100-watt smile, and I felt myself automatically smiling back. Out of the corner of my eye I caught Yuri's Cheshire grin. On the way out of the building he started humming, "Fly Me to the Moon."

CHAPTER 15
MOON MUSIC

YURI WAS ALREADY in the pit when I arrived Thursday morning. "Call me CJ" he said loudly.

"Not funny."

"Want in on the pool for the day and time he's going to call you with something he remembered?"

Adele looked up from her computer and said, "I didn't place a bet." Her professional demeanor was in direct contrast to Yuri's playfulness.

Will yelled from his corner desk, "I've got a dollar on today by 5:00." His wide grin said it was all in good fun.

I consider Grant our level-headed mentor, so I was surprised when he came over and handed Yuri a dollar right in front of me. "Tomorrow by noon." Then he gave me a big smile. "He sounds like a catch. Although I've been rooting for Detective Connolly."

I looked around the room; I needed to end this right now. It was bad enough that my mother and Yuri both kept trying to get me back into the dating world, but if all of my colleagues joined in, I would have no peace. "No one has to root for anyone," I said as firmly as I could. "I'm perfectly happy being a single mother." Glaring at Yuri, I added,

"With an untrained, unnamed dog, a live-in mother and two teenagers. Life is complicated enough."

Everyone applauded. Then Adele came over and handed Yuri a dollar. "Okay, how about tomorrow after noon." She patted my arm. "It can't hurt to have a little fun now and then."

Obviously, it was a losing battle. "And if he doesn't call, I win the pot, right?" I'd aways hated the saying "if you can't beat them, join them." But in this instance, it seemed like the only way to move on.

"If he doesn't call," Yuri said, "you win the pot and I'll buy you lunch. That's how sure I am about this."

After our meeting with Professor King the day before, we had talked with P.W. about whether there was anything else we should do before writing up our report. Clara wasn't paying us to find Rune's killer, and we wouldn't have accepted that assignment anyway. Nor could we see how asking more questions about Rune's womanizing would be helpful to Tilly's defense. On the contrary, it was looking like that line of inquiry might provide more motive for her as the suspect. In the end we decided that P.W. would tell Clara that we would be available if any new evidence or issues came up, but that for now, we had done all we could. Case closed.

I'd finished my part of the report and decided to run out to buy a cookie. Every hand in the room went up when I asked if anyone wanted me to bring them back one, even weight and health-conscious Adele's. On the way out I impulsively asked Blaine if he'd like a cookie. I always feel guilty about leaving him out of everything. He looked at me like I was mad and said, "No thank you." Then, as an afterthought, "It was nice of you to ask."

Still processing his response, I charged out into the mall and headed for Mrs. Field's. Once there I took a minute to study the many cookie options in the glass-covered case. All of them were the same size, perfectly round, all lined up in precise rows, beckoning passersby with their colorful sprinkles or chocolate chips poking up through the crust. Add to that the aroma of fresh baked cookies, and who could resist? I wondered if the cookies actually were baked on site or if some machine pumped out the alluring smells.

When someone stepped alongside me, a little too close for my comfort level, I took a step to the side without looking up. But when the person quickly closed the gap by moving shoulder to shoulder with me a second time, I turned to see what kind of person would do that.

"Ethan," I said, my flight or fight impulse starting to kick in. Surely he wasn't going to attack me in front of Mrs. Field's gourmet, fresh-baked cookies!

"We need to talk," he said. I involuntarily took another step to the side; this time he let me increase the space between us. But he looked ready to pounce.

"Sure. Let me buy my cookies first, okay?" I was biding my time, hoping to get a chance to ring for back-up without him noticing. "There's a table right over there." I pointed. "I'll join you as soon as I get my cookies."

For a moment I thought he was going to say that he couldn't wait for me to buy cookies, but instead, he obediently headed for the table. I got out my phone and punched in Yuri's number as I went over to place my order.

"Guess who . . . I want a dozen cookies . . . Ethan's here . . . an assortment—whatever." The clerk gave me that disgusted look they reserve for irritating customers before getting out a box to process my order.

"How many cookies did you say you wanted?" she asked.

"A dozen," I said quickly before turning back to Yuri. "What should I do? He sees me on the phone. He's coming back." I hung up.

"Do you want an assortment?" the clerk asked. "Or do you want to pick them out one at a time." Her non-verbals, both tone and body language" let me know that "assortment" was the correct answer.

"Assortment," I agreed. Turning to Ethan, I asked, "Did you want me to buy you a cookie?"

"Who were you talking to?"

"My daughter. Why?"

"You have a daughter?"

"Yes. And a son." I didn't mention their names but almost started naming other relatives and pets, I was that nervous.

"How do you want to pay?" the clerk asked impatiently.

I handed her my credit card and we waited in silence for her to finish the transaction. Then I picked up my box of cookies and headed to the table with Ethan. My phone was ringing. I answered and said, "Honey, I'm busy right now. I just picked up a box of cookies and ran into someone I need to talk to. Call me later, okay?" I left the phone on and put it in my pocket.

"We got off on the wrong foot," Ethan said as we sat down.

"Ah, I'd say so."

"You really don't understand about Tilly and me."

I was tempted to say "there is no Tilly and you," but reminded myself I was dealing with an unstable individual. "So, why don't you tell me what you think I should know."

"For one thing, her relationship with Rune was over," he said. "She didn't like him playing around with other women. He was a philanderer. A narcissistic philanderer. She knew he didn't love her the way I do."

Yuri was suddenly standing next to the table. "Cameron," he said. "Everyone's waiting for their cookies."

"Ethan wanted to talk."

Yuri pulled up a chair. "What do you want to talk about, Ethan?"

Ethan glared at Yuri, his eyes telegraphing hate. "You wouldn't understand." He got up and started walking away. Yuri pushed his chair away from the table, but I put my hand on his arm to stop him from following Ethan.

"Let him go," I said. "We don't want any kind of a showdown with all of these people around. Someone could get hurt."

Will came rushing up. "Where is he?" Will had his hand in his jacket pocket.

"Whatever is in your pocket, you won't be needing it."

Will sat in the chair Ethan had vacated. "I wasn't sure if Yuri had his weapon with him." He looked around. "What happened?"

"He didn't want to talk to Yuri," I said. "He just wanted to explain to me that Rune didn't love Tilly the way he does."

"Bizarre," Yuri said.

"Not really," Will countered. "He may think Cameron

would be willing to intercede with Tilly for him. You did say he was delusional, didn't you?"

"He probably knows I called Yuri and wasn't talking to my daughter like I told him," I said. "He may have thought he could use me to advocate for him, but I doubt he sees it that way now."

"We need to call Connolly," Yuri said.

"And you need to start watching your back," Will added. "Both of you."

When we called Detective Connolly and told him about what had happened, he seemed genuinely upset. "Do you think he came to the mall because he knows you work there and wanted to talk to you?"

"I think he's been stalking her, just like he stalked Tilly," Yuri said.

"We don't know that he stalked Tilly," Connolly cautioned.

"You still think Tilly had something to do with Rune's death?" I asked.

"It's an on-going investigation . . ."

"And you can't comment," I finished for him.

"We've talked to a couple of the Full Moon Society members," Yuri said. "And no one seems to think Tilly wanted anything to do with Ethan. Surely your investigators are hearing the same thing."

"I really can't share specifics, but off the record, Ethan seems more than a little unhinged. And we are looking into the credibility of the main witness. As we would do with any witness testimony."

"And you can't tell us who that witness is, correct?" I asked.

"That's right. But I can tell you that she was convincing."

Ah, it was a "she." Had he let that slip deliberately?

"Is the witness also a suspect?" Yuri asked.

"I can't . . ."

". . . comment," I finished for him again, perhaps a bit abruptly. I was struggling to keep my irritation with the process under control.

"If you're considering Tilly as a potential murderer because she was a woman scorned, I assume you are looking at the same possible motivation among his other conquests," Yuri said.

"His relationships with both men and women were complicated," Connolly acknowledged.

"In other words, you have quite a few suspects but are reluctant to give Tilly the benefit of the doubt." I knew I sounded angry, but only because I was angry.

"That's not how a police investigation works."

"We understand," Yuri motioned for me to zip it. That was becoming a theme in our three-way conversations of late.

"I will have someone check on Ethan, but unless you want to make a complaint, there's not much I can do."

"I have no grounds for a formal complaint."

"That about does it then," Yuri said. Now he was starting to get angry.

"Cameron, please be careful," Connolly cautioned. "And don't hesitate to call me if you see him hanging around again."

"I'll put your number on speed dial," I said, making little effort to hide my skepticism.

"I mean it, be careful and try to have someone with you whenever possible."

Did he think I was going to walk down dark alleys on my own with only a shadowy moon overhead? I knew what kind of music they played in a movie when a lone woman did that. And it was music I didn't intend to hear.

CHAPTER 16
A JEALOUS MOON

"WE NEED TO WARN Tilly," Yuri said. "Ethan obviously hasn't given up."

We called Clara's, but Tilly wasn't there. She had gone to the Green Women's headquarters to work on a march they were organizing in the city in coordination with other marches across the country to support climate change legislation. "She is so passionate about climate issues," Clara said. "I didn't think she should go, but she insisted."

"She probably needs a distraction," I offered.

"Is there new evidence?" Clara asked hopefully.

"No, sorry. Just tying up a few loose ends," I said by way of explanation for wanting to talk to Tilly. It sounded lame, but Clara didn't need Ethan to add to her list of worries. "If anything does come up, we'll let you know."

We made our way to the light rail and were lucky enough to hop aboard just as a train was about to leave the station. Fifteen minutes later we were disembarking and headed for the Green Women's headquarters in Pioneer Square. We were panhandled three times before reaching the front door of the aging brick building. Each time Yuri gave the person asking for money a dollar. One man said, "Oh, I can buy almost half a cup of coffee with this. Thanks."

"You need to up your game," I said. "Or give them coupons."

"Point made."

We'd had the discussion before, but I couldn't resist repeating my position. "In my opinion, handing out money on the street is like giving a thirsty person a drop of water." Then I softened my criticism by adding, "Even though I appreciate why you do it. And I know you donate to several nonprofits that support homeless shelters and food banks."

"You know that I sometimes give them two dollars. Maybe even five. I'm a bit short today."

"Two drops of water. Five drops of water."

"You really believe that's worse than no water at all?"

"I'm ambivalent," I admitted.

Our conversation was cut short by our arrival at the Green Women's headquarters. It was Yuri's first time there. After walking up the uneven wood stairs, he paused to examine the polar bear poster on their door. "I find that heartbreaking. I don't understand why everyone doesn't accept that we are facing a worldwide climate crisis."

"I sometimes wish I didn't have kids. I hate to think what it's going to be like for them as things get worse."

We could hear voices inside, voices and activity. When we opened the door, we saw clusters of women distributed around the large room. Some were working on what looked like posters. Others talking in small groups. Before we'd taken two steps in, Raven, the red-haired woman I'd met the first time, came over to ask what we wanted. And not in a friendly way.

"We'd like a few minutes with Tilly." I was looking around but didn't see her. "Her aunt said she was here."

Raven gave Yuri a hard look, then turned to me. "She's in the back room. I'll check to see if she has time to talk to you."

Since she hadn't invited us in, we waited near the door, observing the flurry of various activities. There were so many conversations going on at once that it was impossible to isolate what any one person was saying. Voices blended together in a blanket of sound, like waves crashing on shore. Occasionally a word popped out or a group's laughter skittered across the more serious talk. I had been focused on other news this past week, so I didn't know anything about the upcoming marches. I would have to ask my news junkie son.

Tilly came back with Raven and suggested we step into the hall to talk. If I'd been alone instead of with Yuri, would they have let us talk somewhere inside? Men were not included in their mission and were blamed for much of the climate change crisis. Still, based on the first visit and discussion Will and I had with Lark, the Green Women were apparently willing to take donations from "the enemy." And some of their members clearly had no problem sleeping with "the enemy." Like so many complex problems, there were many gray areas.

"Is there something wrong?" Tilly asked as she shut the door behind her. Physically she seemed fully recovered from her ordeal, but I heard concern in her voice.

"Actually, yes," I said. We moved away from the main entrance before I continued. I hated having to give her more bad news, but she needed to know about Ethan's visit and what Detective Connolly had said. "He's unpredictable and possibly dangerous," I concluded. "You need to take every precaution to protect yourself. Try not to be alone in a place where he could approach you. Try to keep an eye out to see if he's following you. And keep your doors locked."

"I know that sounds grim," Yuri said. "But we wouldn't be here if we didn't feel it was necessary for you to be on alert."

"I still can't believe this is happening."

"I know. But you'll get through this." I tried to sound reassuring, but I felt pretty uneasy myself.

"We also have a couple of questions if you don't mind," Yuri said.

"Sure."

"You know that someone told the police they saw you making out with Ethan, don't you?"

"Yes, they asked me about it."

"Any idea who that witness is?"

"No, I've thought about it and can't imagine who would do that. It isn't true, so why would someone make that up?"

"I'm afraid it's someone who wants to make you look bad . . . or guilty . . . or both," Yuri said.

"It's just so hard to get my mind around any of this."

"This next question is a tough one, but I have to ask."

"Okay." Tilly took a step back as if to ward off a physical blow.

"Do you have any idea who Rune was seeing from the Green Women's group?"

"By 'seeing' you mean 'sleeping with.'" She sounded both sad and bitter.

Yuri nodded.

"I have my suspicions, but I'm not sure I even want to know."

"Think about it Tilly," I said. "Rune and you had agreed on an exclusive relationship, right? Which means he needed to end any other relationships he had. It's possible that the person he broke up with . . ."

"Killed him? Over a break-up?" Tilly shook her head. "I can't imagine that."

"Jealousy is a powerful force. Especially if the person has a mental disorder, a substance abuse problem, or suffers from extreme feelings of rejection, which can turn into depression or anger. The bottom line, their mental make-up may have resulted in irrational choices."

"As I said, I have my suspicions. But I can't think of anyone . . . not anyone like that. I'd rather not name names."

"The problem is that you can't 'see' a mental disorder. And addicts are good at hiding their addictions. They may not show any signs of what I've mentioned; they may be holding it all inside." I was hoping to convince her to tell us who she suspected so we could follow up. But before I could finish my argument, Raven poked her head out the door.

"We could use you inside," she said to Tilly. Tilly immediately started to obey.

"If you think of anyone," Yuri called after her.

"And be careful," I added.

Yuri and I spent an hour working on our final report for Clara Ramsey. We detailed what we had done, but when it came to actual accomplishments, it felt like there were more dead-ends pursued than results achieved. We added another page for the Penny-wise files that included a less customer-focused assessment and listed loose ends. Then it was over. It felt entirely unsatisfactory. There was no closure on anything. We didn't know who had killed Rune. Tilly was still a suspect in a homicide investigation. Ethan was creeping around out there somewhere. And we were concerned that Tilly was only marginally safe. In fact, I wasn't feeling all that safe myself.

When Yuri suggested we make a coffee run, I was all for it. We headed for our favorite kiosk in the mall. Then, while standing in line, Yuri surprised me by asking, "Want to go to the march on Saturday?"

"You mean the climate change march on Washington? The one the Green Women are preparing for?"

"Yeah. The local march starts at Cal Anderson Park around 10:00. From there everyone walks to the Westlake Center. It's only about a mile and a half, but depending on how many people show up, it could take a while. The plan is to hold a rally at noon at the Center. That's where the speeches will take place."

"I hadn't been planning on it."

"You could bring Jason and Mara. It would be a good experience for them."

"You're not suggesting this as some sort of add-on for our already closed case?"

"It's a good cause. And good exercise."

"I'm not really a protest type of person."

"This isn't a protest. It's an attempt to call attention to a global crisis. I've been reading about it. It isn't just extremist groups either, most of the participating groups are mainstream."

We ordered our coffee and stepped aside to wait.

"Instead of starting from Cal Anderson, we could take the light rail directly downtown and attend the main rally," Yuri said. "I could meet you at your place and we could all go together."

"I don't find the march itself very appealing, people all bunched together, being herded toward the Center at herd speed. But attending the rally might be interesting."

"The march is a community event. People talking to like-minded people about their shared cause. Making a statement for the cameras. But I understand your point of view. I'm fine with just the rally."

Okay, I'll see if the kids want to join us. But even if they don't want to, I'll go with you."

My phone rang and I glanced at the caller ID. I could feel the blush working its way up from my neck. "Ah, I need to take this. Grab my coffee when it comes up, okay?" I glanced at the time—Adele had won the pool; it was after noon.

"Hi," CJ said. "Did I catch you at a good time?"

"I'm at work, but now's okay. What's up?" I was trying to be casual, but I could feel Yuri's eyes boring into my back.

"This may seem a little off the wall, but I would like to talk to you about the Full Moon Society, if you're willing. Maybe over coffee or a glass of wine." Coffee or wine, was that some kind of code for whether it was a professional or personal meeting?

"Sure," I said. "Do you want me to check with my partner?" Ouch. That definitely sounded like code.

"I was thinking just the two of us . . . if that's all right with you," he said. Was there a hint of uncertainty?

I wanted to ask if he was married or if he knew I had kids, but that was perhaps a leap too far. Maybe he really did want to talk about the Full Moon Society and thought a one-on-one would be more productive than a threesome. "That's fine," I said, sounding as awkward as I felt. "Maybe coffee after work." If it was code, I wanted to take it slow.

"Tonight? 5:00? I could meet you at a Starbucks near the mall."

By the time we'd made arrangements, Yuri had both coffees and was looking impatient. And a bit worried. Until he looked closely at me. Then he smiled. "Not a problem at home then?"

"No, just . . ." I considered lying but wasn't sure I could pull it off. Yuri knew me too well. "Adele wins the pool, But," I added quickly, "it was about the case."

"So, you informed him that we are no longer officially investigating anything related to the Full Moon Society and you will therefore not need to see him again. Do I have that right?" Yuri's eyes were making fun of me from behind his thick glasses.

"Not exactly."

"You are going to see him again then?"

"Just for coffee and to talk about the Full Moon Society."

"Want me to join you?"

"Very funny."

"He asked you for coffee under the guise of talking about the group—is that how it went down?"

"Not exactly."

"Now you have my attention."

"Okay, I admit he gave me a choice between coffee and a glass of wine."

"And you, very unwisely I may say, chose the safe option."

"I don't know if he's even single. And he doesn't know if I am. Just because neither of us wears a ring . . ."

Yuri interrupted, "Oh, you checked out his ring finger? For professional reasons no doubt."

Ignoring him, I continued. "Nor does he know that I have two teenagers and an untrained dog. And he really is studying extremist groups. So, yes, I took the safe route."

"You may be right, but the others are going to be disappointed."

"You don't have to tell everyone, do you? What if he's married, has a flock of kids, and just wants to talk?"

"Then, let me just say, we'll all be disappointed."

CHAPTER 17
HOLDING MOONLIGHT
IN YOUR HANDS

I CALLED MY MOTHER to tell her I would be late getting home and asked if she could make sure the kids got something to eat. She's used to me having last-minute work things come up, so she didn't ask why I would be late, and I didn't tell her. My work colleagues had already given me a bad time about my coffee "meeting"; I didn't need any more questions or innuendos, subtle or pointed. Someday I would make Yuri pay for creating the pool that spotlighted what could easily turn out to be a total non-event or, worse yet, a total disaster. And whatever happened, everyone would expect some kind of report. Thank heavens my mother didn't know about CJ and the pool. And if Yuri let it slip to her, I would make him pay double.

Adele stopped by my desk to tell me not to take the teasing seriously. "But it sounds from Yuri's description that he's a real looker."

"I don't know anything about the man other than where he works. And that he keeps his desk clear of clutter. For all I know, he may be married. And he said he wanted to talk about the Full Moon Society; he didn't suggest it was a date." Well, maybe the reference to meeting for a glass of wine implied that it could be a date, if that's what I had chosen.

"Hey, just test the waters, but don't be afraid to swim if the opportunity arises. You can always return to shore." As she went back to her desk, I couldn't help wondering how many times she had gone swimming. And if she regretted any of those times . . . or if her regrets were for the times she hadn't. It was a side to her I hadn't thought about before.

I arrived at Starbucks a few minutes early and was tempted to stay out in my car until five after so I wouldn't look too eager. Even though I kept telling myself it wasn't a date, I regretted what I had chosen to wear that day. My orange sweater and brown slacks had seemed appropriate for a casual fall day in the office, but orange isn't my best color, even though I'm fond of it. It makes me look washed out. On the other hand, this might not be a date, so what was I worrying about?

At one minute to five I saw CJ enter Starbucks. I counted to ten and then followed. It was 5:00 straight up. So much for being fashionably late. Although maybe that was out of fashion these days. It had been a long time since I'd done anything even slightly social.

He turned, saw me and gave me a warm smile. At least it felt warm to me; I didn't know if that was his intention. I gave him a return smile that was supposed to be pleasant but noncommittal. Then I joined him in line and we exchanged hello's and how are you's before falling into an awkward silence.

"So . . ." we both said at the same time, then laughed.

"I wasn't sure if it was appropriate to ask you for coffee," he said. "But you aren't wearing a ring . . ."

"You're getting right down to the facts, aren't you?" Good. Once the rules were clear, I could hopefully shed the insecure woman act and be myself. "You aren't wearing one either."

"I'm divorced."

"I'm widowed."

"Oh, I'm sorry."

"Don't be. If he'd lived, I'd be divorced by now." Why on earth had I told him that?!

"Kids?"

"Two barely teens, a girl and a boy. You?"

"One teenage boy with an attitude."

I couldn't help but laugh again. "All this personal information and we haven't even ordered yet."

The next two hours went by so quickly I was surprised when I glanced at my watch and realized what time it was. We'd had several refills, split a sandwich and devoured two heated brownies that the warming process had rubberized slightly. By the time we were reluctantly saying goodbye, I knew a fair bit about him and he about me. We'd even talked some about the Full Moon Society, and I'd brought him up to speed on what we had learned and how the case had limped to a close.

When he suggested dinner Saturday night, I told him I was attending the climate change event with my kids and anticipated we'd want to go out to eat after. Without missing a beat, he suggested the following Saturday for our first official date. We left time and place loose; he said he would call to make arrangements. The instant he said the word "arrangements," it occurred to me that if he came by to pick me up, I would have to explain to Mom as well as to the kids who he was. I didn't want to offend him by suggesting we meet at a restaurant, but I wasn't sure I wanted to expose him to my entire household before getting to know him better. Especially not to my mother. She's been trying to ring wedding bells for me ever since Dan died. I preferred Adele's advice, take a swim with a good-looking man and see where it goes. One date or many. Either way, I didn't need a wedding planner.

The kids were both on their computers in their rooms when I returned. They barely looked up when I checked on them. Now that they were getting older they relied on me less and less for companionship. I'd become more like the captain of a large ship, steering the vessel but not controlling anyone onboard. What I missed most were some of our quiet times together, especially the early years of reading to them while they sipped hot chocolate and hung on every word.

Sadly, when I relived memories from when the kids were young, Dan was seldom part of the equation. He'd been there for vacations and holidays, but he'd missed out on most of the day-to-day stuff with Mara and Jason. It seemed as though he was always at work, and I'd accepted that as normal.

I was looking in the refrigerator for something to eat— the half a sandwich and a brownie hadn't filled me up— when my mother appeared in a long green robe and faux-fur slippers. She was carrying a plastic container. I quickly asked myself how hungry I was. My stomach wasn't up to experimentation.

"Thought you might like a snack," she said as she handed me the container. "I could have a glass of wine while you eat."

"I'm not very hungry," I lied. "What is it?"

"Spanakopita. It's a new recipe. Rather good, I think."

"Oh, sounds good." It really did. I love spanakopita, even a healthy version couldn't be bad, could it? I popped it in the microwave and got out a plate and two glasses while Mom went through my refrigerator looking for wine.

"This one will do," she said. She's more of a wine connoisseur than I am. In fact, I don't think I could be considered a connoisseur even in my fantasies. But I can tell a really good wine from the ones I usually buy.

When the spanakopita was warm, I turned it onto a plate and took a bite. "Yummy. Really yummy," I said, relieved to be telling the truth.

"Yummy enough to earn me an update on what's happening with the Full Moon Murder as the local press has labeled it?"

"Not much to tell, I'm afraid." I quickly filled her in on the encounter with Ethan, downplaying the fear I'd experienced. I also told her about our visit to the Green Women's workplace and our chat with Tilly about Rune's indiscretions and ended by explaining how unsatisfying it was to end a case without closure.

"You saved Tilly from Ethan. That was definitely worth doing."

"But Ethan's still out there, and Tilly is a suspect in a murder."

"Someone said, time moves slowly but passes quickly. You feel this way now, but in a year, you will have moved on."

Not to be outdone, I said, "Yuri is fond of saying, time flies like an arrow; fruit flies like a banana."

"Groucho Marx," Mom said. "He stole that line from Groucho Marx."

"I didn't know you were a Marx fan."

"I'm not. But at one point I dated a man who was. Fortunately, I came to my senses in time."

"I vaguely remember that Dad liked Monty Python." I knew my mother wasn't a fan of dark humor and anything she might label "silly."

"That was an acquired taste after we'd been married for quite a while."

"Otherwise?"

"It's hard to think of the 'otherwise' alternatives after years spent together."

I suddenly wanted to ask about their marriage, to verify or vanquish my suspicion that it hadn't been the best of marriages, but I hesitated, finally deciding to change the subject.

"There's a climate march and rally scheduled for Saturday," I said. "Yuri and I are going to the rally in the Center. He suggested I take the kids. What do you think?"

"If they want to go, I can't see any reason why they shouldn't. But you should probably keep a close eye on them. Crowds can turn ugly in an instant."

In addition to never having talked to Mom about her marriage to my father, it hadn't occurred to me that perhaps she had participated in marches and protests when she was younger. I had her securely labeled as the middle-aged woman I called Mom. Or the irritating mother who still posted the occasional article on my refrigerator even though we had agreed upon a moratorium on information about the ways in which kids of single moms suffer, statistics about a woman's age and her chances of remarrying, and suggestions on careers other than the one I had chosen.

"Did you get involved in any causes when you were young?" I asked. That seemed like a safe question.

"The issues then didn't seem as engaging to me as what's happening now. My generation was sandwiched between anti-war protests and the constitutional and climate concerns of today."

"You sound like you feel cheated."

"Well, we had the Macarena and a few political scandals. It wasn't too dull."

"You are welcome to come with us if you'd like."

She seemed to consider it, then shook her head. "No, I'll donate money to the cause—for my grandchildren's future. But I don't think I'm essential to the rally." She sipped her wine. "I assume you aren't going in order to keep an eye on Tilly."

"I don't even think that would be possible. They're anticipating a large turnout."

"That Ethan fellow wouldn't try anything in a crowd, would he?"

"I don't know what to think about that. He's scary, but I can't imagine him making a move on Tilly with other people around. And we don't know if he's the murderer."

"I don't think he is," Mom said.

"Really? Why?"

"If he's obsessed with Tilly, he wouldn't have used a dagger with her prints on it."

"Maybe he was angry because she didn't respond the way he expected when he told her about Rune's other women. Or maybe he didn't know her prints were on the dagger."

"If he's the murderer, and I emphasize the 'if,' I'm confident he would have wiped the weapon clean if he'd known her prints were on it. And if she is telling the truth and doesn't remember picking up the knife, then someone tricked her into doing it. I can't see how Ethan could have managed that given what you've told me about their relationship, or lack of one."

"I think she's telling the truth about disliking knives. That's what makes her prints on the dagger so puzzling."

"Any chance she helped Rune organize the paraphernalia for the event? Maybe she handled the dagger thinking of it as a prop and not as a weapon."

"I think she would have remembered doing that."

"What about after she was drugged at the ceremony?"

"Seems unlikely but not impossible."

"Maybe she was hypnotized."

"Seems a bit extreme."

"Well, in any case, I still don't think Ethan did it. But you're the detective."

Yes, I was the detective, but my mother's instincts were usually solid. And she was right about it seeming unlikely that Ethan would have murdered Rune and framed Tilly. But that didn't eliminate him from the running. He could have done it not knowing her fingerprints were on the dagger. Either that or someone else was trying to frame her. Or there was an entirely different explanation for why her fingerprints were on the dagger. Sherlock Holmes is often quoted as saying, "When you have eliminated the impossible, whatever remains, however improbable, must be the truth." That of course assumed you had some improbable theories to consider. I had no theories, improbable or otherwise.

As I was falling asleep, I quit dwelling on murder and instead fantasized about my date with CJ. I found myself trying to remember the lyrics to "Catch the Moon." The last thing I remember was a vision of catching moonlight in my hands. It was beautiful and elusive as it lit up my fingers and slipped through them to the forest floor.

Friday morning Yuri was sent out on a stakeout and I was assigned to assist Adele on some background checks for a corporate client. Not an exciting assignment for me, but a good source of revenue for Penny-wise. Most of background check work is done online, although it also involves calls to references and HR people and occasionally in-person visits. The HR reps tend to be very close-mouthed, so I've gone out of my way to curry some rapport by dropping by to meet individuals face-to-face, giving small gifts of food at random times so as not to have the gifts connected with a specific inquiry. I also go out of my way to cultivate potential contacts on LinkedIn and Facebook. I've even gone out to lunch with a few of my favorites. They always want to know about the exciting bits of my job, and I'm interested in the challenges they face with employee issues.

I had just come back from lunch when I got a call from Tilly. She said she hesitated to ask, but there was something she wanted to run past me, as someone familiar with her situation. Could she come by for a few minutes? We agreed to meet in the mall to keep the conversation informal.

She arrived right on time. We sat on a bench near a children's play area where kids were climbing on colorful plastic animals, sliding down plastic slides, and ducking in and out of a tiny plastic log cabin. "At that age you just don't have a clue, do you?" Tilly said.

"You mean about the threat of plastic to our environment?"

"No, about how simple life is at that age."

"Oh, in my experience, kids have their ups and downs starting at a very young age. Although their problems don't involve stalkers or being accused of a crime." I felt like reminding her that we had suggested she didn't go places on her own for a while, and yet here she was, in a mall where Ethan had been sited twice in the last week, and all by herself. Except at the moment, of course, while I was with her.

She took a deep breath before saying, "I need advice."

"I'll be happy to help in any way I can."

"You know about the Green Women and their mission."

I nodded.

"And you know that they sometimes get a little carried away. Do things that are not entirely legal. Which I don't necessarily agree with. But it's for a good cause."

"I understand." And even though I personally wouldn't participate in an illegal act, even one that was only borderline illegal, I really did understand why others engaged in questionable activities in support of this high-stakes movement.

"Here's my issue . . ."

She took another deep breath as if preparing to swim the length of the pool under water. "Something is going to happen at the march tomorrow that I'm uncomfortable with. It isn't really a question of whether it's legal or not—although I'm not sure about that. And no one should get hurt. It may, however, be a bit frightening, at least at first. And I know there will be lots of children there. That's one of the reasons why I'm concerned."

"Can you tell me what they've got planned?"

Tilly shook her head. "I really can't do that."

"Then, what do you want to discuss?"

"I know the police still have lingering doubts about me in connection with Rune's death, and if I end up being connected to another semi-illegal act, well. . . Do you think I'm being stupid?"

"Yes," I said without hesitation. "And the other Green Women shouldn't be asking you to participate in anything of that nature given what you've been through."

"Raven says we all have to stand united."

"Raven is not thinking about your welfare, is she? She's only thinking about the cause. And if you don't participate, it will still take place, right?"

"They don't need me. But Wren says everyone will be disappointed if I don't stand with them."

"What does Phoebe think?"

"She's like you, she feels like I should step back."

"I understand why Raven insists you participate, she's the unofficial leader and wants everyone on board. But why do you think Wren feels that way?"

Tilly seemed to be thinking carefully about her

response. "I'm not sure. I sometimes think she doesn't like me much. Then, she doesn't like anyone much."

"Well, I don't usually like giving advice, but in this instance, I have no hesitation—I definitely think you need to stay away from any potentially illegal acts tomorrow. Or anything that makes you feel uncomfortable. Trust your gut." She seemed surprised by my unequivocal response. "And consider your Aunt Clara for a moment, what she has gone through because of you. If you get arrested, well, she will be devastated. I can't imagine you want to cause her more worry."

Tilly's shoulders drooped. "No, I don't. And I can't believe I hadn't thought about how it would affect her. What kind of an unfeeling person am I?"

"Hey, don't go there. These aren't normal times for you. And, as I said, Raven isn't thinking about what's best for you, and for whatever reason, neither is Wren." After a moment's pause, I added, "But I understand your dilemma. Here's what I would do. Go ahead and meet up with everyone, then the first chance you get, fade away. You can always claim you got lost in the crowd."

"That seems dishonest."

"Then just don't show up. But you'll have to come up with an excuse for not being there if you want to stay in the group. Do you? There are alternatives if your main goal is to fight for climate change legislation."

"I may also have to find new roommates if I don't show or decide to drop out."

"Just take it one thing at a time. And remember, Phoebe is on your side. As am I and your Aunt Clara."

"Thank you. It helped to talk about it."

"You're sure you don't want to give me a head's up about tomorrow? I'm going to be there with my kids and don't want to put them in any danger."

Tilly had started to get up and abruptly sat back down. "It probably won't be a problem, but I know that any time you have unexpected loud noises in a crowd it can cause a panic." She thought for a minute. "Look, you didn't hear this from me, but you might want to give the pinata the Green Women erect at the Center a wide berth, okay?"

CHAPTER 18
MOONLIGHT PINATA

FRIDAY EVENING Yuri and I had a long discussion on the telephone about how we should respond to the information Tilly had shared with me. I admit to being primarily concerned about my own family, whereas Yuri kept bringing up our responsibility to other participants in the march. I reminded him that Tilly had said it wouldn't be dangerous, just unexpected noise that could startle people. From her warning to stay away from the pinata, we concluded that there was something going off when they hit the pinata—firecrackers or party poppers or even special sound effects. "A ploy to attract attention and get news coverage," I concluded.

"Shouldn't the police be made aware of this?" Yuri asked.

"They are already going to be on alert," I argued. "After all, they know the Green Women organized the march, and they have to be aware of their reputation."

"I'm just saying . . ." Yuri couldn't think of a solid reason to betray Tilly's trust, but he desperately wanted to. "What if she told you so that you would report it and get it stopped?"

"I don't think that's the case. She only told me after I mentioned that my kids were coming with me. And she assured me that, whatever they have planned, it's not something dangerous. Maybe they'll make some loud announcement, whap the pinata, and something will fall out."

"The body of a dead endangered animal?"

"That could spook the crowd. At least, it would spook me."

"But she did say they weren't doing anything obviously illegal?"

"She did. That eliminates firecrackers—they're illegal within the city limits. Not sure about dead animals. Maybe the pinata contains pictures of endangered species that will be scattered about when they strike the pinata."

"Leaflets wouldn't surprise too many people. Although it would disappoint those expecting candy to fall from the sky."

After going over the same ground for the umpteenth time, we finally decided it was probably safe to let the kids come with us, but we agreed that we weren't going to get anywhere near the pinata. We did, however, also agree that we were going to check out who was standing in its vicinity. Although we weren't sure what our criteria was for changing our minds about not saying anything to the police or warning people away. We even selfishly decided that we would stay near the edge of the crowd when that part of the event took place. If people panicked and started running away, we would be able to make our own exit more easily. I just prayed that nothing happened to make us regret our decision to stay mum.

At breakfast Saturday morning, Mara and Jason talked excitedly about the day ahead. "We're on the right side of history," Jason said several times. It seemed like a strangely adult thing to say. Although we've often talked about climate change, and they were both familiar with the depressing statistics about the impact of climate change on water tables, rising sea levels, food production, increased storms and wildfires . . . and all of the rest of the calamitous predictions that suggested it was the beginning of the end of life on our planet as we know it.

We'd also discussed the complexities of addressing climate issues. Still, in spite of the dire forecasts and challenges of finding and implementing solutions, I had a hard time accepting that these things were really going to come to pass. I imagined it was like being on death row with ten minutes left, waiting for the governor's call to stop your execution. You know it could happen, you pray it will happen, but at the same time, there is an inner voice that says your fate is in the wind, you may have run out of miracles.

As we were getting ready to leave, I was more nervous than I cared to admit. I think I would have been on edge even without the added burden of having my kids along. When you know something is going to happen but you don't know what that something is, it's hard to focus on anything but that unknown something. It's like waiting for the jack in the box to pop up as someone slowly turns the handle and the tinny voice sings.

Mom saw us off, cautioning us to "stay safe" and "enjoy." I hadn't told her about Tilly's warning; if I had, I knew she would insist we stay home.

Yuri drove. He was in an upbeat mood and got the kids to sing along with lyrics to a song they all seemed to know but I didn't recognize. I felt myself starting to relax.

It was a gorgeous fall day. The sun had found its way out from behind a line of clouds and the temperature was in the 50s. As we passed a stand of stunning maples next to a tall fir that reached out over the road, Jason said: "Did you hear about the study that found poor communities in cities have fewer trees than wealthy communities? There were aerial pictures in the Nature Conservancy magazine."

"That means it will get hotter where there are fewer trees, right?" Mara asked.

"It will be the difference between frying an egg on the sidewalk and drinking a mint julep in the shade," Yuri said.

"I might want to be a climatologist someday." Jason said.

"You think you can save the planet?" Mara chided.

"Someone has to."

We parked a fair distance from the light rail entrance due to heavy traffic in the area and joined the throngs of people skipping the march but heading straight downtown for the rally. If what we'd encountered so far was any indication, it was going to be a big turnout. Anxiety started to tickle my conscience again.

When we arrived at Westlake Center, it was already filled with people milling about, many of them carrying signs or wearing strange hats with barely readable messages written on them. There was also a heavy police presence. Most of the officers were standing near buildings, watching the people as they arrived. Probably assessing possible troublemakers and keeping an eye out for weapons. That was both reassuring and a bit disconcerting.

There were also a few TV vans on the outskirts. There were probably reporters milling about looking for a story. That was what the organizers of the rally, and certainly what the Green Women were counting on.

A helicopter flew over as we were jockeying for a good position back a ways and off to the side, with a good view of the stage. Mara and Jason wanted to get closer, but Yuri convinced them we were in a good spot. On the other side of the square a handful of counter protesters bookended by police waved signs and shouted. I wasn't sure if the police near them were there for their protection or to keep them from the rest of the crowd. But except for glancing at their signs, everyone seemed to be ignoring them. CLIMATE CHANGE HOAX! SCIENTISTS LIE! NATURAL CYCLES not GLOBAL WARMING! I ♥ MY CAR!

"We should have made a sign," Jason said, frowning at me like it was my fault we weren't going to be on TV.

"Just don't wander off," Yuri said. "We need to stay together. I don't want you to get lost in this crowd." He suddenly sounded grumpy, like he, too, was having second thoughts.

"Look," Jason shouted, pointing at the pinata. "Extra."

"Extra?"

"Cool to you," Jason explained.

The pinata was near the stage that had been set up for speakers. It was perched on top of a tall pole. The rainbow colors of its globe shape demanded attention. Tassels hung from bright red cones sticking out from the sides of the globe. Was it supposed to represent the world? The whole thing was high enough in the air that it was going to require a long stick to reach it.

"Let's go get a closer look," Mara said to Jason. Yuri reached out and grabbed Jason's arm at the exact moment I grabbed Mara.

"No," we said in unison. Then I quickly added in a less urgent tone, "We need to stay together."

Yuri said, "You will have a better view of it from here when they break the pinata."

We were saved from further argument by two men heading up the steps to the stage. A momentary hush fell over the square. The main event was about to begin.

"Yuri," I said, pulling him aside and keeping my voice low. "Do you think they are going to hit the pinata with a stick? Seems kinda high for that."

"I was wondering the same thing. Could be remote controlled."

"I hope they give the crowd some warning."

In spite of the loud speakers, we could barely hear the speeches being given. After the initial lull, the noise level of people milling about, talking and yelling slogans dominated the scene. Nevertheless, some of the messages got through and people responded by hooting, yelling encouragement, and occasionally repeating some phrase that caught their fancy. All I had to do was look at the faces of my children to know that the collective passion was more important than any words being spoken on stage. It was chaotic and exciting. You couldn't help but feel you were part of something important—the right side of history.

The handful of protesters on "the wrong side of history" were occasionally booed but kept in one location by their police "escorts." They waved their signs and added their voices to the cacophony.

When Raven took the stage, I found myself bracing for what was about to happen. Yuri also seemed to tense up. That was when I saw Tilly. "Oh my god," I said. Then I turned to Yuri. "Stay with the kids. I'll be right back."

Before he could stop me, I rushed off to where Tilly was standing with a group of Green Women all with interlocked arms. I reached her at the same time I heard Raven say something about the pinata. "Tilly," I screamed as I grabbed her arm.

The woman next to her tried to push me away. "It's your Aunt Clara," I improvised. "She's been taken to the hospital—you need to come now."

The woman trying to get me to leave Tilly alone hesitated. Tilly said "Sorry" to the women on either side of her.

But it was too late. The pinata exploded.

CHAPTER 19
MOONLIGHT BEHIND BARS

THE EXPLOSION included some starburst fireworks, streams of weaponized color flying in all directions. If the crowd had anticipated fireworks, and they had been the only thing coming out of the pinata, the display might have been greeted with oohs and ahs rather than fear. But there were also glittering comets shooting straight up, making whistling sounds like bombs being dropped from a World War II airplane. And there were firecrackers mimicking rapid gunfire. Flying sparks and debris pelted the crowd as they shoved and screamed, trying to escape.

I held onto Tilly, pulling her arm to extricate her from the other Green Women, but the women on either side of her held on, like fighting over a piece of clothing at a sale. Then Phoebe appeared out of nowhere and yelled at the women to stay in position. They closed ranks and started chanting: "WOMEN UNITE! SAVE OUR WORLD." Tilly and I were dragged in with them.

The next thing I knew, the police had us surrounded and someone on a bullhorn was telling us to kneel on the ground. I wanted to explain that I wasn't a member of the Green Women, but it was clear no one was listening. There was too much noise, too much confusion. I obediently knelt alongside Tilly, the two of us silent, while the other women continued to shout slogans.

When my phone rang, I went to reach for it in my jacket pocket and was struck by something hard across the shoulders. I fell forward, hitting the pavement with the side of my head. Tilly yelled something I didn't understand just as someone stepped on my hand. Then I was kicked in the ribs. The next thing I knew a male voice was ordering me to get up and telling Tilly to stay where she was. I managed to get to my knees before a hand reached out and yanked me to my feet. I thought I heard the phrase "butch bitches" as I was shoved toward the other members of the group that officers were busy handcuffing. Even in pain and feeling out of kilter, I couldn't help noticing that the handcuffs being used on the group were a flat black color, like something off of Batman's utility belt.

I desperately wanted to explain to someone that a mistake had been made. I was on the side of law and order; not a law breaker. I avoided jaywalking and picked up after my dog. I had attended the Civilian Police Academy and had eaten cookies and made small talk with the presenters from local law enforcement. I respected the police and their role in the community. They shouldn't be arresting me for something I wasn't responsible for.

My hand was throbbing and I didn't feel all that steady on my feet. When an officer ordered me to put my hands behind my back. I made another attempt to explain my situation. When he repeated his command, I obeyed but asked him to be careful because someone had stepped on my hand and I thought something might be broken. Unfortunately, he wasn't in the mood to listen. Pain shot up my arm and radiated out through my fingers as he pulled my hands together and put cuffs on me.

My phone rang again, but there was no way I could answer it with my hands cuffed behind my back. "My phone is ringing." I looked around and tried to catch the eye of a female officer with a kind face. "I need to answer my phone," I yelled. She glanced in my direction. "My phone," I shouted. "It's probably one of my kids. Can you let me answer it so I can let them know I'm okay?" Not that I was feeling at all okay. My hand was really hurting, my arm ached from being yanked to my feet, and my ribs felt like I would have expected if kicked with sharp toed shoes. That had never happened to me before.

"Sorry, no phones now." She didn't sound unsympathetic, but she nevertheless walked away.

Once we were cuffed, the officers ordered us to line up. Still slightly dazed, I tried to think about what options I had, if any. Poor Yuri. He must be frantic. Did he know what had happened to me? Had he and the kids got away safely? There was a lifeline to friends and family, right there in my pocket. If only I could answer my phone. But it was out of reach, taunting me by ringing and ringing and ringing. Well, actually, it was playing music, but the message was the same. Someone was trying to get me to answer and reassure them that I was alright.

The arresting officers might have been more sympathetic, but many of the Green Women were cursing and spitting at them. I took a gob on one arm and watched as it adhered itself to my jacket sleeve. My eyes kept going back to it, willing it to go away. But it didn't. It hung there, a disgusting reminder of the animosity between the opposing sides.

I looked around for Tilly, but couldn't see her. I caught sight of Wren and Raven near the front of the line. An officer was holding Raven by the arm as she appeared to be yelling at him while trying to wrest herself free.

Officers spaced themselves out and started herding us toward some transportation vans off to the side of the square. There was still too much hubbub and noise to talk to anyone about my situation. Surely when we got somewhere quiet I would get the opportunity to explain that my arrest was a mistake. In the meantime, all I could do was follow along with the rest of the group.

There were ominous sirens getting closer, but I couldn't see any ambulances. It was then I looked around and noticed small clusters of people kneeling next to individuals on the ground. OMG. Had anyone been seriously hurt by the explosion? Or trampled by people trying to get away? Where were Yuri, Mara and Jason? Why had I agreed to bring my children with us? And why had I agreed to come in the first place?

The trip to jail was almost as unpleasant as the arrest. The Green Women continued to provoke the two officers riding in the back of the van with us by swearing and spitting at them, practically begging to be mistreated. Where did they get all of that saliva? My mouth felt dry, as if my silent screaming that I was innocent had sucked all the moisture out of my system.

As I watched, I was awed by the restraint the police were showing. Someone had shoved me down, but I wasn't sure it was an officer. And given how the Green Women were acting, if I'd been one of the arresting officers, I might have been tempted to throw my weight around some too. These snarling, spitting women had set off a barrage of illegal fireworks and caused a large group of people to panic. From my point of view, their message would have been much stronger if flyers instead of fireworks had been let loose from the pinata. And the police would not have become involved.

The more I thought about it, the harder it was to accept that Tilly had labeled the event as "not dangerous." Was she simply naïve about crowd behavior? Had the powerful eruption been intentional, a deliberate incitement? Or had whoever set it off miscalculated the impact of the warlike noises and the amount of rubble that spewed forth? These questions hammered away at me while I mentally relived the aftermath of the explosion. The fleeing crowds in the distance, the angry Green Women, the determined looking police, and the smattering of people who were lying or sitting on the ground, either stunned or injured or both.

The van bumped along the city streets. Most of the women had calmed down a bit, but there was still lots of grumbling and complaining. I didn't recognize anyone in the van and was feeling too insecure to ask questions anyway. I had never been arrested before and didn't know what to expect when we reached the jail, which is where I assumed we were going. I had visions of jailers brandishing nightsticks while patrolling barred cages of criminals. So far it was like being an extra in a bad movie. A very bad movie. Why should I expect it to be any different when we reached our destination?

We'd been Mirandized at the scene. It had been hard to hear the actual words, although I was pretty sure the officer delivering the rote message said that calls could be made after processing. That didn't seem fair to me and my circumstance, although with so many arrestees, I didn't see how I could make myself heard over the cacophony of complaints. I kept telling myself that once we got to the jail, I'd be able to get someone's attention and explain my situation.

Even though I'd been at the tail end of the group arrested, I somehow ended up being in one of the first groups to begin the intake process. As they removed my handcuffs I explained that I needed to call my children to see if they were safe. "My phone is in my pocket," I said.

"Hand it over, and empty your pockets."

"But . . ."

"It will all be safe; everything goes in a locker."

My phone started playing Clair de Lune. "Can't I answer and tell them I'm okay?"

"Sorry, we can't let you keep anything that could be used as a weapon."

Did they think my phone was a laser gun in disguise?

"You'll get a chance to make a call soon."

I finally gave up protesting, handed over my cell, relinquished the rest of my belongings—including my clothes and shoes—and changed into the uniform provided. It didn't fit—the legs were too short and the shoulders too big. And it smelled of disinfectant. I wasn't going to make the "best dressed prisoner" list.

Then I was put in a holding cell along with a handful of other Green Women. It was a fairly large space, about 15x20 feet, and not terribly crowded, but hearing the door click shut made me feel the full weight of my situation. I was trapped. I couldn't leave until someone gave me permission. And I had no idea when that would happen.

How long would it be before Yuri or my mother or P.W. found out where I was? I reminded myself that I was innocent and that P.W. would know what to do once she found out that I'd been arrested. Meanwhile, I had to be patient and calm. Patient and calm. Patient . . . and calm.

The other women in my cell and the adjoining cells were chatting as if this was a normal event in their lives. Maybe it was. I sat down on a bench and repeated to myself: patient and calm. Just as I was starting to let go of my irate sense of injustice, an officer motioned for me to come. He let me out of the cell and led me to one of those places in a jail that I never thought I'd get to see in person. While I continued protesting my innocence, they took my photo and my fingerprints. I was officially and unequivocally in the system.

Then I was put back in a cell and some time passed before I was again summoned to a room for still another stage in the processing. A representative from the municipal court explained the charges against me and was filling out a form and taking down personal information when a shadow passed by the door and a women yelled, "Don't let her fool you, she's a Green Woman." I didn't actually get a good look at the person who had yelled at us, but I was fairly certain it was Wren's voice.

"I don't know why she said that, because I'm not."

"Doesn't matter. You'll get your chance to explain." It was the processing mantra. Just wait until later . . .

When I was returned to the holding cell again, I felt the full weight of my arrest. My last hope for a quick exit had been dashed. I had no idea what would happen next or how long it would take.

A woman I vaguely recognized come over to me and said, "I don't know you."

"That's because I'm not a member of your group."

"But you were at the rally. I remember seeing you when we got arrested."

"I was just trying to give Tilly a message about her aunt."

"You're a friend of Tilly's?"

"I know her Aunt Clara." I wasn't sure that being a friend of Tilly's was good for Tilly's reputation in the Green Women, and calling attention to the connection wouldn't probably do me any good either. But it was the truth.

"And you got scooped up. Lucky you."

"I was with a friend and my two kids, and they won't let me call to find out if they are okay."

"They're probably fine. How old?"

"My son just turned 13 and my daughter is 14."

"Teenagers. I wouldn't worry. Kids are resilient."

"I just hope they didn't see me get arrested."

"Why? You ashamed of being associated with our group?" Her tone had quickly shifted from sympathetic to unfriendly, from oboe to bassoon.

"No, I believe in your mission, but not in your tactics."

"Maybe you think we should just sit down in front of government offices and wait to be dragged off or go on hunger strikes to get noticed? How much attention do you think we'd get for that these days?"

"I do understand your motivation," I said. "But what if someone was hurt today because of the explosion?"

"Hey, don't talk to her," someone shouted from the next cell. "She could be an undercover cop."

Several other women in the cell moved closer to listen in on our conversation. I saw them approach, all dressed alike, like a sports team in cheap, hand-me-down uniforms. And they were all aware that although I was wearing the team colors, I wasn't a player.

"What did you think was going to happen when the pinata exploded?" I asked. It might be a tactless question, but I was truly curious.

The woman hesitated before responding. "I didn't realize it was going to be like it was."

"I've been thinking about it," I said. "With all of the stuff inside the pinata, you had to have known it was going to frighten the crowd and likely injure those who were standing close to it."

"It was a malfunction," someone off to the side said.

"Sorry, but that was not a malfunction," I said, turning to face the women who were now within spitting distance, a thought I found disconcerting having witnessed their spitting skills. I knew I should shut up, but I really wanted to know the truth about what had taken place.

"Look, no one realized it was going to be like that," someone said.

"No one? How about whoever loaded the pinata and set it off?"

The women glanced at each other.

"You do know who put it together, don't you?" I persisted.

Again, they looked at each other but didn't say anything. If they did know, they certainly weren't going to tell me. I peeked up at a camera in the corner of the cell and wondered if it was also capable of recording what we were saying. Maybe that's why they were being cautious.

"You do understand that all of you will be blamed for what happened, for everything that happened. And I'm fairly certain there were injuries. What if some children were hurt? What if someone lost an eye?" I don't know why I threw in the bit about the eye, but at least one woman cringed at the thought.

"We'll have to wait and see what happens." The women moved away, as if I was contaminating them with possibilities.

The woman I'd initially been talking to was still there beside me. "How long does this all take?" I asked. She seemed relieved to have the topic changed.

"A couple of hours before you get a hearing. Maybe longer because there are so many of us. Do you have any priors? That can affect how your hearing goes."

"No, this is the first time I've been arrested."

"Then you need to get involved more," someone eavesdropping on our conversation said. Her comment was followed by snickers and laughter from the others.

"I'm Cameron, by the way," I said to the only woman still willing to talk to me.

"Marty," she said. I noted it wasn't a bird name. Unless it was a nickname for a martin.

"What happens at the hearing?" I asked.

"You'll either be released or they will set a bail hearing."

An officer passed by with Tilly and Raven in tow. They did not look happy. Tilly kept her eyes straight ahead as they passed, but Raven gifted me with a malicious smile.

Tilly was probably disappointed that I'd tried to save her. Especially since I'd failed. I hoped she knew my comment about her aunt being in the hospital was a ploy to get her to go with me. As well as to give her an excuse for leaving that would be palatable to the other Green Women.

When I finally got a chance to make a phone call, I called Yuri and almost cried when he answered. He was my lifeline to the real world. I heard myself babble about being in jail and needing a lawyer and asking about the kids.

"Don't worry, Cameron. It's all under control. P.W. got you a lawyer. We're here now. As soon as we get you out, I'll fill you in on what happened."

I wanted to ask a zillion questions, but I became acutely aware that there were people listening in on my end of the conversation. "Any idea how long it will take? I asked.

Yuri said he didn't know. "Just hang in there, Cameron. We'll have you out as soon as we can."

Knowing Yuri and my lawyer were working on getting me out made me feel somewhat calmer, but not the kind of calm one experiences in more pleasant situations. Everyone else seemed bored, standing or sitting around, not talking much. I wondered if any of them had children. Maybe they had planned ahead for their care, anticipating they might spend the night in jail.

When my name was finally called and I appeared before the judge, it all went so quickly I didn't have time to do more than listen to the charges—Obstructing Public Officer and Reckless Endangerment—claim I was not guilty and acknowledge that the information on the form filled out earlier was true. Given my ties to the community, the fact that it was my first offense, and that I was not considered a danger to the community, the judge declared I could be let out on my own recognizance. I wanted to add that the fact that I was arrested by mistake should figure in there somewhere. But I wasn't given the chance. It felt like a scene out of the old "Night Court" television show. The scripts were already written, and the goal was to move people through the system as quickly as possible.

After I changed back into my own clothes and retrieved my belongings, and after what seemed like an eternity of standing there at the gates of hell, I was unceremoniously ushered to the door and sent on my way.

CHAPTER 20
WANING MOON

YURI WAS WAITING for me. He ran over to me and gave me a big hug. A man in a navy-blue jacket, light blue shirt and gray slacks was with him. "Thank god you're okay," Yuri said, taking a step back to make sure he was right about that. Then he looked alarmed. "What's that red spot on your forehead?"

"It's nothing," I said. "I'm fine."

The man in the jacket said, "Let's get out of here." He ushered us into the lobby before saying more. "P.W. called me in case you needed help or bail. We haven't met before." He handed me a card. "But you can call if you have questions or concerns." He glanced at my face, "How did you get that bump on your forehead?"

"It happened when I was arrested. I'm not sure who pushed me down. But someone struck me with what felt like a stick across my shoulders, and I hit my head when I fell. Then someone stepped on my hand." I held out my swollen fingers. "And I was kicked." It felt whiney to say it out loud, but it was true. And I was feeling admittedly a bit sorry for myself.

"Do you want to issue a complaint?" the lawyer asked.

His matter-of-fact tone suggested he considered my physical complaints not in terms of pain but as legal issues.

"No, I just want to go home."

"Well, fortunately, you are free to do just that."

"Our client's niece is still in there. Is there anything we can do for her?"

"If she's never been arrested before, she will probably get out on her own recognizance fairly soon. Otherwise, she will have to post bail. That will take longer."

"What's next for me?" I asked.

"The prosecutor will decide whether to file charges or not. If they do, it will be another couple of weeks before you are officially charged with a crime. Then a pre-trial date will be set. That usually takes a few months."

"Months?"

"Sorry, that's not something you need to think about right now. Just go home and try not to worry about it."

"Not worry?"

"I don't mean to be glib, but chances are you won't be charged. But if you are, there will be plenty of time to prepare your defense."

"But I was arrested by accident."

"Once you get in the system, you have to play it out. I know that sounds cumbersome, but that's the way it is. Fortunately, you have me to defend you." He smiled, a confident, reassuring smile that almost convinced me not to worry. Almost. Then he left.

"My car is in the lot next door," Yuri said. "Let's get out of here."

"Thank you for coming to get me. Sorry you had to wait so long."

As we walked to the car, I finally got to ask the question that had been on my mind all evening: "What happened to you and the kids when the pinata exploded?"

"Well, as you know, it turned from a crowd to a mob in an instant. No one was sure what had happened or if some of the sound effects were gunfire. So, while you were being arrested, Jason, Mara and I joined the exodus away from the Center. Although to their credit, they didn't want to leave you behind. But I saw the police moving on the group and you trapped with them, and I thought it was best to assure the kids that you would catch up with us as quickly as you could and get them out of there. I didn't think they needed to see you being arrested. Besides, knowing Jason and Mara, they probably would have tried to rescue you."

I almost smiled at the thought of Jason and Mara throwing themselves at the police. If there had been reporters around, that would have made a good picture and story.

"Was anyone hurt badly?" I asked.

"From the reports I've heard so far, there were no serious injuries and no deaths. But there were plenty of minor injuries, including to some kids. It isn't going to get the Green Women any good press."

"For the record, I don't think most of the Green Women had a clue how bad it was going to be."

"If Tilly knew and didn't warn you, then she loses my sympathy vote."

"I can't believe she knew how big an explosion it was going to be. She mentioned 'unexpected loud noise,' I'm not sure if she was thinking fireworks or some other sound effects."

"Like trains in the distance or whale noises?" Yuri said sarcastically.

"More like broadcasting some slogan over a speaker system. Not intended to scare people, but startling enough to make the news."

I got in the car and felt what little energy I had left leave my body like a balloon deflating. I was so exhausted I didn't even care that Yuri was behind the wheel. I just wanted to get home, wash the stink of the jail off me, and have a glass of wine before falling into bed. When Yuri swerved to avoid hitting a parked vehicle, I didn't even flinch.

"Some of the stuff that came out of that pinata was like shrapnel," Yuri said. "I think your Green Women friends may be in for some serious fines. Maybe even jail time. They were just damn lucky it didn't turn out worse than it did."

"I was charged with obstruction and reckless endangerment, and I assume the others were charged with the same. Both are misdemeanors. But reckless endangerment. That doesn't sound like something that goes away with a fine and community service."

"Community service wouldn't be too bad," Yuri said.

"I'd be more than happy to do community service if that would expunge the charge. But I don't think that's how it works."

"Well, your arrest was a mistake. That should be clear enough at some point. But Tilly, I'm not so sure. It depends on how involved she was with the pinata disaster. Any ideas who was responsible?"

"I have no idea, but I heard one woman say she'd been expecting the pinata to spray everyone with candy in customized wrappers with climate slogans printed on them, not fireworks."

"Well, let's say they didn't realize what was really going to happen—were they upset with the outcome?"

"Hard to tell. Their goal was to make the national news. And between the blast and the arrests, I'm pretty sure that will happen."

"All to call attention to the cause," Yuri mimicked.

"I do think some of them believe the adage 'there's no such thing as bad publicity.' Although I'm not sure that includes injuring innocent people. Especially children."

"They may find out just how wrong that philosophy can be."

"Oh," I said suddenly. "Do you think P.W. called Clara? Or should I?"

"You know more than P.W. does, so even if she did, I think you should call her."

I had her number in my cell, and she answered on the first ring.

"Are you calling about Tilly," she asked anxiously.

"Yes, don't worry, she's fine."

"P.W. said she'd been arrested."

"She was, and still is, in jail. But she wasn't hurt. She may have to put up bail though. That could take awhile."

"Why didn't she call?" Clara asked.

"The police probably took her cell phone. They took mine."

"Why'd they take yours?"

"Because I was arrested with the group. I had just spotted Tilly and was trying to get her away when the explosion occurred."

"Oh no I'm so sorry. P.W. didn't mention that."

"It's okay. I was released on my own recognizance. I'm on my way home now. The police have a lot of people to process; I'm sure Tilly will get in touch soon."

"What I don't understand is why she was with them today. I thought she had decided not to march."

"I think the other members put a lot of pressure on her. From their point of view, it was an important event. And they had no idea things would go sideways." I found myself defending her even though I was upset with her myself for being there.

"I saw excerpts on TV. It looked like a mess."

"It was."

"Why were you there?"

"Yuri and I believe in the cause and thought it would be a good experience for my kids."

"Your children were with you?" I wasn't sure if Clara's tone was incredulous or critical. Both reflected my own feelings.

"Fortunately, Yuri got them out of there when I was arrested."

"Not quite the experience you anticipated."

"No, but they weren't hurt, so in some ways it was probably instructive. Anyway, I just wanted to let you know Tilly's situation."

"Thank you. It's a relief knowing she's okay. Even if she's in jail."

I clicked off. "Poor woman. Tilly's not making it easy for her."

Yuri sped up to get through a yellow light, not quite making it and causing a chorus of honks.

After my heartrate returned to normal, I said, "There's one thing that bothers me."

"Only one?"

"Well, one thing I find particularly puzzling. Why would Wren claim that I was a member of the group? Was she hoping to make it tougher on me? I'd already been arrested."

"If I had to guess, I'd say it's because she's a despicable and mean person."

"Maybe someone told her I was trying to get Tilly out of there. Whatever . . . I agree that she's not a nice person. I'm going to give Phoebe a call tomorrow. I've sensed she disapproves of Wren, and I would like to hear why."

"Well, if I were Tilly, I'd find a new roomy," Yuri said.

"Maybe after today she'll do just that."

When we arrived at my house, I asked Yuri if he wanted to come in for a drink, but he laughed and said, "No thanks. I'm not facing your family a second time. The kids threw a fit when I told them I had seen you get arrested. They didn't buy the 'it's what your mother would have wanted' argument I made about why I lied to them. And your mother called as soon as I dropped them off demanding to know what was going on. You sort it out before I visit again, okay?"

Feeling somewhat apprehensive myself, I made my way down the path to my house. It was so peaceful I almost convinced myself the worst was over. Then I went inside and all hell broke loose.

CHAPTER 21
BAD MOON RISING

THE MOMENT I set foot inside, No-name went crazy, his black and white body shaking with passion, his floppy ear flopping around while his other ear remained rigidly upright. It was almost like he knew something bad had happened and he wanted to get in his two cents worth. The kids rushed me and gave me a double bear hug. Mom hung back, but it was clear she would have a few things to say about what had happened when given the opportunity in private.

As soon as the kids saw that I was alright, they shifted gears. They wanted to hear all of the gritty details about my arrest, what it had been like in jail, and what was going to happen next. I saw Mom glance at my forehead and tried to casually brush some hair over the bump. The kids didn't need to know about that, at least not yet.

I explained that I had been trying to get Tilly away from the Green Women when I got mixed in with them and was arrested as part of the group.

"Why didn't you tell them you weren't a Green Woman?" Jason asked.

"I tried, but things were pretty chaotic."

"We saw a clip on television," Mara said. "It looked like all the women were on their knees and being handcuffed. Were you handcuffed?"

"Yes, I was handcuffed."

"I read they've replaced the old steel handcuffs with more comfortable versions. Were your handcuffs comfortable?" Jason asked.

"I wouldn't describe them as comfortable, I did notice they were black and not silver."

"They're aluminum," Jason said. "They aren't supposed to pinch your wrists like the old ones did."

"Well, I'm sorry I wasn't arrested before they changed over so I could tell you how much they've improved."

Jason smiled and then got serious. "Why didn't you call us?" he asked. "Yuri kept trying to get in touch."

I explained that initially my cell phone had been in my pocket and I wasn't able to get to it while handcuffed. Then it had been taken away. That they have to process you before you get to make a call.

"He saw you being arrested," Mara said, sounding angry. "And he didn't tell us until we were on the light rail headed back."

"He knew I wouldn't want you to watch what was happening to me."

"But you're our mother," Jason said. "We should have tried to help you."

"The best way you had of helping me was to make sure you were safe. I'm thankful that Yuri got you away from there."

"Why were all the Green Women arrested?" Jason asked. "What did they do?"

"They were responsible for putting up the pinata that exploded."

"Was the explosion on purpose?" Mara asked. "I thought something went wrong. Who would want to do that?"

"I'm not sure if that's what they were trying to do or not. Although I'm fairly certain that not everyone in the group knew what to expect. At least one person thought there was going to be candy released, like a normal pinata."

"The press is speculating about that," Mom said, suddenly joining in. "Trying to decide who was responsible."

"Really? Most of the talk I overheard in the cells implied it was either a malfunction or a stupid mistake. But they were careful not to name names."

"Maybe whoever did it didn't tell the rank and file," Mom said. "Some of them might not have approved. People, including a few children, were hurt. It even caused some damage to one of the nearby buildings. Those Green Women were lucky; it could have been even worse. When crowds are startled like that, anything can happen." She looked at Mara and Jason. "Let that be a lesson. If you get involved in a group that engages in criminal activity, you will be blamed for their actions whether you had a hand in them or not."

"Will you be in trouble?" Jason asked me, eyes wide with the possibility that his mother would be labeled a criminal.

"I don't think so." At least my fingers were crossed that I wouldn't be. The fingers on my undamaged hand, that is.

"The police should apologize to you," Mom said.

"Unfortunately, one of the women said several times that I was part of the group, although I'm not sure that her assertion registered with anyone official."

"Didn't she know you weren't?" Mara asked.

"Yes, she knew."

"Then why did she say you were?"

"I'm not entirely sure." But I was definitely going to ask her the first chance I got.

Just as I anticipated, Mom came down with a bottle of wine after the kids went to bed. She poured two glasses and said, "I've been thinking about why someone would want the police to think that you were part of the group."

"And . . .?"

"My first thought was that they were mad that you tried to spirit Tilly away. They wanted her to get in trouble with the rest of them. After all, she was part of the group that helped plan the event. Even if she wasn't one of the saboteurs."

"I get why someone might try to get me in hot water in the heat of the moment. But after we were in the holding cells, why still claim I was with the group? And why didn't anyone speak up for me?"

"Who was saying that you were one of them?"

"I think it was Wren, Tilly's roommate."

"That's interesting."

"Isn't it. Maybe it is all about Tilly. Maybe she was told I was trying to get Tilly out of there before the explosion."

"Or, maybe she thinks Tilly is guilty of murder. Or . . . maybe she wants Tilly to be blamed because she killed Rune."

"Why would Wren kill Rune?"

"The woman scorned perhaps."

"Wren doesn't like men much."

"Maybe she doesn't respect them, but that doesn't mean she's celibate. And if she's truly evil, maybe she's the one responsible for the pinata explosion."

As usual, my mother had given me a new slant on a crime I had been struggling to unravel. I fell asleep cradling my swollen fingers in my comforter and picturing Wren attacking Rune from behind, casting a dark shadow in the pale light from the moon.

Sunday morning I made blueberry pancakes for everyone to signify that things were back to normal. Even though the lawyer had told me it could take months for true normal to return. Mom poked her head in long enough to say that she was headed out for brunch and might be a bit late in getting back. Her Sunday brunches often lasted most of the day. Not for the first time, I wished I had a group of friends I enjoyed spending time with. When you move away from what has been your home base for years, it isn't easy to build new relationships. Especially when you worked full time and had two children to raise. At least that was my excuse.

Yuri called as I was cleaning up, checking in to make sure I was okay and to see how the kids were doing.

"They're mini ghouls," I said. "They wanted to know all about what getting arrested and being in jail was like."

"Little concern for mom's welfare, huh?"

"They didn't notice my forehead or my fingers. Although No-name tried a couple of times to lick my hand. That isn't something he normally does. It makes you wonder . . ."

"Do you need to get your hand x-rayed?"

"I don't think so. I can wiggle my fingers, so I don't think anything's broken."

"I still think you should have it and that bump on your forehead checked out."

Ignoring his advice, I changed the subject: "The kids are mad at you for making them miss the real live arrest."

"I was conflicted," Yuri admitted. "On the one hand, I wanted to try to help you, but on the other, I felt responsible for your kids."

"You did the right thing. They would probably have arrested you for interfering. Especially after someone claimed that I was part of the group."

"Yeah, I've been thinking about that."

"Me too. Mom thinks Wren was trying to deflect suspicion away from her own murderous motivation."

"Wren the roommate?"

"Yeah, she thinks Wren may have stabbed Rune."

"But why?"

"I'm not sure, but I think I'm going to have a little talk with Phoebe. See what I can pry out of her. I'm not sure Wren would be willing to talk to me and even less sure that she would tell me the truth if she did."

"Want me to go with you?"

"No, I think this is a woman-to-woman situation."

"Well, give me a shout if you need anything." Before he hung up he added, "And get that head looked at.

Phoebe was home when I called and agreed to meet me for coffee later in the afternoon without pressing about the reason for my request or commenting on our recent jail experience. The kids both had plans with friends for the day, so I didn't have to be home until dinnertime. I got a few chores done around the house and took No-name for a walk. Well, not a walk in the normal sense. He bolted after every bird or squirrel or imagined critter and paused frequently to mark his territory on neighbors' bushes. I kept having to reel him in on his expanding leash and jerk him away from bushes. "If you want me to walk you again," I threatened, "you'd better behave." He gave me that wounded look that dogs use to control their owners, but I wasn't about to let him become the Alpha in our relationship. Maybe we should name him Beta to remind him of his place in the family pecking order.

I arrived before Phoebe at the coffee shop and was enjoying a cranberry scone when she got there. "I wasn't sure how you liked your coffee," I said, "so I didn't get you any. But I got an extra scone and a cookie. Take your pick."

"Don't eat that other scone, and I'll be right back." She returned shortly with a cup of coffee in hand.

"You must take your coffee black," I observed. "I'm always amazed at how long it takes to create their fancy drinks."

"I go with my mood."

"Not sure what a black coffee signifies," I said with what I thought was a lighthearted tone, but Phoebe frowned.

"Not much to feel good about these days."

"Were you released on your own recognizance?" I asked.

"No, I had to post bail. Most of us did. I was one of the first to get out, around midnight."

"That long . . . sorry."

"You were one of the lucky ones I understand."

"Yes, I got processed early and got out early. After what seemed like forever though."

"Yeah, time goes slow when hanging out in a cell."

"You've been arrested before?"

"A couple of times. But never for reckless endangerment. We're all a bit concerned about that. I assume you got the same charges as the rest of us."

"Yes. Initially I was surprised by the reckless endangerment charge, but in retrospect it makes sense, given the injuries to people and property."

"Several of the women seemed to think you were sympathetic with the police," she said.

"Well, I didn't agree with the name calling and the spitting."

"Yeah, that was tacky. But emotions were running high."

"I know. Someone shoved me to the ground." I pulled back my hair and showed her the bump on my forehead. It was already starting to turn purple. "And my hand was stepped on." I held out my swollen and bruised fingers. I didn't bother mentioning being kicked in the ribs. I had some bruising but little soreness.

"Ouch," she said, looking first at my hand, then at my forehead. "Did that happen during the arrest?"

"Yes, someone stepped on my hand after I got shoved to the ground and hit my head. It could have been an accident. I didn't see who it was."

"Yeah, probably an over-zealous police officer. But everyone was pretty wound up after what happened with the pinata."

"Was that planned?" I asked the question as casually as I could, hoping she wouldn't feel the need to lawyer up before responding.

"Some of the fireworks, maybe. The rest of it, I don't think so."

"But you know who put it together, right? And it must have been done with a remote control device—did you see who set it off?"

Phoebe hesitated. "I'm not sure. I know who was on the planning team, but we haven't had a chance to debrief yet."

I could tell by her tone that she wasn't about to reveal any names to me, but before I could change the subject, she did.

"Wren was pretty mad about you getting released ahead of us."

"Well, I was pretty mad that she tried to convince the police I was a member of the Green Women. Not because I don't believe in your cause, but I could lose my license over this if I get convicted. Any idea why she would say I was a part of your group?"

Phoebe stared at me wide-eyed. "You have no idea?"

"No. I only met Wren when I came to your house to check on Tilly. I don't know anything about her."

"It's because of Rune."

"But I didn't know Rune either."

"She did though. And she sees you as aligned with Tilly." Phoebe looked at her scone, broke off a piece and popped it in her mouth.

"Are you suggesting what I think you're suggesting?"

"She was sleeping with him."

My mother was right. "It sounds like almost everyone was sleeping with Rune."

A hint of color crept up Phoebe's pale face. "I wasn't."

"That was smart of you." I sipped my coffee. "Did Tilly know about Rune and Wren?"

"Not at first, but eventually. Ethan told her."

"Ethan is the wild card in this drama, isn't he? Do you think he stabbed Rune to put him out of the picture?"

"Why would you murder someone for that reason? If the person doesn't love you back, they aren't worth it, are they?"

"Do you think Rune loved Tilly?" I was having a difficult time diagramming the love connections. Definitely more than a triangle. A very dark, many-sided polygon.

"They were sleeping together."

"It sounds like you didn't think it was 'true love.'"

"I'm not sure there is such a thing for most people. But there has to be more than physical attraction."

"As someone whose marriage wasn't the greatest, I definitely agree."

"Are you divorced?"

"Widowed."

"Seeing anyone?"

"Actually, next weekend I'm going on the first date I've had since I can't remember when."

"Is he someone you think you could love?"

"I have no idea. At this point I'm just worried about what to wear." I laughed. "And what to tell my kids."

"You have children?"

"Yes, they were at the rally on Saturday. But the friend I was with made sure they were safe."

"I understand you were trying to get Tilly to leave with you when the pinata exploded. Why were you trying to get her away?"

"Because I knew it would upset her Aunt Clara if Tilly was arrested."

"But that was Tilly's choice, wasn't it? We all make choices that we have to live with."

"I know. Sometimes I'm overprotective. I think it comes from being a mom as well as being in a profession where the goal is to try to solve people's problems."

"Do you like your job?"

"Yes, it's interesting, and I work with a great group of people."

"Do you usually solve your cases?"

"Most of the time, yes. But there isn't always something to solve. We do background checks, employee complaint investigations, that sort of thing."

"What about Rune's murder?"

"Oh, that's not in our bailiwick. We were hired to find Tilly when Ethan kidnapped her. And we were lucky to succeed. But we don't do murder cases. We leave that to the police."

"Oh, then why did you call me?"

"Curiosity, I'm afraid. Even though our official role is over, I'm still trying to tie up loose ends in my mind. To quote Sherlock Holmes: 'It is a capital mistake to theorize before one has data.' And I can't seem to stop theorizing in this instance."

"That sounds like trying to solve the murder to me."

"No, seriously. I would like to know more about the players. But tomorrow I will be moving on. New week; new case."

Phoebe downed the last of her coffee and wrapped the rest of her scone in a napkin and put it in her bag. "Yes, tomorrow we'll all move on. Although the climate crisis will still exist. We'll just have to find new ways to address the problems." She stood. "Thanks for the scone."

I sat there a few minutes after she left, going over our conversation. She had interviewed me as much or more than I had interviewed her. But it struck me that she, like my mother, believed Wren had a motive for murder.

CHAPTER 22
MOONSHINE

MONDAY MORNING was more chaotic than usual. It was the first day of school, and both Mara and Jason were acting like they'd never had to get ready for school before. I had to remind myself that the first day of school was a big event in their lives. The end of summer, seeing friends you hadn't seen for a while, new teachers, and all sorts of deadlines involving everything from when to get up to turning in assignments on time. It was a huge shift in routine and priorities—for them as well as for me.

Mara fretted over what to wear, ignoring my suggestions about her new outfits, of course. Finally choosing something a bit too flattering for her developing shape from a mother's point of view. But I had given it my blessing when she first brought it home, so I could hardly change my mind now. Especially if I wanted her to get to school on time.

Jason complained about his lunch and his old lunchbox that he felt wasn't age appropriate anymore, so I gave him money to buy what he wanted at school and promised him either a new lunchbox or brown paper bags going forward—his choice.

Then No-name started barking for no reason that I could see and wouldn't be quiet. Every attempt to corral him or get him to shut up ended up with him darting away and increasing the volume of his excited attempts to vocalize whatever he was trying so desperately to communicate.

"He doesn't want us to go," Jason said loudly.

Mother suddenly appeared in the doorway. "What's going on?" she asked.

"Everything's fine," I assured her. No-name begged to disagree with several yips and a yowl.

"Puppy, be quiet," my mother commanded from the doorway. No-name instantly laid down and put his head on his paws.

Irritated that No-name obeyed her but not me, I set it aside and took the opportunity to point to the cereal I'd set out for breakfast. "You don't have much time," I said. "You need to eat something."

Mara frowned at the cereal choices, ones I was pretty sure she had picked out at the grocery. "I'll have a banana," she said, staring at the bowl of bananas I'd put on the table to go with the cereal. Several of them had brown spots. If no one ate them soon, I'd be torn between making banana bread or feeling guilty for tossing them.

"Me too," Jason chimed in, his hand hovering over the bowl, evaluating his options.

"Okay, have as many bananas as you want." No-name's head came up. Did he know the word "banana?"

Mom stepped into the room. "You need to eat more than a banana," she said to my two hyped up teenagers. They obediently sat down and poured some cereal into their bowls and splashed on milk. Jason added more sugar than he should have, but I kept my mouth shut and sent my mother a silent "thank you."

"Now then," Mom said, directing her attention at me. "I think you mentioned it before, but tell me again when you will know whether you are charged with a crime or not." She sounded matter-of-fact, but I knew she was as worried as I was and that she was most likely in denial about the timeframe I had originally laid out for her.

"It's my understanding that it could take up to two weeks."

My two children froze with spoons halfway to their mouths. Then Jason dropped his spoon and milk splattered the table. "Could you go back to jail?"

"No, I could end up going to court. The lawyer is handling things."

"Two weeks isn't so bad," Mom said. I knew she didn't mean it but was saying it for the benefit of Mara and Jason.

"The good news is that I'm out on my own recognizance. I think that means I can do anything but leave the country."

"Not funny, Mom," Mara said.

"Think of it as the two weeks at the end of summer—you know how fast that goes." They could think of it that way, but for me it was more like two weeks in the dentist's chair.

The lawyer P.W. had hired to represent me called to tell me that he had filed a motion to dismiss based on "insufficient evidence to establish a prima facie case of the crime charged." He explained that while it was up to the prosecuting attorney's office to decide whether charges would be filed or not, and a dismissal at this point was not common, there was reason for hope. He believed the affidavits from Yuri, P.W. and Tilly stating why I was there and that I wasn't and had never been a member of the Green Women were collectively convincing. Like I had been saying all along, my only crime was being in the wrong place at the wrong time—the charges against me were moonshine, absurd, and nonsensical. Unfortunately, the facts needed to be clothed in the right legalese to be effective. I was thankful that P.W. considered my act as one committed on behalf of a client so that Penny-wise was covering legal costs that could otherwise be a serious hit to my bank account.

As soon as I got to work, I went into a conference room and called Tilly to see how she was doing and to talk with her about my conversation with Phoebe.

"You were lucky to get released from jail so quickly," Tilly said. "I managed to get out on my own recognizance, but it took forever. Well, until almost midnight. And for the women who'd been arrested before, it took even longer to get released. Apparently arranging for bail and getting it processed was a hassle. Some of the Green Women were there until mid-afternoon."

"I heard someone say that the Green Women have 'a' lawyer. Are you all going to use the same lawyer for your court appearances? Is that a good idea?"

"Aunt Clara wants me to get my own lawyer. I'm going to wait to see how things progress first. Some of the others are talking plea deals, but I don't want to go that route."

"My lawyer told me that 90 percent of misdemeanors are disposed of with guilty pleas and that only a small number go to trial."

"Whatever you do, as I understand it, the process takes a long time. After you're charged it can take months before a pre-trial date is set, then you have to wait for the court date. Then there's the trial. The whole thing can take years!"

"Being in limbo that long would be painful." I secretly prayed that wasn't what was going to happen to me. And I also hoped it wouldn't be what happened to Tilly either. She might deserve it, but her Aunt Clara didn't.

"Just being arrested was bad enough, but being associated with an act that injured innocent bystanders, supporters of the cause, that's depressing. Have you seen the press coverage? They've been interviewing people who were hurt, including an adorable little girl who had a piece of metal pierce her cheek. An inch higher and she might have lost an eye."

My nightmare scenario in which someone lost an eye had fortunately not come true, but the little girl's injury sounded horrible. What if it had been Mara? "It would be helpful if the perpetrators were identified. Then the prosecutor might drop the reckless endangerment charges for everyone else."

"I don't know who's responsible. And it's caused a lot of dissension within the group. Obviously, most of the members don't mind getting arrested for their beliefs, but that doesn't mean they want to be accused of putting supporters, including children, in harm's way."

"The other problem as I see it is that a fair number of your cohorts were not only verbally disrespectful to the police, they spit on them. That might be considered a form of assault." I wanted to ask if she had cursed or spit on any officers, but didn't.

"I know. It was truly ugly. I couldn't believe how some of the women got so carried away. Most of them aren't like that. Even so, my Aunt Clara thinks we're all going to get tarred and feathered with the worst of the group."

"Are you still staying with your aunt?"

"Yes, for a few more days. As much for her as for me. She's worried that having a misdemeanor charge on my record will have an impact on my future employment. Whereas I'm worried I might end up with jail time."

"My guess is that conviction will most likely result in a fine and possibly community service rather than jail time. Unless they are able to prove the explosion was deliberate and not an accident. And if they can't identify who was responsible. But your aunt is right. Any misdemeanor conviction will show up on a background check. I should know, I do them all the time. But a lot of companies will give you a chance to explain. It is, however, one more hurdle to overcome in the job search process."

"Yeah, and I confess that I resent getting blamed for someone else's actions."

I finally had the chance to ask the question I'd been wanting the answer to since our first conversation about the rally. "What did you anticipate would happen when you warned me to stay back from the pinata?"

"I didn't know for sure, but from what was said in our meetings, I thought it would be a few fireworks. Like those exploding stars. High in the air. Startling but not harmful."

"But you knew even the fireworks were illegal."

"Yes, but I didn't think they would arrest all of us on the spot. I thought the group would be fined."

"Any chance Wren was involved in what actually happened?" I knew my dislike of her prompted the question; Tilly had already said she didn't know who was responsible."

There was a moment of silence. Then: "I admit I've wondered. She has a lot of bottled-up anger, and she obviously doesn't feel loyalty to anyone."

"Sorry, I shouldn't have brought her up."

"No, that's one of the reasons I haven't returned to the house though. Especially since Phoebe is staying at her parents' cabin. She said she needs some alone time. I can certainly understand that."

That evening Mom cooked what she labeled as a "celebratory dinner." When I asked what we were celebrating, she said, "Not having my daughter in jail wearing an orange jumpsuit. Orange is not a good color for you."

"It's for our first day of school," Mara said. "Isn't that what you told me, Grandma?"

"We all have something to celebrate today, don't we?"

Dinner was a vegetarian lasagna, a compromise between healthy eating and comfort food. Paired with a very nice merlot and well-behaved children, it was an excellent meal. Even No-name was on good behavior, hovering at first, then finding a comfortable out-of-the-way spot on the floor to settle in with what was left of his ring-tailed lemur. Since it was hard to hand off lasagna bites to a dog without creating a mess, I assumed his behavior was due to the fact that he wasn't getting table food from any of the usual suspects.

Over dinner, Jason confirmed what Tilly had told me about the group getting bad press because of the explosion. He said that local newspapers were obsessed with the picture of the little girl with the cut on her face. Someone got a shot of her crying, with blood running down her check and staining her flowered T-shirt and peasant skirt. In addition, TV reporters not only interviewed a string of people who described their experience with passion and total lack of sympathy for the Green Women, they kept re-playing footage of the arrest as well. The spitting looked pretty ugly, he said, and most of the screaming had been censored. Which made it seem even worse. He thought he'd caught a glimpse of me in one of the shots, but he wasn't sure. Maybe I'd need to find videos taken by bystanders to prove I hadn't engaged in the cursing and spitting. I hoped it wouldn't come to that.

Mom surprised me by giving me a stiff hug before returning to her upstairs apartment. I wondered if it was motivated by love or relief. Maybe a bit of both. Having a daughter in jail wasn't something she could brag about to her friends. As for me, I was experiencing a recurring nightmare while wide awake. In it I was being charged with a crime that would take years to come to trial. A crime of which I was innocent and that could cost me my livelihood. How was I supposed to live my life with that hanging over my head?

I was just about to get into bed when my cell announced there was a call from Detective Connolly. I can't say I had a premonition, but for him to call me at that late hour, something was wrong.

CHAPTER 23
BLOOD MOON

"CAMERON," Detective Connolly said. Even though he used my first name, his official tone suggested that what he was about to say was not good news. I tightened the grip on my cell phone and stood perfectly still. "You knew Tilly Jamison's roommate, Wren Davies, didn't you?"

"Knew?"

"Yes. I'm at their place now. The reason I'm calling is to inform you . . ." He hesitated as if trying to remember why he'd called me. Finally, he abruptly finished his sentence. ". . . that she's dead."

"Dead?"

"She's been murdered."

"Murdered?" What was wrong with me? Couldn't I put together a coherent thought?

"Are you okay?"

"Yes." At least this one-word response was not an echo. "When did it happen?"

"We don't have a time of death yet, but most likely within the last few hours."

"And you called me to tell me she's been murdered, why?"

"Actually, I'm calling to see if you know Tilly Jamison's whereabouts."

"I do. I talked to her earlier. She's been staying with her Aunt Clara. I can text you her number if you'd like."

"That would be great. I don't suppose you know where the other roommate is?"

"Tilly mentioned that Phoebe had gone to stay at a cabin her parents own. She wanted to be alone for a while. I have no idea where it is, but I have her phone number too. I'll text it to you." I knew the police could look up phone numbers in a flash, but I wanted to be as helpful as possible. I might need a friend on the inside in the future.

"Thanks, this saves me some time." He paused. "And, I wanted to tell you that I'm sorry you were arrested at the rally. Things like that happen unfortunately."

"Thank you. It was an interesting experience. The arrest, getting shoved to the ground and stepped on, the handcuffs, the jumpsuit, the fingerprinting, the mug shot. To say nothing of hanging out in a cell with members of a group that I don't belong to." Why had I listed the unsavory highlights of my arrest and let sarcasm creep into my voice? If only he hadn't said "things like that happen." Things like that shouldn't happen. Not in my world. Not in anyone's world.

"I am sorry," Connolly added. In spite of my rude response, he sounded sincerely sorry.

Self-interest aside, I knew I should have acknowledged his contrite, if too late, apology on behalf of his role as an officer of the law with less cynicism. Like the unyielding officers at the rally who had been provoked by the indignity of being cursed and spit upon, he had a job to do. I owed him an apology. It was on the tip of my tongue when he abruptly ended our call: "Thanks for your help. I'll contact Tilly." My cell phone turned dark.

I wasn't sure if I was angry that he had cut short our conversation or relieved that I didn't have to corral the complex thoughts and emotions swirling in my head to put together the explanation and apology he deserved. The pain of my arrest and not knowing what was going to happen next was obviously clouding my ability to think rationally about the situation. Realistically, I knew I was fortunate to live in a community where what happened to me was the exception rather than the rule. But I needed some distance on my personal injustice before I could let go.

Tuesday morning I awoke with the taste of guilt in my mouth. Detective Connolly had always been fair with me, and if his role as an officer sometimes didn't align with my personal preferences, what right did I have to be rude to him? And although the anger about my arrest continued to bubble just below the surface of consciousness, I knew that if the roles had been reversed, I might not have reacted kindly to a group of people who were screaming obscenities that the media would have to bleep out. To say nothing of having disgusting gobs of spittle lobbed at me from all directions like toxic hailstones.

Policing issues are larger than any one person's experience; nevertheless, it's hard to see things from another person's perspective when your own emotions are gripping you by the throat. I knew I should call Connolly and extend an apology, but I put it off, telling myself he was busy with the case and I shouldn't be bothering him simply to assuage my guilt. On the other hand, if I apologized, maybe he would share some information about Wren's death, something I wouldn't find in the news. There was nothing wrong with combining being contrite with a personal agenda, was there?

At noon Yuri and I went to the Food Court to grab some lunch. I sniffed in about 50 calories trying to let my nose decide what I wanted to eat. I couldn't make up my mind, so I followed Yuri to the pizza place that sells it by the slice. I wasn't sure if it was freeing or confusing to be able to order any topping I wanted. When I pointed to a slice with spinach and goat cheese, I briefly wondered whether my mother's cooking was actually changing my eating habits. If so, I'd be careful not to let her know. She had left an article on my refrigerator sometime during the night. For once it wasn't on parenting or how hard it is for single women to meet single men after a certain age. Instead, it was an article on the Green Women—their checkered past as do-gooders and criminals. I wasn't sure what the hidden message was, or even if there was one. Maybe it was simply informational.

Wren's murder made the headlines in the local news, both in the papers and on television, but there weren't many details. The police were quoted as saying they had a suspect but no one had been arrested yet. While quickly attacking our pizza, Yuri and I speculated about who the suspect might be. To be sure it wasn't Tilly, I gave her a call while we were finishing up our meal. She assured me the suspect wasn't her. She had not only been at her Aunt's when the murder allegedly took place, but she had been on the telephone off and on talking with other Green Women members about the charges against them and sharing information about lawyers.

"How about the other roommate?" Yuri asked, pushing his empty paper plate aside.

"She wasn't home either. Tilly told me she went to her parents' cabin for some alone time. In any event, I can't imagine what her motive would have been to kill Wren. Normal people don't kill someone just because they are a lying, mean-spirited, despicable . . ."

"I believe the word you're searching for is 'scumbag.'"

"Scumbag," I said. "Wren definitely deserves, ah, deserved that label."

"But I'm not sure I accept your assertion that normal seeming people don't kill people. Ted Bundy for example. And how about during a Blood Moon? Did you know . . . "

"Nooo." I held up a hand. "Please stop with the moon trivia."

He reached out and slapped my hand "And stop snitching my fries!"

"They're cold anyway," I said.

My phone rang. It was Mara. She wanted to know if she and some friends came by the mall after school if she could get a ride home with me. "Sure," I said. "Just come by the office. I should be leaving on time tonight."

It was almost 4:30 when I got another call from Mara. When I saw it was from her, I half expected her to tell me she had a ride home with someone else. Instead, what she said surprised me, shocked and surprised me.

"Mom, there's a man here who wants to talk with you, but he doesn't want to come to your office. He says he knows you, and it's personal, not professional."

"Who is it?" I felt a tingle of unease, but didn't see it coming.

"His name is Jones." Panic gripped my throat with strong fingers.

"Where are you, Mara?" I managed to keep my voice calm, but images of Tilly in Ethan's bedroom flashed across my mind.

"In the mall. Mr. Jones recognized me from some pictures he saw somewhere."

"You're with Mr. Jones right now? In the mall?"

"Yes, why do you sound so strange?"

"Tell me exactly where you are." I kept my voice calm so as not to frighten her; I was frightened enough for both of us.

"We're in front of Cinnabon. Smells yummy."

"Are your friends with you?"

"They're just down the way, why?"

"Hand your phone to Mr. Jones for a moment, okay?"

"Sure."

Ethan came on with a "we're old friends" camaraderie: "Hi, Cameron. I was hoping we could meet for a few minutes."

"Listen to me very carefully," I said. "Give my daughter her phone back and let her walk away. When she tells me she's rejoined her friends, I'll come to meet you. Not before. Do you understand?"

"Of course. That sounds good. But just you, not that friend of yours. And right away. Not ten minutes from now. Do you understand."

"Yes. Now hand my daughter her phone."

"Your mother wants to talk to you, Mara," Ethan said. Him using her name made me want to throw up. Yes, I understood; the message was gut wrenchingly clear.

"Mara, I know this sounds strange, but I would like you to leave Mr. Jones where he is and catch up with your friends, got that?"

"Sure, right now?"

"Yes, start walking and keep talking to me."

I heard her say, "Bye, Mr. Jones." Before coming back to me. "This is strange. What do you want to talk about?"

"Is he staying put? Or is he following you?"

"Ah, he's watching me, but he hasn't moved. Why? What's this all about?"

"Don't react to what I'm about to say. I'm not telling you this to frighten you; you're not in any danger. But Ethan Jones is the man who held Tilly hostage. So, I want you to go find your friends and stay with them until I call you back. Is that clear?"

"I heard him say he didn't want your 'friend' to come with you when you meet with him. Did he mean Yuri? Will you be okay?"

"I'll have back-up, don't worry. Now I have to hang up so I can make arrangements and not keep him waiting too long. But I'd like to have you pretend you're still talking to me a little longer. To give me some time. Got that?"

"Sure. I'll just keep talking, no problem. Call me as soon as you can."

I immediately went to Yuri and Norm and quickly briefed them on the situation. "I have to hurry," I said. "I'll leave my phone on. Yuri, stay out of sight. Norm, give me a head start." I rushed to the door and turned toward Cinnabon. Ethan approached almost immediately and waved me in the other direction. I tried to act like it didn't matter, hoping Norm would track my phone and not head for Cinnabon.

"What do you want?" I asked instead of saying what I really wanted to scream at him: "Stay away from my family!"

"I won't keep you long. The police are looking for me, and I assume you told one of your fellow agents to call them and let them know I'm here."

"No, I didn't know you were wanted. Is it in relation to Wren's death?" I found myself staring at his empty hands and wondering if he had a weapon with him.

"Yes, that's why I'm here. I want to tell you what happened."

"Can we sit?"

"No, keep walking."

"I won't go outside the mall with you," I warned.

"You won't have to. This won't take long."

"So, tell me your version of what happened."

"It's not my version, it's the truth. Anyway, I got a call from Wren last night. At least I thought it was from Wren. Now I'm not so sure. She told me we needed to talk about Tilly. That she had something to tell me that I would be glad to hear. And she suggested I come by."

"You were there last night? At their place?" No wonder the police were looking for him.

"Yes. She told me she was doing some work in the kitchen at the back of the house and that I should not bother knocking at the front door because she might not hear me. She said to come directly around to the back door."

If he was making this up, it was quite the story. "So that's what you did?"

"Yes, but the lights were out. I wasn't sure what to do. I tried the door, but it was locked."

"Why did you try the door?" I had to ask.

"Because when I knocked, no one answered. If it had been open, I was going to stick my head inside and call out for her." He stopped walking and turned towards me. "Isn't that what you would have done?"

"Under the circumstances, probably," I admitted.

He continued walking toward the north entrance, and I fell into step beside him. "Next I tried to call her, but there was no answer."

"Did you leave a message?"

"No. I was ticked. But even though I didn't leave a message, there should still be a record of my call to her."

We were getting close to the north entrance to the mall. I slowed down and asked, "Why are you telling me this?"

"Because . . . because . . . I think you're willing to fight to discover the truth. And I'm telling you the truth."

"You're not my client. You almost shot me. How can you possibly think I'd help you?"

"I'm not asking you to like me or to approve of what I did to Tilly. I . . . I know I've got some relationship, ah, challenges. But I'm not a killer."

"You didn't kill Rune?"

"No, I didn't. I was with Tilly."

"You know how farfetched your story about last night sounds, don't you?"

"That's why I'm here. You've got to believe me—I'm telling you the truth."

"Let's say I do believe you . . . what do you expect me to do?"

"Find out who did it." He made it sound so simple.

"The police are already trying to identify the murderer. Besides, Penny-wise doesn't handle murder investigations."

"The police think I did it. They won't be considering other possibilities. I'm just asking you to give it your best shot. Whoever killed Rune probably killed Wren." Suddenly he glanced back the way we had come. "That's one of your partners, isn't it?"

I looked and saw Norm meandering toward us, pausing to look in shop windows. "Go," I said. "I'll think about what you've told me. If I find anything, how can I contact you?"

He didn't bother responding and was gone almost before I could finish my sentence. Obviously he didn't intend for me to get in touch.

Norm came up to me and asked, "Should I follow him?"

"No, he spotted you."

"I must be losing my touch."

"I need to call Connolly," I said, pulling out my phone. "Let's go back to let Yuri know everything's okay. And you won't believe why he said he came by."

It only took two rings to get Connolly on the line. I didn't bother with preliminaries. "If you're looking for Ethan Jones, he just left the mall from the north entrance."

"Thanks. But . . . how did . . .? I'll call you back."

Back at the office, Yuri, Norm and I huddled together in the conference room, and I gave them a blow-by-blow account of what had transpired.

"Weird," Yuri said.

"Did you believe him?" Norm asked.

"I didn't want to," I admitted. "I can't get what he did to Tilly out of my mind. But my gut says he may have been telling the truth."

"That story about you being a fighter for truth, that's crap," Yuri said.

"I beg your pardon!"

"I mean, it's crap coming from him. He almost shot us, if you remember."

"Oh, I haven't forgotten what he did. And I'm pretty sure there's some name for the kind of mental disorder he has, but . . ."

"But that doesn't make him a murderer," Norm finished for me.

"It certainly makes him a violent looney-tune," Yuri said. "And he has not only stalked you since that night, now he has stalked your daughter."

"I need to call her." I picked up my phone just as it rang. It was Detective Connolly.

"I have a couple of questions," he said.

Yuri signaled for me to put him on speaker. "Sure, but I'm going to put you on speaker. Norm and Yuri are here with me."

"Okay." He sounded reluctant to be on speaker but didn't say no. He had to know that whatever he told me I would pass along to my colleagues.

"Do you want me to go first? Or do you want to start with your questions?"

"How did you know we were looking for him?"

"I guess that means you want to start. Well, I knew because he told me."

"You talked with him?"

"Yes, but first I need to explain what happened. Then if you still have questions, you can ask." With that I launched into an overview of how I came to be talking with Ethan in the first place and what was said during our conversation, ending with a question of my own. "Is his story consistent with what you know about his movements last night?"

"I can't comment . . ."

". . . on an open case," I finished for him.

"It's nothing personal."

"It feels personal when a suspect in a murder investigation uses my daughter to get to me. I think that entitles me to a little information."

"Okay, I get it. A neighbor saw him go around back, but she didn't see him leave."

"What does that mean?"

"Just what I said—she didn't see him leave. Then she started to worry and called the police."

"Why was she worried? Did she hear something? Did he act suspicious?"

"She thought he might be a burglar. There were no lights on, and she didn't think anyone was home."

"That makes sense. But you don't know for sure that he went inside." It was part statement, part question.

"We've barely begun our investigation."

Yuri jumped in. "Is he still a suspect in the Full Moon death?"

"Ah, you've been reading the headlines. They love that label, don't they?"

"Is he?" Yuri repeated.

"We haven't ruled him out."

Norm asked, "What would you advise us to do?"

"Let the police investigate, and stay alert," he said without hesitation.

"You are open to the possibility that Jones may be innocent," I said.

"We'll go where our investigation takes us."

After he hung up, Yuri, Norm and I were silent, each with our own thoughts. Finally, Norm summed up what I was also thinking, "Ethan Jones is either a very clever, manipulative criminal or he's an innocent man accused of murder."

CHAPTER 24
THE MOON ON A STICK

THE NEXT MORNING, the news was full of Ethan Jones' arrest on suspicion of not one but two murders. In spite of what he'd put Tilly through and everything else he'd done, I was surprised to feel a teensy bit sorry for him. A very teensy bit sorry.

While taking a shower, I kept going over what Ethan had told me, again and again. *Splash, splash.* Trying to find some fact to grab onto, something I could twist into a theory. *Splash, splash.* Considering all of the angles. *Pitter-patter*, raindrops keep falling.

I agreed with Yuri's assessment that he had some serious mental problems, but I wasn't convinced he was guilty of either murder. I switched off the water and got out, none the wiser.

My mind turned to what I knew about Wren and her complicated relationships. Then there was the phone call Ethan claimed he got from Wren. Or later suspected the call that may not have come from Wren but from someone trying to frame him. If he was telling the truth, the police would be able to determine whether there had actually been a call, probably from a burner phone. But even if he was able to show he got a call in the timeframe he mentioned, that wouldn't exonerate him.

Once dressed, I followed the aroma of fresh coffee and found my kids already eating breakfast in the kitchen, No-name was sitting at attention next to the table, looking hopeful. "Thank you, Mara," I said. There was no way Jason had made coffee for me. Although maybe I should show him how.

"You're welcome. Thought you might need it today."

"Mom," Jason said with his mouth full of cereal, "Mara said she talked with that killer guy."

"Alleged 'killer guy,'" I said, pouring myself a coffee in my favorite mug. It had a picture of Jason at 5 years and Mara at 6, a Christmas present that I cherished. Although their pictures had faded patches from years of being in dish washers.

"He didn't seem that bad," Mara offered. "Maybe a bit weird."

"He definitely has a weirdo gene," I said. "And some anger issues. And . . .," I hesitated to mention to my kids that he might be a sexual predator. "And he's obviously dodgy. But . . ."

"But . . .?" Mara prompted.

"I'm not sure he's the killer."

"But the police arrested him," Jason said.

"Jason." Mara glared at her brother. "You read enough news to know that they sometimes arrest the wrong person." She nodded in my direction. "They even arrested our mother by mistake."

"Statistics show that most murder charges end in convictions," Jason countered.

"That's because they don't charge someone without solid evidence. But it still isn't 100 percent, is it?"

"Mom, what do you think?" Jason asked. "Is he guilty?"

"I'm not sure," I said. "Rune's murder could have been a spur-of-the-moment thing, but if it was, whoever did it took some big risks. Even if the dagger was already there, I'm not sure Ethan had enough time. Besides, I think the night of the ceremony he was focused on his abduction of Tilly. That was definitely planned, very carefully. To have pulled off both that evening, he'd either need to be a criminal genius or unbelievably lucky."

"Maybe there are two murderers," Mara said. "Maybe someone else killed Rune, but Ethan killed Wren."

"One of the reporters said there's a witness who identified Jones at the scene of the Wren murder," Jason said.

"Actually, the man admitted to Mom that he was there," Mara said, obviously pleased to know something her brother didn't. On the drive home the night before, I had shared most of what Ethan had told me with Mara. But it hadn't been a topic of dinner conversation when Jason was present.

"Why didn't you tell me that?" Jason asked.

"Because it wasn't a big deal. He was hardly likely to confess to me, was he? In theory, he just wanted to give me his version of events."

Jason chewed his Grape-nuts slowly, considering my statement. I could hear his teeth pulverizing the crunchy nuggets even when he kept his mouth closed.

"Even though Mom thinks he's a creep, she's keeping an open mind. That's why he wanted to talk to her. He asked her to prove he didn't do it."

"You going to try to prove him innocent?" Jason asked.

"That's up to the police. He's not a client."

"But if you think he's innocent—" Jason bit down hard on a spoonful of Grape-nuts.

Mara also took a bite of Grape-nuts, and now I was hearing crunching in stereo. Maybe I should make a recording. It might be the kind of sounds that could help some people sleep, the steady rhythm of muffled chomping like the distant sound of footsteps on gravel. It was an effect you couldn't achieve with softer cereals.

"What are you thinking, Mom?" Mara asked.

"I was thinking about—" oops. I couldn't admit I was in a cereal chewing trance. "—about the dead dog." I improvised. The memory had been lingering on the edge of my consciousness since the night of Rune's death.

No-name suddenly yowled.

"Mom," Jason said accusingly.

"Jason, he wasn't responding to my comment."

"He understands a lot more than anyone gives him credit for."

At that moment my mothered joined us. No-name yowled again, like a court herald announcing the entrance of the queen.

"Stop it," Mom scolded. No-name cowered down and went under the table. Mom poured herself some coffee and sat down. "So, have you already discussed the arrest?"

"Yes," Mara and Jason said in unison. Then they giggled. I'm always amazed at how quickly they can become best buddies after squabbling.

Even though my mother and I had an agreement that I would keep her up-to-date on my cases or anything I was working on that could have an impact on the family, I had not yet told her about Mara's conversation with Ethan Jones and my subsequent talk with him. I wasn't trying to keep it a secret, well, maybe I was avoiding the topic, but I definitely hadn't asked Mara to keep mum, and I had been pretty sure she would tell her grandmother at some point. Apparently this was that point. Mara began the tale and then turned it over to me to finish up. It was clear that my mother was not pleased with what had happened, and the fact that I hadn't mentioned it to her, but it wasn't as if I had done anything to make him contact me. And he hadn't actually threatened Mara, saying just enough to nudge me into action.

"Tell me again why he came to you to confess?"

"He didn't confess, Mom, he explained his situation."

"And he expects you to prove him innocent, right? Otherwise, why bother exposing himself like that?"

"He wants the moon on a stick," I said.

"What does that mean?" Jason asked.

"According to Yuri, it's an idiom for wanting something that's difficult to get."

"What's an idiom?" Jason asked.

I silently cursed myself for using one of Yuri's trivia expressions in the first place; Jason usually requires a surfeit of examples before accepting a definition, and I wasn't in the mood. Fortunately, Mara jumped in with an explanation, her superior tone like a young spelling bee contestant who had won a first-place trophy. Rather than encourage her to show off more, Jason backed off.

The kids finished their cereal and put their empty dishes in the sink. Now that the first day of the new school year was in the past, they were already settling into their school routine. Everything was going smoothly and on time. They were eager to be off to see their friends, and, hopefully, excited about a few of their classes too. I felt confident their teachers and classes would soon be topics of dinner conversations.

I finished my coffee and stood up. "I'd better get going."

"I'll just sit here a few moments and finish," Mom said. As I started to leave, she added, "By the way, I've been thinking we need to put a spare key outside somewhere. There have been several times when I've . . ." she hesitated before finishing her sentence. ". . . when I've had to step outside with No-name and almost locked myself out."

I smiled. "Admit it, you cater to him behind our backs."

"There are times when it's nice to have a dog in the house. Even though I'm not convinced he's much of a watchdog." Mom took a sip of coffee and I started to leave. Then, Columbo like, she added, "And I've ordered one of those expanding gate things to block his access to the stairs." In the future No-name would be able to visit my mother by invitation only.

Clara Ramsey called as I was walking to my car. I had parked out front and was enjoying the winding brick path lined with trees and tall bushes that led to the front of the lot and the ornate wood gate. The golds and orange of turning leaves made me think of pumpkin pie and cornucopias. I don't actually care for pumpkin pie and have never decorated with a cornucopia, but Hallmark cards had imprinted a positive impression of them in my subconscious.

"Isn't it terrible?" Clara said.

"I assume you're referring to Wren's death."

"Wren's murder, you mean. By that horrible man who kidnapped Tilly."

"He hasn't been convicted yet." I don't know why I felt compelled to defend him.

"I'm confident he will be. I've heard there's a witness. But that's not why I called. It's about Tilly."

"Is she okay?"

"She says she's okay, but the uncertainty of whether she will be charged with reckless endangerment or not is wearing on her. And on me. If she's convicted of a misdemeanor, even if she doesn't do any jail time, it will stay on her record. It seems to me that her best chance is to prove she didn't have anything to do with the explosion."

"Tilly told me she doesn't know who's responsible." I reached my car, unlocked it and got in to finish our conversation.

"That's what she's told me too. Although I think she has her suspicions. I don't understand why someone in the group doesn't out whoever did it."

"Do the police have any leads yet that you know of?"

"Not that I've heard. And, I'm convinced that the only way to prove for sure that Tilly wasn't involved is to find out who did it."

"I'm sure the police are all over this investigation."

"Tilly seems to feel like they are inclined to condemn the entire group. That they consider all of them guilty even though they must realize that only one or two people were involved in actually building the device that exploded. Tilly wouldn't even have known how to do it."

"Well, they probably think everyone is involved, at least in the planning. And the press coverage of the arrests didn't do the group any favors."

"That's why I'm calling. I've asked P.W. to have you and Yuri look into it. You've met some of the Green Women. And you know Tilly wouldn't have done anything to endanger people at the rally. But P.W. said I needed to talk to you first. She pointed out that working on the original case was quite an ordeal and that you've been under a lot of stress. That, and because of pending charges against you, she thought you might want to bow out. I will understand if that's the way you feel. I know you have your own family to consider."

My mind went to the conversation with my children this morning, and I could hear Jason's voice saying: "But if you think he's innocent . . ." How do you pass on righting an injustice? Or a perceived injustice? Even if it's the last thing you want to do.

"It's okay, Clara. I'm willing. And I'm sure Yuri will agree. I'll tell P.W. when I get to the office. I'm about to leave right now."

"Thank you. I'm so grateful. And thank Yuri for me."

Yuri wasn't in the office when I got there, and Adele had some follow-up for me to do on the background checks I'd completed for her. It was after lunch when Yuri returned and I had a chance to tell him about Clara's request. He was thrilled with the assignment. "Let's go rock that moon," he said immediately.

"What does that mean?"

"Just what you'd expect—shake things up."

"Please stop with the moon idioms," I pleaded. "No one talks like that, and once I get one of those in my head it starts infiltrating my conversations. I actually referred to a 'moon on a stick' this morning when talking with my kids. So, stop it." How long was it going to take for me to stop thinking in moon images?

"Afraid you'll tell your professor that you want to 'dance in the moonlight' with him or that thoughts of him 'send you over the moon' or . . ."

I stood up. "That's it. I'm headed out . . . want to come?"

"Where are we going?"

"To talk to some Green Women. One of them detonated the device. Not that I would expect anyone to confess. But someone may have seen something. Maybe something that at the time did not seem suspicious. It's up to us—the Moon Detectives—to figure it out."

"Hey, I like that," Yuri said as he grabbed his jacket.

CHAPTER 25
THE MOON DETECTIVES

WE COULD HEAR voices and laughter as we got out of the elevator and headed for the Green Women's headquarters. When we opened the door, it was clear there was a celebration going on. The large room was filled with women. It was mid-week and mid-afternoon. I wondered how all of them managed to be there. Didn't they have jobs? Raven was standing at the back of the room, her red hair luminous under a strong overhead light. Everyone fell silent as she raised a glass in the air and made a toast: "To us, the Green Women who are going to save the planet for the next generation."

"To us!" everyone echoed cheerfully.

Phoebe went forward, stood next to Raven, and raised a glass. "Last year was the deadliest on record for those of us defending our diminishing natural resources. But we will not be stopped. No one—no politician, no cop, no man— no one can stop us. We will not be stopped!"

"We will not be stopped!" "We will not be stopped." "We will not be stopped." A dog near the front of the room joined in with sounds halfway between a howl and a bark, perhaps a dog's version of a chant. The crowd's rhythmic repetition of their commitment to mission broke into laughter as attempts were made to placate the dog.

Yuri whispered to me, "Kinda reminds me of 'lock her up'."

Several other women went forward to make short toasts accompanied by more shouted slogans before the group transitioned from a somewhat formal celebration to a casual party atmosphere. It was then that Raven noticed us and came over. "You again," she said. "This is a private gathering."

"We came to give our condolences about the loss of one of your members," Yuri said solemnly.

Raven had the decency to look somewhat embarrassed, but only slightly. "We must look rather hard-hearted under the circumstances," she conceded. "Of course we are all going to miss Wren and are upset by her demise, but at the moment, we are celebrating the fact that we are out of jail and have a good shot of winning at trial."

"But you are willing to go to jail for the cause, right?" Yuri said. He wasn't exactly being his usual flirty and congenial self with Raven. But then, I didn't think she would be susceptible to his charm anyway.

"Getting arrested was sufficient publicity. For now. But we'll go to jail if it serves the cause."

"Does that mean you have plans for more disruptive behavior?" Yuri asked.

"You don't like us much, do you?"

"I supported the march by being at the rally. But I don't approve of stampeding and pommeling innocent people with flying debris. I don't see how that serves anyone's cause."

Several other women had gathered around, like good soldiers awaiting the command to attack.

"We understand that the majority of Green Women didn't know about the explosion in advance," I said. "And it was definitely bad publicity for the group. A peaceful demonstration would have been better for furthering your, our, mission."

"You talk the talk but you don't walk the walk," someone yelled. Others murmured agreement.

I turned to address the entire group instead of just Raven. "I brought my two children with me to the rally. They are part of that generation you claim to be advocating for. And you put them in danger. How am I supposed to feel good about that?" We hadn't planned to get confrontational, but maybe it would bring some dissenters out in the open.

"Hey," Yuri said. "Sorry—we aren't here to cause trouble or to play the blame game. We just want to talk to a few of you about Wren."

"Are you investigating her murder?" someone asked.

"No," I said. "But there's the possibility that someone in this group, perhaps even someone in this room, wanted her out of the way." Heads moved from side to side, no one making direct eye contact but obviously considering the possibilities.

"We all liked Wren," Raven said. Murmurs of agreement rippled around the room.

"But Wren discovered who detonated the pinata, didn't she?" I threw out the challenge wondering who, if anyone, would make a counterargument.

"Why do you say that?" Raven asked. She was too clever to take the bait.

"Let's just say we have an inside source." I'd lobbed a second grenade into their midst.

"It was an unfortunate accident," Raven said. "But it got attention from the press."

"Putting that much firepower into a pinata wasn't an 'unfortunate accident.' And when Wren discovered who did it, that made her a target."

The women were inching toward us, intent on my exchange with Raven. The idea that Wren discovered who had sabotaged the pinata must have at least flickered across their minds before now. Unless they all knew who was responsible and were committed to keeping it secret. But the thought that there was an "inside source" must have been disquieting. When I'd mentioned it, quite a few women had turned to look at Phoebe. She was standing off to one side, deflecting their sudden misgivings with a steely glare. "Don't look at me," she said loudly. "I was Wren's roommate, but I'm not an 'inside source.' You all know I wouldn't hesitate to do something illegal if necessary, but I certainly wouldn't kill someone to hide it."

Eyes moved away from Phoebe but continued to look around at the other members of the group, wondering, weighing. Clearly this was an unresolved issue for all of them.

Raven turned away from us. "Come on," she said to the group. "This is a party. Or a wake if you want to call it that. But it isn't a time to turn on each other. We're in this together. Now fill your glasses, grab some food, and enjoy yourselves!"

The group around us slowly moved away and small conversation groups started gathering. Raven waited until the din of talk suggested the party was on again. Then she looked at me and said, "You're not welcome here. Please leave."

"What are you afraid of?" Yuri asked.

"Nothing, but you're putting a damper on festivities. Wren may be dead, but the rest of us are going to continue with our fight for policies that can save our world."

"But someone in your group saw fit to violate your own rules about engaging in criminal activities and brought the police and the press down on you. Don't you want to know who did that?"

"It's done. We just want to move on."

We were interrupted by a disturbance at the side of the room. I looked over and saw Phoebe backing away from a large German Shepherd. "Get him away from me," she said, sounding both angry and a bit frightened.

"Give him that sausage roll in your hand and he'll go away," I heard someone say.

The dog lunged for her hand and Phoebe dropped the roll on the floor. "Stupid dog," she said as the dog devoured her sausage roll in one gulp and turned toward her to see if there was more where that came from. But Phoebe was in full retreat.

Raven turned back to us. "You're welcome to leave any time now."

"We'd like to mingle and ask members a few questions," Yuri said.

"Not today. As I said, this is not a good time for amateur detectives to be snooping around."

The "amateur" label stung. I motioned for Yuri to come with me, and the two of us left. Once out in the hall, Yuri said what he always says in situations like that: "That went well, didn't it?"

"I didn't realize the plan was to antagonize everyone in the room. But if it was, we were successful."

"No one was going to tell us anything once Raven interfered. I thought a few shots in the air might flush out some truthsayers."

"For a moment there, I thought they might shoot back."

"It's hard to get true believers to break ranks."

"That's it then."

"Not necessarily. I could tell there were women there who wanted to know more about what you were saying. And they didn't necessarily fall for Raven's deflections. If we can figure out how to reach a few of them when they aren't with the whole group, we might learn something."

"I wish I shared your optimism."

We were half way down the hall when someone called, "Cameron, wait." We turned back to see Phoebe headed in our direction. "If you were looking for Tilly, she didn't show up today. I thought she'd be here. I hope she's okay."

"I'm not sure where she is, but that wasn't why we came by. We really did want to talk to some of the members about Wren. We're fairly certain that either she helped rig the pinata or she knew who did it. We wanted to see if anyone could verify our suspicion, maybe even give us a name. What do you think?"

"She might have been involved or knew who was, but, as I already told you, she didn't say anything to me."

"But did you suspect her of being involved in some way?"

"Not really. And even if she was, I'm not sure that was why she was murdered. I just assumed . . .," she began, then abruptly stopped.

"Assumed what?" I asked.

"That Wren had something on Ethan, something about Rune's death, and that's why he killed her."

"Wouldn't Wren have gone to the police if she had evidence that Ethan had killed Rune? She was sleeping with Rune. She must have had feelings for him."

Phoebe's neck turned pink. Some blonds blush like that. "But she wasn't in love with him. I'm not even sure she was all that upset about his death. It wouldn't surprise me to learn that she thought she could take advantage of the situation by blackmailing Ethan. Make a few coins off of Rune's death. Or simply because she liked to see people squirm."

"The affair was just an affair? You're sure Wren wasn't serious about Rune?" She'd hinted at that when we'd talked before, but I sensed there was something more to it.

"Wren only cared about herself," Phoebe said with a pinch of bitterness.

"And you think she was capable of blackmailing someone?" My antenna was up and quivering, but before I could ask another question, Phoebe turned away.

"I should get back. Raven will wonder where I've gone."

We watched her leave, then headed down the stairs. "That was interesting," Yuri said.

"I would say 'strange.' You don't think Phoebe was another one of Rune's women, do you?"

"You think Rune was sleeping with all three roommates? That sounds like a real Agatha Christie moment. Maybe they figured it out and all three conspired to snuff him."

I got out my cell phone.

"Who are you calling?" Yuri asked.

"Tilly."

"To ask her what?"

"I'm curious why she isn't at the celebration. And she might be able to give us the names of some Green Women we could call."

When Tilly answered I explained that we had just left the Green Women's headquarters and asked why she wasn't at their gathering.

"Because Wren is dead and no one seems to care. And even though they let us out of jail, we don't know that we won't be sentenced to jail time at our trial. So, I'm not sure there's anything to celebrate. To be honest, I'm disappointed with their reaction to what happened at the rally, and I'm not sure I trust any of them anymore."

"So, any new speculations about who detonated the pinata?"

"No, whoever did it is staying mum."

"Well, I have another question for you. It's a bit delicate, and I don't want to upset you, but I feel like I have to ask."

"Go ahead."

"Do you think Rune was sleeping with Phoebe?"

"Phoebe and Rune? I suppose it's possible, but before all this happened, I would have thought it more likely that Phoebe was sleeping with Wren."

CHAPTER 26
THE DARK SIDE OF THE MOON

WREN AND PHOEBE? Wren and Rune. Phoebe and Rune. Maybe even Wren, Phoebe and Rune? The more we learned about Tilly's roommates, the more questions we had. We needed to get in touch with some Green Women without having Raven there to monitor responses. In spite of their alleged anti-male agenda, it was possible Yuri's charm would work on a few of them. We could also try shaking out information with a hard glimpse of their upcoming legal troubles. Or maybe we could leverage latent guilt by mentioning the injuries to innocent bystanders. One way or the other, we needed to find a weak link and do some prying.

We'd been hoping Tilly had a list of members and volunteers with their contact information, but she didn't. And we could hardly ask Raven for one. Tilly was, however, able to give us a fair number of names, and we found telephone numbers for all but one. We waited until the end of the day before calling anyone, not sure whether their celebration was still in progress. Had they told employers they were attending a funeral or a wake? Or did they get time off for volunteer work? The fact that they were there celebrating anything annoyed me.

When no one answered our calls, we weren't sure if the celebration was ongoing or if they saw who was calling and had been warned not to talk to us. We left messages and stayed late in case someone called back. When not a single person returned our calls, rightfully or wrongfully, we blamed Raven.

At the end of what I could only label an unproductive work day, I headed for home. On the way I remembered my mother saying that we needed to have a spare key made, but traffic was bad, I was tired, and it didn't seem particularly urgent. Still, it got me to thinking about spare keys in general, which in turn led me to wondering about who had a key to Rune's condo. Did he give them out to all the women he slept with? If he had, his place could have been pretty crowded at times. If he'd only given them to a select few, had Wren been favored with a key?

Had Rune's dog been in the car with them the night of the ceremony, or had someone else taken him from the condo and then to the park? Perhaps using the dog to lure Rune to the woods. I could imagine Rune bending down to comfort his dog and someone taking that opportunity to knock him out. And then killing the dog.

Then there was the question of how Tilly's prints got on the dagger. I'd given it a lot of thought and had one niggling suspicion that wouldn't go away. I started to pick at my theory, turning it this way and that, putting it under a microscope, zapping it with laser analysis. Finally, I couldn't stand it any longer. There was something I wanted to know now. I pulled over and called Tilly. Fortunately, she was always good about answering her phone.

"Tilly, I have a strange question for you."

"Go ahead."

"Do you ever take sleeping pills?"

"No, never."

"How about Wren or Phoebe?"

"Phoebe has problems sleeping. And I think she has pills. I vaguely remember Wren asking her for one once when she was having some sleep issues."

"Is there any chance you could have been fed sleeping pills some night before the ceremony?"

"You mean deliberately by someone? In something I ate or drank?"

"Yes, probably by one of your roommates."

"But why would they do that?"

"To put your fingerprints on the dagger that killed Rune." There. I'd said it.

After only a moment's hesitation, Tilly said, "You think Wren could have drugged me and placed my fingerprints on the dagger while I was asleep?"

"What do you think?"

"I'm a really sound sleeper anyway." She paused. "I do remember having difficulty waking up one morning. I think it was about a week before the ceremony. But I don't have anything to compare it to, so I can't say whether it was drug induced grogginess or not."

I didn't know how many pills you would have to take to be dead to the world, but someone who took them on a regular basis might know. It would be interesting to see what was in the medicine cabinet at their house.

"Another thing," I said. "Did you have a key to Rune's place?"

"No, he offered me one, but I was holding off. Our relationship was escalating a bit too fast. I know everyone thinks I was crazy about him, but I did have some misgivings."

I didn't exactly have an aha moment at that revelation, but I could feel some ideas start to click into place, a timeline of events slowly emerging from the swirl of possibilities.

I said goodbye, started the car and headed for the house where the three roommates had shared their "independent entity" lives. If Phoebe was there, maybe she would be a bit more forthcoming on her home turf.

When she answered the door, she was wearing a sweatpants outfit the color of oatmeal; it was not at all flattering to either her figure or her complexion. It gave her skin a "locked up too long in a castle away from the light of day" pallor. And the sweatpants had lost their shape and hung unevenly from her full-figured frame. Her smile was friendly though, and she didn't look at all surprised to see me. In fact, she acted almost like she'd been expecting me.

Without any hesitation, she invited me to come in, offered me a glass of wine and suggested that I join her in the kitchen while she finished making a casserole she was fixing for her dinner. "I like casseroles," she explained. "I don't mind eating leftovers, and I like the idea of not having to cook again for several days."

"With a growing boy at my house, we seldom have any leftovers," I offered. I followed her into the tiny kitchen and took a seat at the bar while she poured us each a glass of wine. I took a few sips while she chopped an onion. Chop, chop, chop. The motion with the knife was swift and efficient. She didn't say anything, apparently waiting for me to take the lead. Instead, I asked if I could use her bathroom.

"Sure, it's down the hall." She pointed with the knife. It was a chef's knife with a long, pointed blade.

"It must have been challenging with three women and only one bathroom," I said, hoping that she would tell me how many bathrooms there were in the house.

"When this house was built, one bathroom was the norm," she offered. That didn't mean they hadn't added a second bathroom, but it sounded like there was only one.

I went down the hall, closed the door and peeked in the medicine cabinet. It was too easy. There was a bottle of prescription sleep aid pills with Phoebe's name on it right up front. It was half full, or half empty. The date on the bottle was fairly recent, but even if I counted how many were in the bottle, I wouldn't know what that meant. Phoebe might not take them every night.

I flushed the toilet, paused long enough to wash my hands, and returned to the kitchen.

There was a carton of eggs on the counter next to a hand mixer. "What kind of casserole are you making?" I asked.

"It's a version of macaroni and cheese. It was one of Wren's favorites."

"Did you know Wren a long time?"

"Yes."

"I know you said that you didn't intrude on each other's private lives, but you still must have talked about things that were happening, right?"

"We talked a fair amount, yes."

"And you knew about Wren and Rune. Do you know whether Rune had given her a key to his house?"

She stopped what she was doing. Something Yuri had said recently found its way back to me: Everyone is a moon with a dark side. We'd argued about it. Yuri was convinced it was true, but I believe most people don't have a dark side. Not in the sense of harboring evil deep inside. But in that moment, I detected the presence of an ominous darkness that pleasant-faced Phoebe kept turned away, out of sight, residing somewhere in an inner recess of her being.

"I need a dish," she said as she came around the end of the counter, still gripping the chef's knife.

I'm always impatient with characters on TV or in a movie who wait too long to react to an aggressor. I wasn't sure if I was making the right call or not, but I tried to smile as I slid to the edge of the stool and tensed my muscles for action. Okay, Will, I said to myself. If I'm right about this, I hope your training pays off. And if I'm wrong . . .

I didn't actually see her raise the knife for an attack, but something told me she was about to do so. I leapt up and threw myself at her, punching her in the stomach and following through with an uppercut to her chin. She staggered back as I got in close and shoved her hard. She lost her balance and fell. The knife clattered to the floor and skidded away, and I grabbed the hand mixer off the counter and hit her with it. Then I rolled her over, pulled her hands behind her back and wrapped the wire from the mixer around her wrists.

It was all over in less than thirty seconds.

Still dazed, she started to struggle. I knelt on her back and pressed the slightly pointed beater from the hand mixer in between her shoulder blades. "Stay still or I'll shoot you. Don't think I won't."

"Let me go!" she screamed. "What do you think you're doing?"

I poked her harder with the beater. "Shut up." I'd slipped my phone out of my pocket and hit Connolly's number, feeling uneasy about what I'd done and incredibly relieved when he answered. I explained where I was, that I had Phoebe tied up and was holding her at gunpoint. "You might want to send someone over immediately," I concluded. I had to give him credit—he didn't ask questions, he simply said he would have an officer there within ten minutes and to keep my phone on. Phoebe had remained quiet during my conversation with Connolly, but when it was over she came to life.

"Get off of me!" she screamed, bucking like a wild horse. I pressed down hard with all of my weight. The instant she calmed down, I texted Yuri. Then Connally came back on the line and said two officers were on their way. Apparently realizing the phone was on, Phoebe started yelling again: "She attacked me. She's crazy."

I bounced on her back to shut her up. "I'll explain everything when the officers get here," I assured Connolly, wondering if I would be able to offer a convincing explanation. I had either acted precipitously or just in time. It would depend on whose story they believed.

"She's got a gun!" Phoebe sobbed. "She's going to shoot me."

"I'm not going to shoot her," I said to Connally. "Unless she tries to get up." I jabbed her again with the beater on the hand mixer.

I sensed Connally didn't know what to say. And I wasn't sure what to say either. I couldn't prove my suspicions. They were just that —suspicions. And I had attacked Phoebe. Although I was prepared to lie about that, to say that she had attacked me. After all, it was what I thought was about to happen. And if I didn't lie, I might end up back in jail, and Phoebe would go free. If my analysis was correct, I couldn't take that chance.

"Why are you doing this?" Phoebe asked, suddenly completely still, like a cobra about to strike. Or like someone getting her story together. Acting the part of the victim. Aware that my phone was still on, I responded, more for Connolly than for Phoebe. This was my chance to lay out my case for Phoebe as murderer.

"I know you were in love with Wren but you also had a thing for Rune. I don't know exactly what happened for you to turn against Rune, but I know how you killed him"

"I didn't—"

"Let me finish." I jabbed her again. "Wren had a key to Rune's house. You made a duplicate and used it on the night of the ceremony to steal his dog. You used the dog to lure him to the edge of the woods where you clubbed him to knock him out before dragging him to the altar and stabbing him. That probably upset his dog, so my guess is that you killed him too. That wasn't a problem for you because you hate dogs. But it was a big mistake. Ethan would never have killed the dog. Nor would he have had access to the key."

"You can't prove any of this." Her speech was unnaturally flat, all of her former anger and passion gone. But I didn't for a moment believe that she was about to confess.

"The police found a dead dog at the scene, and my guess is that it's Rune's. You also have sleeping pills that you could have used to drug Tilly so you could put her fingerprints on the dagger. She remembers feeling particularly drowsy when trying to wake up one morning a few days before the ceremony. We all assumed the dagger used to kill Rune was one he brought with him for the ceremony, but I'm confident the police will be able to track down where you bought it.

"Finally, when Wren figured out you had used her key and concluded you had killed Rune, you had to get rid of her too. And since you could no longer pin it on Tilly, the only woman Rune loved, Ethan became your scapegoat."

"Rune didn't love Tilly." Apparently, that little fact had broken through her calm; her voice was tight and had increased in volume.

"Maybe not, but he certainly didn't love you." Take that. "And Wren didn't either."

When she started rocking and cursing, I knew I'd hit the mark. "Damn you," she repeated over and over. "Damn you to hell."

"Poor unloved Phoebe. Did they laugh at you?"

She heaved her body up, trying to throw me off. "Bitch," she screamed. "You don't know anything."

In that moment, I knew I was right. But if she hadn't killed two people, I might have felt sorry for her. She had been rejected, denied love, possibly ridiculed. I just hoped Connally and his team would be able to get a confession or prove her guilty some other way.

"Police, open up," a male voice yelled.

"Come in," I yelled back, too afraid to get up until there was someone else there to keep her under control.

"It's locked." I heard someone say.

"Knock it down," I shouted.

"Don't!" Phoebe screeched.

I don't know if they heard me or were just determined to find out what was going on. It took them several tries before the door flew open, but it finally did, with the crackle of shattered wood and a bellow. Three officers burst into the room and one of them yelled, "Put down your weapon and put up your hands."

Happily, I set aside the hand mixer, held up my hands and stepped away from Phoebe's prone figure.

When Phoebe turned to one side, saw the hand mixer and realized that was my "weapon," she went berserk. "You witch," she hissed, like a real witch casting a spell. I hoped she didn't have an eye of newt or toe of frog handy.

Actually, being called a witch didn't seem all that damning under the circumstances. If our situations had been reversed, I might have managed some epithets that would have turned the air red. She'd been attacked without warning, held at mixer point, and had her secrets revealed while a homicide detective listened.

Suddenly, the full weight of what I had just done hit me. My entire body began to quiver, and I wasn't sure I could remain standing.

One of the officers frisked me for weapons while the other untied Phoebe and helped her to her feet. "Where's your gun?" he demanded when he didn't find one on me. It felt like they had our roles in this drama backwards.

"There's no gun," I said. "But there's the knife she attacked me with." I pointed to the chef's knife next to the officer's feet. He took a quick step back and exchanged questioning looks with his partner.

Then, like an angry animal issuing a threat, Phoebe pointed at me and demanded: "Arrest her!" When the officers didn't act on her command, she became hysterical, feverishly yelling: "She assaulted me. Arrest her, dammit! Arrest her."

"Her prints are on the knife, not mine," I said. Hint, hint. Preserve the evidence. As if he heard my silent command, the officer who seemed to be in charge motioned for one of the other officers to secure the knife.

I was about to suggest they should be arresting Phoebe, not me, when Connolly came in and rushed over. "Are you alright?" It was the concern in his voice that did me in. I felt my knees start to cave. He reached over and pulled me into his arms, and I collapsed against him. "Hey, it's going to be all right. You're safe now."

Apparently sensing the situation wasn't going the way she'd hoped, Phoebe lurched toward us, and it took two officers to restrain her. "I'm the victim, not that bitch," she said loudly. Then she stopped struggling and stood upright and said, "You can let go. I'm fine now." The officers took a step back but remained poised for action.

I could sense Phoebe's mind at work, calculating her strategy. She wasn't sure whether I was a "witch" or a "bitch," but she was smart enough to see that Connolly was on my side. That had to give her second thoughts.

Suddenly Yuri came flying into the room and yelled my name. Connolly stepped back, keeping his hands on my shoulders to steady me.

"Him!" Phoebe screamed. "He put her up to this!" Her rubber band of control was snapping back. The two officers grabbed her again. She began flailing her arms, making it hard for the officers to keep her restrained. I noticed that one of the officers had a hand on what looked like a taser. I was hoping he would use it. Given her behavior, I wondered whether in addition to sleeping pills she had other medication for some mental disorder. Medication she had failed to take before my visit.

Connolly released me and took another step back. Then he looked me in the eyes and said, "I assume you can explain what happened here."

CHAPTER 27
MOON RIVER

THE SONG "MOON RIVER" is said to be about the future and the past simultaneously. I'm not sure how that's even possible, but in the aftermath of my alleged assault on Phoebe, time did seem to blend past and present in a bizarre and jumbled way. Looking back, it's a series of moments in my mind rather than a coherent chronology.

Given how things turned out, I'm glad Will's training kicked in and that I charged Phoebe before she was able to attack me with her knife. If I had waited until she'd made her move, I'm not sure I would still be around to remember the moments. My chronology would have ended with a chef's knife.

Then there was the central lie that I decided to tell. I stuck to it during the initial exchange with Detective Connolly and through the many later interviews with other officials. I held onto the lie like it was a life preserver and I was stranded offshore in a churning sea. "She attacked me," I told Connolly and the other officers, repeating it over and over until I almost believed it myself. I did, of course, tell Yuri the truth the minute we were alone. Although he argued that it was a "split second decision" rather than a lie, he also said that the police and the justice system have difficulty discerning the difference between the two. He therefore encouraged me to keep lying. In the interest of justice and self-preservation.

Meanwhile, once Phoebe realized she was actually being arrested on suspicion of murder and that our entire exchange had been not only overheard by a detective, but had been recorded by him, she seemed to have had some kind of mental breakdown. Instead of continuing to maintain her innocence, she became incoherent and mumbled about perceived wrongs, interspersing her ramblings with screaming complaints about me and what I had done to her. Connolly told me they would most likely end up having her competency to stand trial evaluated.

Since I didn't have anything concrete to back up my conjectures about how Phoebe had managed to get away with not one but two murders, I realized I could be wrong about some of the details. On the other hand, I had obviously come close enough to the truth to push Phoebe over the edge. In addition, several Green Women came forward and shared some fairly damning tales of altercations between the two roommates, confirming that Phoebe's dark side had surfaced on numerous occasions in the past. Others confirmed her obsession with Wren and her infatuation with Rune.

Although unrequited love may have been strong motivation for retaliation, ridicule and humiliation could have been the final indignity. Almost everyone knew that Wren and Rune laughed about Phoebe's passion for them behind her back. Several Green Women admitted to feeling sorry for Phoebe because Wren and Rune were so cruel, each of them deliberately stringing her along as a joke. My guess is that at some point Phoebe caught onto the joke and decided to take her revenge. I almost couldn't blame her. Although she would have been better off adhering to the motto "revenge is a dish best served cold." A clever and less tormented mind might have come up with something to eventually humiliate her persecutors publicly, tormenting them as they had tormented her.

My memory of what happened once the officers and Connolly arrived remains a bit vague. I was apparently suffering from shock, shock at what I had done as well as shock at what had almost happened. I do remember Detective Connolly's response to my situation. Of course, some of that memory might have been shaped by Yuri's teasing. "I thought I'd walked onto the movie set of some chick lit film," he'd said. "There the two of you were, locked in an embrace that would have thrilled Jane Austin fans."

Another memory moment was the look on Phoebe's face as she was being led away in handcuffs. I'd always thought of her as pleasant looking and approachable. But as they walked her out, an officer on either side, she looked back at me and bared her teeth in an aggressive, insane "smile." Like a Jack Nicholson ad for The Shining. The transformation was terrifying. But I'm confident she would be her old self at the time of her trial. Her lawyer would see to that. My hope was that, under cross-examination, she wouldn't be able to entirely hide her dark side from a jury.

After the police took my statement and released me, Yuri drove me home. He had a brief, whispered conversation with my mother while I went into the kitchen to pour myself a glass of wine. When I joined them, Mom didn't

miss a beat, informing me that she would take the kids out
to dinner to give me some space. Yuri offered to stay and
keep me company, but I begged off. All I wanted was a
long soak in the tub and an evening of mindless TV. But
not a cop or detective show.

While the tub was filling, I gave P.W. a call. Yuri had
updated her on most of what had happened, but she wanted
to hear some of it from me. Including why I'd gone to see
Phoebe in the first place.

"I had this idea about Tilly being drugged in order for
someone to put her fingerprints on the dagger. I wanted to
know if there were sleeping pills in the house that could
have been used for that."

"How did you make the leap from finding pills to
concluding Phoebe had killed Rune and Wren?"

"I didn't really know for sure until . . . we, ah, fought
over her knife."

P.W. paused ever so briefly, then didn't press for more
details. Instead, she said, "Your instincts were good" and
quickly moved the conversation along. When I reached
the part where they took Phoebe away, P.W. said she was
satisfied that she knew enough to handle any questions that
might arise. She warned me not to talk to the press and
reminded me that I could call my lawyer if any issues came
up that I wasn't sure how to handle. Then she suggested I
take a few days off to recover, and I happily agreed.

Mom must have told the kids not to talk to me about
what had happened because when they came home they
went to their rooms and left me alone to choose whatever I
wanted to watch on TV. That was a rare treat. Although I
found myself channel hopping for a long time before ending

up watching Seinfeld and Mash re-runs. Exaggerated normality and laughter was what I needed.

The next morning I gave Mom and the kids the pollyannaish version of what had happened, leaving out the part where I attacked first and making light of Phoebe's resistance. I did admit I tricked her into thinking the mixer beater was a gun, and they howled at that. And even Mom cracked a smile when I told them that when the police arrived they'd ordered me to put down your weapon.

Most of Thursday was a blur of inactivity. Except for the phone call I got from Ethan Jones thanking me for getting him off the hook. I ungraciously pointed out that I didn't do it for him and that I felt like he needed to see a therapist. The call did not end on a friendly note.

Yuri called to take my emotional temperature every chance he got. Clara called to thank me. Tilly called to thank me. I even had an unexpected call from Raven. She wanted me to know she had no idea about what Phoebe had done. Why she cared what I thought wasn't clear to me. But if, as I suspected, she was one of the people Rune and Wren had laughed about Phoebe with, she may have had a fleeting human moment and experienced at least a pinprick of guilt. After all, Phoebe had been a loyal and hard-working member of the Green Women.

That evening my mother came downstairs with a good bottle of wine and a lot of questions. I considered coming clean with her about everything. After all, I had promised honesty and transparency about my work in exchange for her support. But I was concerned that it would make her worry more, and I couldn't see any upside.

"I don't understand why you didn't have backup with you," she said at one point.

"Because we didn't suspect Phoebe," I admitted.

"So, what was the tipping point?"

"Your suggestion that we needed a spare key," I said. "It made me wonder about who Rune gave keys to his place. Someone took his dog using a key. And, it was also a matter of what you said about jealousy making people do terrible things."

"I helped you solve the case?" She seemed very pleased at the thought.

"Yes, in this instance, jealousy and being ridiculed turned Phoebe into a killer." A very human motive with grievous results.

"Now if you could figure out who was responsible for the pinata explosion, you could close the book on the case."

Was that my mother's way of saying "good job" or was she telling me I wasn't done yet? I could have asked, but instead I put it back to her. "I'm waiting for more inspiration from you."

"Well, all I can tell you is that my money would be on that Raven woman you've talked about. Maybe with a little help from Wren."

"I agree. Raven is selfish enough to let everyone be punished for her criminal act. And I think Wren was too. What I don't see is Raven confessing to any wrongdoing."

Friday, I started feeling normal and bored. I took No-name for a walk and threatened to start calling him Obnoxious or Loser if he barked at another shadow or tried to catch one more squirrel. Although he probably knew I wouldn't do either because Obnoxious was too hard to say when reprimanding him and there was something about calling a dog Loser that seemed to reflect badly on the owner.

That afternoon I cooked up a storm only to discover both Mom and Mara had plans to eat out and that they had told me about it the day before, but I had forgotten. I let Jason watch the news while we ate our fill of enchiladas verdes and Mexican rice. I put the leftovers in plastic freezer containers for a night when I was in a hurry and wanted something to microwave for dinner.

Saturday was a re-run of Friday . . . a slow day which ended in a flurry of indecision as I tried to choose what to wear on my first date in eons. I didn't want to look like I was trying too hard. But I didn't want it to seem like I didn't care how I looked. I had a dozen or so options laying on my bed when my mother poked her head in and said, "What's going on here?"

"Just sorting some clothes."

"Cameron . . ." She has always been able to detect a fudged truth. That's why I'd been surprised when she didn't call me out on the big lie I'd been telling about Phoebe's capture. Maybe I just needed to think bigger. Or maybe it was something she didn't want to know.

"Okay, so I have a date and I don't know what to wear."

Showing incredible restraint, she came in and started going through my choices. I knew she wanted to grill me about the who and where, but she held back, waiting for me to break down and tell her on my own. "This is nice on you," she said, holding up a jacket and matching turtle neck in a deep teal. The jacket had a black collar and a black strip down the front. "With black slacks it would be appropriate for most places."

"Go ahead," I said.

She turned innocent eyes on me, then grinned. "Are you going to tell me about where you're going?"

"Out to dinner."

"And . . .?"

"With someone I met during the case."

She looked almost alarmed. "Not someone from the Full Moon Society, I hope."

It was my chance to needle her for a change. "As a matter of fact, yes."

"Cameron." Her tone said "how could you?"

"You're always saying I should get 'back out there,' that I shouldn't let the 'best days of my life' pass me by.'"

"But the way you've described the people in this group, I guess I'm a bit surprised."

"And disappointed?"

"Well, I have been hoping that you and that nice Detective Connally would get together."

"Someone I don't even call by his first name . . ." And didn't even know his first name. Or if he was single.

"So, what's tonight's date's name?"

"He goes by CJ."

"Cute."

"His first name is Carter."

"Hard to get a nickname out of Carter, I admit."

Since she was trying so hard to be nice, I relented and filled her in on CJ. Her relief was almost amusing . . . almost. I was a bit irritated that she had doubted my choice of men in the first place. Although given the disaster of my marriage, perhaps I deserved that. But this was just a date, an evening out. I didn't want her to make more of it than it was. And I intended to try very hard to do the same.

CJ and I had agreed to meet at a nearby neighborhood restaurant, convenient for me and with no pressure on either of us to deal with my family. He was there waiting at a candlelit table near a window with a gorgeous view of a wooded ravine that would one day probably be a housing development. It always surprised me when steep hillsides became housing sites. But with the housing shortage in Seattle, there were apparently no obstacles that couldn't be overcome to turn what used to be considered unusable land into rows of look-alike condos or boxy apartments.

The first few minutes were spent oohing and aahing over the view. From that, the transition to real conversation was awkward for me. I was definitely out of practice. I didn't know how I was supposed to act on a first date. And I couldn't seem to land on "normal." CJ, on the other hand, made comfortable small talk, slowly getting me to relax.

We managed to order drinks and hors de oeuvres before the inevitable topic came up. Having practiced the laugh lines on my family, I was able to regale him with the amusing highlights of Phoebe's capture without dwelling on any of the less flattering aspects. The best line was the officer demanding me to put down your weapon.

"Were you afraid?" he asked at one point?

"Of course. Who wouldn't be?"

"But you still managed to take her down. I'm impressed."

"One of my colleagues taught me the basics of self-defense," I said.

CJ laughed. "Remind me not to pick a fight with you."

I suddenly found myself getting serious. "When I took the job with Penny-wise I never thought that I might be putting myself or my family in danger. Coming to grips with that has been a struggle."

"You can run into nasty people anywhere," he said. "You should read some of my student reviews." Then he reached across the table and put his hand on my arm. "I don't mean to make light of the risks you take. But I have confidence in you."

The rest of the meal was filled with lighthearted talk about our respective families, our hobbies, what books we liked—all of the normal topics of conversation people have when they are getting acquainted. We lingered over coffee and dessert as if we didn't want the evening to end. I know I didn't. I was more relaxed than I'd been in a long time. And I liked sitting across from a handsome man who seemed interested in what I had to say. Maybe Adele was right, a test swim wouldn't hurt. I could always go back to shore.

We had agreed that after we left the restaurant, he would see me home. I wasn't sure if the offer was code or an act inspired by the gender protection myth. Not that sometimes women didn't need protection. But sometimes men did too. Either way, I had a few fantasies about how the evening might end.

He parked his car behind mine out front, and together we made our way down the narrow path to the carriage house. The walk was filled with shadows from the waning moon peeking through the trees. As we drew near, I silently cursed the bright light over my door and wished I'd thought to put in a dimmer bulb for the evening.

He stopped me at the outer ring of light, and we turned toward each other to say goodnight. I found myself mesmerized by his gaze, a deer caught in the headlights. More than anything I wanted to pull his face down and kiss him, but I didn't need to. He reached over, put his hands on my face and kissed me so tenderly I almost swooned.

Our kiss ended abruptly when loud barking protested our presence there. Why on earth had No-name taken this opportunity to finally play watch-dog?

Then the lights on Mom's deck came on and I heard her sliding doors open.

"It's me, Mom," I called up to her.

"Cameron?" I saw her peek over, then pull back. "Goodnight," was all she said.

No-name was still going at it, the sound of his high-pitched yapping penetrating the otherwise still evening. CJ was laughing as he touched the side of my face with his fingers. "To be continued." He turned and disappeared into the shadows on the path.

EPILOGUE

MONDAY MORNING at work I had to force myself to concentrate. It was as if my brain was haunted. Without warning I'd flash on Phoebe's look of hatred as she was hauled off by the police. Then I'd switch to being almost kissed by CJ only to flip back to images of being arrested. Everything was all jumbled together, the good and the bad, popping up when least expected, like those ads that appear out of nowhere on your computer screen. How I regretted ever Googling dog toys at work—the gods of retail had apparently decided I was the answer to their sales goals for the year, bombarding me with ads.

Adele had me working on background checks for a company that needed special high security clearance for some of their employees. It made me think about the potential threat to my own livelihood if, in spite of my lawyer's confidence, I was convicted. And what about Tilly? Would Clara's fears for her niece come true if the charge of reckless endangerment stuck?

What's interesting about doing background checks is that people do all sorts of creative and stupid things to maximize their chances of getting a job they want. They lie about past job titles to make themselves sound more important. They find ways to characterize their education to suggest a degree they never completed. There are frequently inventive explanations for gaps in job history that have to be checked out. Or suspicious justifications for a history of short-term employment engagements. Then there are the repeated traffic violations. Careless speech on social media. On and on it goes. All of these little indiscretions and lies have to be unearthed and catalogued so the client can make a decision about the applicant.

In the end, it isn't always easy to know whether to give someone a clean bill of health or not. How do you interpret a tiny exaggeration—is it "putting your best foot forward" or a "lie?" Does job hopping mean the applicant is adaptable or unable to commit? What constitutes an indiscretion on social media? And how do you assess those bad or carefully "qualified" letters of recommendation? Especially those from people the applicants themselves have requested. How we characterize these things can make the difference between a person getting a job or not. We are hired by the client, but we don't want to be unfair to the applicant either. As someone who spent a long time trying to get back into the work force, I perhaps sympathize too much with the job applicant.

When my phone rang and I saw that it was Detective Connolly, I thought he was probably checking in to see how I was doing. But I was wrong.

"I have something I want to tell you in confidence," he said.

"That sounds mysterious."

"I think you've earned the right to a few details, and I trust you to keep them to yourself."

"I can't even tell Yuri?"

Connolly sighed. "I'd rather you keep this to yourself for now. Can you do that?"

Keeping secrets was becoming a habit. Not one I was pleased about. But how could I say "no" under the circumstances? If my curiosity was the puck on the strength tester machine, Connolly had hit the bell. But I wanted to be honest with him. "Will whatever you are about to tell me eventually be made public?"

"Yes."

"Then I can keep my mouth shut." For now.

"Good. I thought you would like to know that we have information that will most likely impact the charges made against the women arrested at the rally, including you."

"You know who is responsible?"

"We believe we do. We managed to get some fingerprints off the pinata."

"But you can't tell me the name or names?"

"No, but I wanted you to know that the reckless endangerment charge will most likely go away for everyone except those responsible."

"The word 'those' suggests more than one person."

"Don't read too much into that, okay? And by the way, I know your lawyer is trying to get you off completely, and I want you to know that I will put in a good word for you."

"I appreciate that."

"You should also be aware that our investigation may have a ripple effect. If the Green Women connect you to our identification of those responsible for the explosion, they may not be too happy with you. I know that doesn't make sense, especially since it will get most of them off the hook for reckless endangerment. Still, I'm fairly certain they will see it as a betrayal, by Phoebe and by you."

"True believers can be scary," I said.

"But if not for you, we wouldn't have made it this far with the investigation. So, I thank you."

"Thank you for thanking me. And I appreciate you sharing this with me; I will definitely not tell anyone else until it becomes public."

"Hopefully we can make an arrest soon. I'll give you a call when we do."

After I hung up, his words about putting in a "good word" for me turned bleak fears into rays of sunshine. Surely having him speak up for me would carry some weight with the prosecutor. It was tempting to call my lawyer and ask, but I knew he wouldn't be able to promise me a particular outcome, so why bother?

Connolly hadn't named names, but Yuri and I were convinced the main person responsible had to be Raven. She wouldn't have let someone else make important decisions about the event, and how the pinata was used was definitely an important decision. The only question in my mind was whether she was able to do it all on her on. And if Wren had also been involved.

I was curious about whether Phoebe played a role in discovering who was responsible for the explosion. If she had any proof, it seemed likely she had traded information for something, although I couldn't imagine what kind of quid pro quo the prosecutor could offer a person accused of two murders. Capital punishment had been abolished in our state, so that was already off the table.

Now the test for me was whether I would be able to refrain from telling Yuri before an official announcement was made. I intended to try. Otherwise, if Connolly asked, I would have to lie again. I was getting tired of lies.

Yuri had been out of the office most of the morning but returned at 11:00 and pulled a chair up close to mine and whispered: "Will and I are going to do something after work that I think you might want to join us for." He leaned even closer. "I got a peek at P.W.'s calendar. She has a hair appointment at 4:00. We thought we might follow her home from there. What do you say?"

I've participated in a number of the attempts to learn more about our mysterious boss, even though I'm iffy about whether we should be doing it. On the one hand, not knowing anything about her background or even where she lives is a puzzle that screams to be solved. Like how did they build the pyramids? Or who and where is D.B. Cooper? Or what's with Area 51? Or what happened to Malaysian airlines flight 370? On the other hand, P.W. has made it clear that there are some things she wants to keep private. Who are we to violate her trust by treating her like the object of an investigation?

"Count me in," I whispered back. I'd deal with my guilt later.

Yuri and the others had made half-hearted attempts to follow her home before, but with no success. Today, given the information gleaned from Yuri's clandestine look at her calendar, he and Will were convinced we had a shot at it. But in light of our many discussions as a team about whether this was a legitimate pursuit or an unjustifiable intrusion, we decided to keep it between the three of us. That made it seem less invasive, at least that's what we rationalized. If we discovered where she lived, we could decide then whether it was something to share with the others.

The rest of the day didn't exactly speed by. I went into the mall for coffee twice. Bought a dozen cookies for the group and ate three myself. Adele sniffed them and gained a pound. Will took his time choosing just the right one. Norm grabbed one as he was passing by, not even looking at what it was until after taking a bite. And Yuri managed to scarf down the rest before either Will or Norm had a chance to return for seconds.

At 3:00 Yuri waved me into the conference room. As soon as we were seated, he said, "Okay, I've been patient, trying to give you your space. But it's time you talked."

For a moment I thought he was referring to my conversation with Connolly, but then it hit me. "Talk about what?" I said with mock innocence.

"Come on. I'll admit that holding a pool about when CJ would call was tacky, but I really do want to know how your date with him went. Not because I'm some kind of relationship voyeur, but because I care about you."

"Relationship voyeur—that's an interesting term."

"I've been very patient so far . . . and you know that I can blackmail you into telling me anything I want to know."

"But you wouldn't do that."

Yuri's dramatic sigh could have qualified for an Emmy. "You're right, I wouldn't. But I thought it was worth a shot."

"If you weren't such a good friend, I'd tell you to make like a tree and leave."

Yuri blinked. "I can't believe you said that."

We both laughed. "I think I read it on a popsicle stick not too long ago."

"You eat popsicles?"

"I've been known to."

"Another thing we have in common."

"Like curiosity." It felt good to be sparring with Yuri, teasing him more than he was teasing me for once.

"If it didn't go well, that's okay," he said, obviously trying to bait me.

"Okay, you win. I give up. You can haul in your hooks." I paused for a drumroll, tapping it out on the table. "It was a great evening, and we'll probably go out again." I was tempted to tell him about how No-name had interrupted a perfect ending, but decided to save that for another time.

At 3:30 Will, Yuri and I slipped out and got in position to follow P.W. to her appointment. Will was driving. When Yuri had offered, Will had calmly said his car was less distinctive so better for tailing. The words came out so quickly and smoothly I had no doubt he'd planned in advance what he was going to say if Yuri offered to drive.

It was 3:40 when P.W. drove her grey BMW sedan out of the parking lot. It was an expensive car but not a flashy one, as if it didn't want to compete with its owner for attention. The address associated with the car license was a PO Box. That's legal as a mailing address, but state law requires a physical address as well. Somehow P.W. has managed to use our business address for that purpose. We weren't sure if that was entirely legal, but we certainly didn't want to be responsible for calling attention to it, so we've never pursued the issue. Besides, we worried that any poking around on our part would get back to P.W.

Instead, we've chosen more creative ways to try to uncover her secret life. Like what we were doing this afternoon by tailing her to her hair dresser's. Even though none of our previous attempts have succeeded, you never knew when success would be thrust upon you.

Will followed at the appropriate distance, making an effort to keep his driving consistent and conservative. Fortunately, P.W. didn't speed or change lanes a lot or run yellow lights, so she was easy to follow.

When she pulled up in front of a bakery and got out, we were surprised; there wasn't a lot of time left for her to get to her appointment. We parked a few cars away and waited, expecting her to come out within minutes carrying a bag of pastries. We waited some more. It was approaching 4:00, and she still hadn't come out. We started to wonder whether there was a back room where someone cut hair. Like a hidden gambling game room. Or maybe there was a back door and she'd sneaked out, a car waiting to pick her up in the alley. We considered all sorts of crazy possibilities as we continued to wait.

We were all getting a bit antsy when a man wearing a white apron came out of the bakery carrying a pink cardboard box. He walked down the sidewalk in our direction. Was he looking at our car? Yes, he was!

We were all watching intently as he stepped over to the passenger side and motioned for Yuri to put his window down. Yuri hesitated, but the guy didn't go away. He just stood there holding the pink cardboard box. Finally, Will switched the engine on so Yuri could roll down the window, but Yuri was so rattled that he put the back window down first and had to try a second time.

"This is for the three of you," the man said as he handed over the box. He didn't wait for us to respond but headed directly back in the direction of the bakery.

"What do you think it is?" Yuri said. He was holding the box in his lap, staring at it as if it contained something scary. Like it was filled with vipers or tarantellas or . . . a bomb.

"Should we be checking for explosives?" I asked.

"In a pink box?" Will said.

"I don't think there are any rules about bomb containers," I said.

We stared at it for another few seconds before Will broke down and ordered Yuri to "Open it!"

Yuri's hands were shaking as he clumsily pulled up the lid. When nothing exploded or leapt out, we all leaned over to look inside.

There were three individual pecan tarts in aluminum pans. And a note with our names on it.

"I doubt those are incendiaries," Will said. "What does the note say?"

Yuri opened the folded piece of paper and read out loud: "Enjoy. It's signed, 'P.W.'"

"That tears it, she saw us," I said. "I can't believe it."

"I guess she beats us in the detective department," Will said. "Again."

"Definitely disappointing," Yuri said before reaching into the box and snagging one of the tarts. "Might as well celebrate our failure. Want to stop for coffee on the way back?"

As Will started the car, he said, "At least the note didn't say 'You're fired.'"

ABOUT THE AUTHOR

IN A WORLD FILLED with uncertainty and too little chocolate, Charlotte Stuart has always anchored herself in writing. As an academic with a Ph.D. in communications, she wrote serious articles on obscure topics with titles that included phrases such as "summational anecdote" and "a rhetorical perspective." As a commercial fisher in Alaska, she turned to writing humorous articles on boating and fishing. Long days on the ocean fighting seasickness required a little humor. Then, as a management consultant, she got serious again. Although even when giving presentations on serious issues she tried for a playful spin: Stress—Clutter and Cortisol or Leadership—Super Glue, Duct Tape and Velcro.

Her current passions include pro bono consulting for small nonprofits and writing lighthearted mysteries. A curious mix of problem solving; pragmatic and fantasy. Charlotte lives and writes on Vashon Island in Washington State's Puget Sound and spends time each day entertained by herons, seals, and eagles and hoping the deer and raccoons don't raid her vegetable garden.

ACKNOWLEDGMENTS

I'VE ALWAYS FOUND the ways in which people coalesce around ideas fascinating. Differing views and the desire for power in groups are the perfect storm for a mystery novel. The Full Moon Society and The Green Women are fictional organizations based very loosely on historical reenactment and protest groups. My apologies for showing their potential dark side.

This is the fourth book in the Discount Detective series. I continue to be grateful to Kristina Makansi, Laura Robinson, and Lisa Miller of Amphorae Publishing Group and to my agent, Donna Eastman. Their on-going support has made this series possible.

Most of all, I want to thank you for reading this book. Please take a few minutes to write a short review. Reviews are every author's best friend.

Visit my website at www.charlottestuart.com.
Or contact me on twitter and Facebook:
- https://twitter.com/quirkymysteries
- https://www.facebook.com/charlotte.stuart.
mysterywriter